"John...you do know what you are, don't you?"

He shrugged, not quite understanding what Alanna was getting at. "I'm a man, but I guess that much is obvious. Well, ah...I was in the mining business in Nevada, ranched in Arizona and got into the oil game in California. Why?"

"John, look...there's something I have to tell you. It's going to come as a terrible shock, and I'm sorry about that, but...oh, there's just no good way of putting this. John, you're dead. You're a ghost."

Alanna DeRain, John decided when her words sank in, would be better named Alanna Deranged. But he wasn't about to suggest that while she was the one with a gun, so he just said, "Ma'am, I'm definitely not dead. In fact, I'm not even feeling a mite poorly."

Dear Reader,

John McCully appeared as a secondary character in each of my three previous time travel Superromances. After that, he put his foot down and demanded a story—and a woman—of his own.

Once he'd met Alanna DeRain, though, he had serious second thoughts. She was the most aggravating, ornery, infuriating woman he'd ever come across. And there he was, trapped alone with her in a ghost town. Alone, that is, except for a few ghosts.

When I saw the initial fireworks that erupted between John and Alanna, I began to wonder if I'd made a mistake. Could a cowboy from 1887 and a paranormalist from 2014 really find happiness together?

It turned out they could. All they needed was a little help from their friends.

I hope you have as much fun reading John and Alanna's story as I had writing it.

Dawn Stewardson

Dawn Stewardson
Gone with the West

Harlequin Books

TORONTO • NEW YORK • LONDON
AMSTERDAM • PARIS • SYDNEY • HAMBURG
STOCKHOLM • ATHENS • TOKYO • MILAN
MADRID • WARSAW • BUDAPEST • AUCKLAND

ISBN 0-373-70615-4

GONE WITH THE WEST

To the romance lovers who made my previous
time travel Superromances award-winners.

And to John, always.

CHAPTER ONE

EVEN CONSIDERING the sweltering heat, the town below seemed unnaturally quiet.

Nestled near the base of the mountain, surrounded by scrublands of semidesert stretching into the distance, the place was a sprawling metropolis that had to be home to three or four thousand people. But he could see no sign of life.

Wiping the sweat from his forehead, then adjusting the brim of his hat to protect his eyes from the sun, John headed forward once more.

By the time he reached the level plain, he was sure the place was deserted.

The only living thing in sight was an enormous turkey vulture, sitting on a weathered sign that marked the city limits. As he drew closer, the buzzard gave a lazy flap of its wings and flew off.

Pausing, John gazed at the sign it had been perched on. Chester City, Nevada, it read. Founded, 1888.

When he started off again, Chester City seemed to become more dilapidated with each step he took. Many of the cabins lining the side streets had collapsed over the years, and the buildings on the main street were in little better shape. There had once been stretches of boardwalk in front of the larger structures, but they'd decayed long ago.

He trudged past the first business establishments he came to—several saloons and brothels, one hotel, a general store, two blacksmith shops and a bakery.

They were all in various stages of decay, some merely sagging shells without windows or doors, nothing more than shady spots for lizards and rattlers to hide. Their corrugated metal roofs, creaking now and then in the heat, provided the only sounds to break the silence, other than the soft thud of his boots on the dirt street.

Then the tinkle of a piano drifted through the still air, stopping him in his tracks. He wasn't alone, after all. Bizarre as it seemed, someone was playing the piano in the Miner's Saloon.

For a minute he stood listening to the sad, haunting melody, then he turned and followed the sound.

The Miner's Saloon still had doors—swinging ones that squeaked in protest when he pushed them open. The final notes of the song died as he stepped into the semidarkness.

The air inside was stale and the atmosphere spooky. The room was still furnished—half a dozen round tables surrounded by roughly built chairs. A couple of pool tables stood near one wall, as if waiting for players to enter and rack the balls.

And there, on the far side of the front window, was the piano. But its stool was empty and the cover was pulled down over the keyboard. He looked around slowly, seeing no sign of life.

Dust particles floated thickly in the dim light and dust blanketed every surface—including the piano and stool. It was disturbed only on the floor, where tiny trails had been left by mice.

Puzzled, he wandered farther into the room. Cobwebs covered the walls and linked the row of dust-dry bottles that stood behind the bar.

Seeing them made him think of how thirsty he was, so he looked away. He walked along the bar to where a calendar hung on the wall. It was gray with grime, the print so faded he couldn't make out the year. He brushed it a little cleaner.

It read *1897*. But how long had the calendar been hanging there? *Exactly* what year was it?

There was no clue in the Miner's Saloon, so he'd have to look elsewhere for his answer.

Then, just as he was about to leave, the swinging doors squeaked again.

Over the sound a woman said, "Move an inch and you're dead."

He didn't move a muscle—simply stood listening to his heart pound.

ALANNA WAITED, needing time to calm down enough to think clearly before she tried to say anything more.

It was a good thing that ghosts reacted to situations as if they were still alive, because threatening to shoot one had been ridiculous.

But ridiculous or not, she'd managed to startle him. And until he began thinking straight again she had the upper hand. She needed those few minutes to establish whether or not he could be trusted. Not all ghosts could be, not by any means.

Besides, as long as he was busy worrying about getting shot, it wouldn't occur to him to simply drift away on her. And she certainly didn't want that. He was the most magnificent specimen she'd seen in all her years of studying the paranormal. He had to look almost exactly as he'd done more than a century ago.

"Don't turn around," she finally said. "I want you to take your gun out of its holster. Slowly... and put it on the floor... then slide it away from you."

Apparition or not, what she could see of that old revolver looked deadly. And it was all too common for a ghost to do something that surprised the devil out of her.

This one, though, did exactly what he'd been told.

She watched as he slowly bent down. When she first noticed him through the window, he'd seemed so alive that she hadn't been sure what she was dealing with.

And even up close he looked incredibly real—from his broad shoulders, past his pattable-looking behind, to those long, lean legs.

If it weren't for his clothes, she might have believed he was flesh and blood. But his outfit was a dead giveaway—definitely manufactured in the late 1800s.

A pale blue shirt of roughly woven cotton, worn with faded jeans, a black Stetson, dusty black cowboy boots and a hand-tooled leather gun belt.

Individually, no one item screamed out that it hadn't originated in today's world. But add them together and the message was unmistakable. There were too many subtle clues in the fabrics and tailoring for her trained eyes to miss.

"All right," she said as he stood up again, his back still to her. "Now, tell me who you are."

"My name's John McCully, ma'am."

Ma'am. That sounded like more solid evidence he'd lived a long time ago. Either that, or he was from the South. Looking at him, she doubted the latter. And his revolver, she noted, glancing over to where he'd slid it, was a frontier-model Colt.

Everything added up to John McCully's having met his maker near the end of the 1800s. And, undoubtedly, he'd died right here in Chester City. Why else would he have materialized here?

"Ma'am?"

"Yes?"

"Do you reckon I could turn around? It feels kind of strange, your being just a voice and all."

"All right," she agreed, curious to see if his face was as clearly defined as the rest of him.

It was. All rugged planes and angles, with just enough creases to make it interesting.

His skin was a sun-kissed shade of gold that had become unthinkable after people realized the dangers of UV, and he had a granite jaw, pronounced cheekbones and a straight nose.

The only softening features were his dark brown eyes and the most sensuous mouth she'd ever seen—on a man *or* a ghost.

All in all, she knew that if John McCully were alive, her hormones would be going into overdrive.

He hesitantly reached up to remove his hat, revealing dark hair with just the trace of a curl. Seeing that, she almost wished he *was* alive.

"Pleased to meet you, ma'am," he said, his eyes lingering warily on her pistol. "But I don't believe you mentioned your name."

"Alanna. Alanna DeRain."

He nodded, then glanced at her pistol again and said, "That's a gun."

She wasn't sure if it was a statement or a question. Her little plastic automatic wasn't something he'd have seen back in his time. And its design was space-age, compared to his revolver's.

"It's a Glock . . . they're made in Austria. And it's a newer model than your Colt."

"Uh-huh," he said, still not taking his eyes off it. "I didn't mean you any harm with my Colt, though, ma'am."

"No . . . no, I realize that now. But when I first spotted you I thought you might be . . ." She caught herself before saying she'd thought he might be alive. Ghosts were often sensitive about their dead status, so she tried not to remind them of it.

"You just took me by surprise," she explained instead. "I'm alone in town."

The instant she said that she regretted it. Admitting she was on her own wasn't smart. But it was too late to call back her words. She'd just have to stay on her guard and hope he wasn't a malevolent ghost.

"I didn't mean to startle you, ma'am. I just heard the piano and came in. You play very well."

"I'm glad you enjoyed it," she said, not bothering to correct his assumption. It would be better to keep the focus of their conversation entirely on him.

He stood watching her with a curious expression, but he no longer seemed afraid. Any minute now, reality was going to kick in and he'd realize her gun couldn't hurt him. He'd also realize that he didn't have to stay. But she needed him to. She just *had* to talk with him. Thus far, fewer of Chester City's ghosts had cooperated with her than she'd initially hoped.

"John . . . I'm going to put my gun away, but will you promise me something first?"

"What's that, ma'am?"

"Promise me you won't disappear? I'd like to talk to you for a little longer."

His expression grew even more confused, but he nodded.

She lowered the Glock and stuck it in the waist of her shorts.

John swallowed hard, his gaze following Alanna DeRain's gun. He'd never seen a woman wearing as little as this one was. Not outside the privacy of a bedroom, at least.

Oh, his friend Will had told him how women's clothing had changed a lot over the years, but seeing it for himself was an entirely different matter.

Those little yellow *things* she was wearing ... well, even his sisters' *bloomers* came down to their knees, and they wore long skirts over them. But those yellow things barely covered the tops of Alanna's thighs, leaving her long, gorgeous legs almost entirely naked.

And her thin white blouse didn't cover much, either. It had no sleeves and was unbuttoned down so far that he could see the tiny bit of lace of the top of her undergarment.

Intensely aware of the way his body was reacting, he shifted his hat, letting it come to rest just below his belt buckle. Then he forced himself to focus on Alanna's face, even though there was far less of it visible than there was of the rest of her.

She had a luscious mouth, pale creamy skin and long, thick dark hair. But the upper part of her face was hidden by the most peculiar spectacles he'd ever seen.

They were goggles, really, with wings at the sides. And the lenses were such a deep purple that he couldn't imagine how she saw anything through them.

He glanced back at the wall calendar, trying to decide how to proceed. He'd like just to come right out and ask her what year it was, but he could hardly admit he didn't know.

She'd ask him why, and he wouldn't have a credible answer for her. Will had told him that even in the future most people didn't believe time travel was possible.

"And those of us who know it is," Will had explained, "make a point of not talking about it. If too many people caught on and started changing events in time, we'd have a cosmic disaster on our hands."

So, John reminded himself, he had to be very careful about what he said. Odds on this woman believing in time travel had to be danged low. And if he slipped up, she'd think he was suffering from some disorder of the mind and pull her gun on him again.

Casually, he gestured at the calendar, hoping she'd be able to see it through her goggles. "That's been hanging there since 1897."

"Yes . . . a long time."

"Uh-huh." Well, so much for that try. He thought for a moment, then said, "You know, I've never been to Chester City before."

"Really?"

She seemed to find that surprising, but it was hard to tell when he couldn't see her eyes.

"You mean not since you . . . ?"

"Not since I what?" he asked.

She cleared her throat, then rubbed her palms on those little yellow things—a nervous gesture that drew his attention back to her naked legs. Anxiously, he checked that his hat was still keeping everything under cover.

"John . . . you do know what you are, don't you?"

He shifted his gaze to her face again, hoping to see a clue to what she meant by her question. But if there was a clue, it was hidden by the goggles.

"Ma'am . . ." He hesitated, not wanting to say anything that might insult her. "Ma'am, I hope this question doesn't sound unmannerly, but I've been wondering if there's something wrong with your eyes."

"No. Nothing."

"Well, then, would you mind taking off those spectacles for a minute? They make it difficult to talk to you."

"Oh, could you try just to ignore them, John? If I took them off, you probably wouldn't seem nearly as clear to me."

An extreme sense of embarrassment swept him. He shouldn't have said a word about the goggles because Alanna DeRain must be partially blind. They had to be some newfangled invention that helped people see. Yet she'd just finished saying there was nothing wrong with her eyes, so—

"John . . . you haven't answered my question. Do you know what you are?"

He shrugged, feeling like a bit of a fool because he didn't understand what she was getting at. "I'm a man. But I guess that much is obvious. And I . . . well, I've been a lot of things. Been in the mining business in Nevada, ranched in Arizona, got into the oil game in California. Why?"

"And when did you do all that? What years, I mean."

"What years?" he said slowly, giving himself time to think. There was something in her tone that was starting to annoy him. She sounded condescending, as if she thought she knew something he didn't.

And maybe she did. Well, actually, there was no *maybe* about it. She had to know a whole lot of things he didn't. Will certainly hadn't told him *everything* there was to know about the future. But regardless of how much Alanna knew, he didn't like her patronizing attitude.

He was almost tempted to tell her the truth. That would certainly shock her out of her smugness.

"John?"

As she said his name, she began nervously rubbing her palms on those little yellow things again. He swallowed hard. Annoying or not, she was having quite an effect on him.

"John, who's the vice president of the United States?"

"Chester Arthur, of course," he said before he could catch himself.

But instead of saying he was crazy, Alanna simply nodded, then said, "Of course. The man Chester City was named for. But look... there's something I have to tell you. It's going to come as a terrible shock, and I'm sorry about that but... oh, there's just no good way of putting this. John, you're dead. You're a ghost."

IT HAD TAKEN JOHN a few moments to realize Alanna wasn't joshing with him. But even with those stupid goggles hiding her eyes, he finally decided she actually believed what she'd said.

Rational people, though, didn't believe ghosts really existed. And they certainly didn't tell perfect strangers—very much *alive* strangers—that they were dead.

And he'd been worried that *she* would think *he* was suffering from a disorder of the mind.

Alanna DeRain would be better named Alanna Deranged. But he wasn't about to suggest that while she had a gun tucked in her waistband and his was lying ten feet away on the floor, so he just said, "Ma'am, I'm definitely not dead. I'm not even feeling a mite poorly."

"Oh, John," she murmured. "I really am sorry to have had to tell you. And I know how difficult it is for you to accept. But if you'd like to talk about your...condition, I'll be glad to help you work through your feelings."

"Work through my feelings," he repeated. What in tarnation was that supposed to mean?

Uneasily, he glanced at her gun again. He didn't have the slightest idea how to deal with a crazy lady. And a crazy lady who was armed was a more worrisome problem yet.

"Don't be frightened to talk about your emotions," she told him with a tiny smile. "I know men didn't do it in your century, but it's quite acceptable today. And I've had extensive training in working with ghosts. And extensive experience. I'm a paranormalist."

"A...paranormalist." The word sounded strange on his tongue.

"Oh, of course," Alanna said, "you don't know what that is, do you? Paranormalism is a relatively recent field. I mean, there've always been people involved in the occult, but paranormalists are trained scientists. Paranormalism is a respectable profession."

John nodded, but he wouldn't be at all surprised if it was a *profession* that existed solely in Alanna's mind. Paranormalism sure sounded like a made-up word to him. Or, if there really was such a profession, he'd put his money on its being one that attracted all kinds of quacks.

"I...I'm sorry if I seem to be staring at you," Alanna was saying. "I don't mean to. It's just that you've thrown me a little. You see, you're the most lifelike ghost I've ever come across."

"Ah, I see." He stood wondering if he should demonstrate why he was so lifelike. But he'd already told her once that he wasn't dead and she'd totally ignored him. Apparently, she wasn't about to let reality intrude into her fantasy world.

And maybe trying to press the truth wasn't the best idea, anyway. She'd only find the details confusing, and she was obviously a danged confused woman already. So maybe he should just follow her lead and play along.

"If we're going to talk about your condition, John, it might be best to start with your final memories of being alive. What year was it when...what year do you last remember?"

"What year is it now?"

"It's 2014."

He silently cheered. What a load that was off his mind. He'd made it to the right year, after all, and now he just had to get out of here and head for Boston.

"And you last recall it being...?" Alanna prompted.

"Well..." Hell, how could he play along when he had no idea what to say? And why should he try twisting the truth in knots for the benefit of a crazy lady?

He considered that for several seconds, then made his decision.

Will might have warned him not to tell anyone he'd come from 1887, but Will had never met up with Alanna DeRain.

Besides, back home, he was known as Honest John. And he damned well wasn't going to start lying now, simply because this woman couldn't tell the difference between men and ghosts.

"This is going to sound mighty complicated," he warned her.

She merely nodded for him to continue.

"Well, I last recall it being 1850. But that's only because I went down the wrong tunnel. If I hadn't, I'd last recall it being 1887."

Alanna took a deep breath, trying to quell her excitement. It was difficult, though, when she just might be looking at an extremely rare case—a ghost so into denial that he was transposing the dates of his birth and death.

And *tunnel*, he'd said. He'd gone down a tunnel. Heavens, that was such an obvious metaphor for the birth canal it would make Freudians jump for joy.

If there were still any Freudians around, that was. Their ranks had vastly diminished over the last twenty years or so.

Focusing her attention on the ghost once more, she said, "So you were born in 1850. And you're thirty-seven."

He looked at her strangely. "No, ma'am. I said that 1850 was the last year I recall. I was born in 1853. February 12, 1853. And I'm thirty-four."

"I see." She spoke the words as calmly as she could, but this went far beyond any textbook case she'd ever read. John McCully thought he could remember the time before he'd been born. What she had here was a ghost not only in denial, but in some sort of dissociative state, as well.

She *had* to get more details before he decided to disappear on her. If she could manage to get enough of his story, she'd be able to write a landmark paper about him. Possibly even a book.

"Ma'am?"

"Yes?"

"Ma'am, you seem to be missing an important point here."

"What's that, John?"

"That I'm not actually a ghost. *That's* why I seem so lifelike to you."

She thought quickly, trying to decide how best to handle the situation without upsetting him. He probably didn't even believe ghosts existed. And she didn't want to push too hard. But he seemed intelligent, so perhaps a rational explanation would be the best approach.

"John," she began, "it's these glasses I'm wearing that make you seem so alive. I thought I'd mentioned that. You see, ghosts radiate auras that are a cooler temperature than the auras of living people."

"Auras?"

"An aura is an emanation of the life force in the atmosphere surrounding a person ... or a ghost."

When he still seemed uncertain, she gestured at the air around herself. "And, as I said, a ghost's aura is cooler than a living person's. The life force diminishes after death. But the lenses in these glasses were specifically designed to pick up the cooler aura and digitize the prior human form from it."

"Ma'am, I just don't—"

"Call me Alanna. Please." He'd begun looking at her as if he was certain she was utterly insane, so she gave him her most reassuring smile before going on. "I know it sounds very confusing, John, but the bottom line is, that if I took off my glasses, I wouldn't see you half as clearly—or not at all if you decided to dematerialize."

He didn't speak, simply stood watching her, his gaze making her a little uncomfortable. He just looked *too* much like a real live man.

"What about touch?" he finally asked. "Can you feel a ghost?"

She shook her head. "If I reached out and tried to touch you, my hand would go straight through where you're standing."

"Try it."

For some reason, that suggestion made her even more uncomfortable.

"There's no point," she said firmly. "I know from experience what would happen."

"Then just do it to humor me. I *don't* know from experience."

"Well . . . promise you won't be too upset? This sort of thing can be very traumatic for a ghost who... Well, it can be very traumatic."

"I promise I won't be upset."

Tentatively, she reached forward.

"Oh, my Lord," she whispered, not sure which was more of a shock—her hand hitting his solid chest or his snatching her gun from her waistband.

CHAPTER TWO

JOHN QUICKLY DIVED for his revolver, grabbing it from where he'd slid it across the floor. Then he tucked Alanna's gun safely into his boot.

When he looked at her again she was clearly terrified, so he holstered his Colt and turned away, giving her time to gain her composure.

He stuck his hat back on his head and pretended to use the mirror behind the bar to adjust it. Actually, the glass was so filthy he could scarcely make out his reflection.

"Who are you?" she finally whispered.

He turned back to her. "I told you, ma'am, my name's John McCully."

"But…but I could touch you…you're not a ghost."

"No, ma'am, I told you that, too. If you took those spectacles off, I reckon you'd be sure of it. You'd still be able to see me perfectly."

Hesitantly, she removed them, then murmured, "You really *are* alive."

"Yes, ma'am."

Her face grew even paler. It was obvious that, for a woman living in the desert, she didn't get much sun. But despite her unhealthy pallor she was beautiful. He'd been pretty sure of that when she'd had the goggles on. And now there was no doubt at all.

She had the biggest, bluest eyes he'd ever seen. And long, thick dark lashes that put him in mind of the dancer Lola Montez, who was billed as the Dark Seductress. He'd seen her perform once, over in Virginia City, and he'd never forget her scandalous spider dance.

Not that he imagined Alanna DeRain was scandalous. Or that she was *intentionally* trying to look seductive. Except for her skimpy clothes, she seemed a proper lady. And gazing into those deep blue eyes of hers, it was tough to believe she wasn't every bit as sound minded as he was.

Except that she still didn't seem entirely convinced he wasn't a ghost. In fact, she looked as if she half expected him to start rattling chains or begin moaning any moment.

"If you're a real man," she said at last, "how did you get here? I didn't see a car. Or hear one, either."

"No, I didn't come by car, ma'am."

"Well, how then? Motorcycle? Horse?"

He shook his head, wondering what a motorcycle was. He didn't recall Will mentioning the word.

"Then how *did* you get here?"

"I walked, ma'am."

"Across the desert?"

"No, down from the mountains."

"But why are you dressed like an escapee from the 1800s? And why do you keep calling me ma'am?"

Her tone told him there was something she didn't like about that, so he said, "Well, I'll stop calling you it, ma'am."

That was easy enough, but how did he explain his clothes? When he'd come right out and told her he'd been born in 1853 it had only confused her—just as he'd expected it would.

And the more he said, the more frightened she seemed of him. So maybe, instead of trying to explain anything, he should do what he could to allay her fears.

"Look, ma'am...Alanna," he corrected himself, "I'm not going to hurt you. I—"

"Then why did you take my gun?"

"Because I don't want *you* hurting *me.*"

"Oh."

She seemed to think that might be the truth, so he decided to satisfy his curiosity. "I was just wondering...would you mind telling me why you were so convinced I was a ghost?"

"I...because that's all I was expecting to see here, I guess. And because of your clothes. And—"

"But *why* were ghosts all you were expecting to see?"

"Because that's the whole reason I'm *in* Chester City. I'm working on a research project. Studying the ghosts here."

"Ah." It took a serious effort, but he managed not to laugh.

She eyed him for a minute, then said, "You seem awfully skeptical. You don't believe ghosts exist, do you?"

"Well...no, actually, I don't."

"So what *do* you think? That people hallucinate them, or something like that?"

"Something like that," he admitted.

Alanna merely shook her head. In the past fifteen years, there'd been so much hard scientific data proving that ghosts *did* exist, she didn't understand how so many intelligent people could discount it.

"You *do* believe in ghosts, though," John said. "Enough so that it's got you living in this deserted town. But doesn't your being all alone out here make your husband danged anxious? If I had a wife, I sure wouldn't let her be staying someplace like this by herself."

"Well, I'm not married, so it's not an issue." She resisted the temptation to add that, if she *did* have a husband, he wouldn't be the type who'd lay down rules for her.

"What about your family, then?"

"What about them?"

"Don't you have a father? Brothers?"

"Yes, I have a father and two brothers. A mother and sister, too. But that's not really relevant to my being here." And none of John McCully's business, either, so she didn't bother mentioning that she was very close to her family, even though they were spread out all over the country now. She didn't want to discuss anything personal with the man.

In fact, there wasn't anything at all she wanted to discuss with him, and she wished he hadn't reminded her she was alone—alone with him. There was something extremely peculiar about John McCully.

Actually, now that she'd gotten over her shock, she realized that there was a *great deal* peculiar about him— starting with his coming down from a barren area of the mountains. What had he been doing up there?

When she asked him, he said, "Camping."

"Oh...camping," she repeated. But he was lying. She could see it in his eyes.

And there'd been those remarks about remembering things from 1850 and 1887. They made no sense at all if he wasn't a ghost. Which meant, to put it in totally unscientific terms, that he must be nuts.

But, oh Lord, he couldn't be! Could he? Surely not this man she was suddenly alone with in the middle of nowhere.

Anxiously, she cleared her throat, then said, "John? Now that we've got everything sorted out, may I have my gun back, please?"

"Well...you know, it's really not a good idea, sticking it in your waist the way you do. How about I just keep it safe in my boot for the moment."

That wasn't really a question, so she simply manufactured a smile and tried telling herself she was far more worried than the situation warranted. After all, John McCully looked perfectly normal.

Only everyone knew that looks were often deceiving. And thinking about that, she just couldn't keep her imagination from running wild.

With all the vividness of a feature film, the adventures of an ax murderer started playing in the back of her mind.

"ALANNA?"

John's voice jolted her back to the moment, just as the ax murderer was crawling through her bedroom window.

"Is something wrong?" he said. "You're looking a mite upset."

"No! No, nothing's wrong. I just..." She'd just about worked herself into a panic. She needed a couple of minutes to figure out whether she might actually be in any danger, and what to do about it if she was—a couple of minutes without John McCully standing watching her.

She held out her digitizing glasses to him. "I was just thinking you might like to try these on."

"You reckon I'll see a ghost with them?"

The smirk that accompanied his question irritated the hell out of her.

"There aren't any ghosts here at the moment," she said coolly. "But you might see an image of a mouse or something. If one's been around in the past hour or so," she added, gesturing at the tracks on the floor.

"Really?"

"Yes. If there's been any recent temperature change, you'll pick up the image of whatever caused it."

He put on the glasses and began slowly walking toward the bar, his gaze on the floorboards, while she tried to calm down and think logically.

Would a sane man be wandering around in the wilds of the Sierra Nevadas, wearing clothes from another century?

The obvious answer to that was *no*. But could there be another answer? One that didn't suggest John was a certifiable lunatic?

One idea came to mind, but she immediately wished it hadn't. What if he'd been hiding out up there? What if he was on the loose from some prison?

And maybe he'd gotten those clothes . . . maybe he'd gotten them right here in Chester City. Why hadn't that possibility occurred to her before?

When the gold and silver had run out in this area, people had left a lot of things behind, rather than hauling them through the mountains to another mining town.

There were old clothes in many of the shacks, and if John had been wearing prison garb he'd have been glad to find *anything* he could change into.

She tried to decide whether she'd rather he were an escaped lunatic or a criminal. It was a toss-up.

Whichever he was, though, she didn't want to be alone with him. But since she was, probably the best thing she could do was try to act as if there was nothing out of the ordinary about this situation.

"John?" she called over as casually as she could. "See anything interesting yet?"

"No, not a thing." He took the glasses off and started back toward her.

She could feel her anxiety level rising with each step he took. Trying to act as if nothing were out of the ordinary, she quickly realized, was well beyond her acting abilities.

What she needed was a Plan *B,* but the only one she could think of was simply trying to convince him to leave.

When he handed over her glasses she took a deep breath and said, "Well, I've really got a lot of work to do. And I guess, now that you've seen Chester City, you'll be wanting to get back up to your camp."

"No, actually I don't intend to go back."

His little news flash did nothing for her equanimity. Nervously, she tried another tactic. "John...would you mind if I explained a little about my research?"

"Not at all."

"Well, I realize that since you don't believe in ghosts, you won't think much of what I'm trying to do, but it's very important to me."

He nodded.

"You see, I'm a lecturer at Washoe University, up in Elko. And if I'm ever going to be made an assistant professor, let alone a full professor, I've got to do some significant work. Something I can write an important paper about. And this research is significant, even though *you* might not agree."

She paused, suspecting she was sounding sarcastic without meaning to. When she was nervous, her voice seemed to take on a personality of its own—sometimes, a rather unpleasant one.

"John...look, I really don't mean to sound rude, but your being here is a serious problem for me."

"That so?"

"Yes. The thing is, it's critical to my study that I'm the only one in town, because living people make ghosts nervous. And the more of us there are around... John, what I'm trying to say is that you've *got* to leave. Otherwise, you'll upset the ghosts and they won't communicate with me."

He didn't look convinced. But he *did* look annoyed.

She really *must* be sounding strident. Trying her best not to, she pressed on. "I guess I really shouldn't have said that you've *got* to leave, should I? After all, I don't own the town, so I can't order you out. But I'd really appreciate it if you'd go. For the sake of my research."

It seemed forever before he spoke. Then he simply said, "Sure."

"Sure?" she repeated suspiciously. "But just a minute ago you said you didn't intend to leave."

"No, I said I didn't intend to go back up to my camp. But I've no mind to stay in Chester City."

His words sent a flood of relief through her.

"I have to get to Boston," he elaborated. "You think I could make it there by tonight?"

"To Boston?"

"Yes...it hasn't disappeared in the last little while or anything, has it?"

"No, of course not. But without a car...John, there isn't an airport within two hundred miles of here."

"Really?"

She nodded unhappily. "The nearest town is Branchwater, and it's fifty miles away. It's only a tiny place, too. There's not even a landing strip, let alone a real airport."

"Ah . . . even fifty miles is a little farther than I'd hoped. But . . . would it be *too* far for you to drive me? Just as far as Branchwater, I mean. I could make my way from there, and I'd be glad to pay you for the ride."

She only wished she *could* drive him. She'd cheerfully drive him two *thousand* miles if it meant getting rid of him.

"John, I'm sorry. I'd really like to give you a ride, but I don't have a car here. And the fellow who comes out from Branchwater to deliver my supplies was just here this morning. He won't be back until Tuesday and . . . No, wait, I think I can arrange something."

"Alanna, I don't want to put you to a lot of trouble. I—"

"No, it's no trouble. I've got an SCU—a satellite communications unit," she added, seeing his blank expression. "And I can easily call my research supervisor. You see, he's responsible for my project and . . . well, I'm sure Chris will be happy to arrange a ride for you."

Actually, Chris was going to have a fit when he heard what she wanted him to do, but he *was* responsible for the project. And there was no way she'd get any work done until John McCully was gone. So, like it or not, Chris was going to have to send in the cavalry.

She just hoped there was cavalry to send. There weren't normally many people around campus the last few days in August—particularly not on the Friday afternoon before the Labor Day weekend.

But surely there'd be *someone* Chris could commandeer to come and take John McCully off to... well, it didn't matter, as long as it was away from her.

She took a step toward the door, saying, "You just wait here, John. I'll go and call right now."

"Alanna? Those supplies you mentioned? My throat's as dry as a lizard baking in the sun. So how about I go with you and get a drink?"

JOHN STRODE SILENTLY down the center of the street beside Alanna, thinking that if he weren't dying of thirst he damn well *would* have waited back at the Miner's Saloon.

After the way she'd been *ordering* him to leave town, he was feeling as welcome as a polecat at a picnic.

Hell, he'd been right smart not to give her gun back when she'd asked. She'd probably have turned around and driven him out of Chester City at gunpoint.

He kicked a stone, debating whether he should tell her she had nothing to worry about—that even if he didn't have to get to Boston he sure wouldn't want to stay here with *her*. She was the most uppity woman he'd ever met, and he'd had more than enough of her company.

If she was a fair example, women had gotten a danged sight less mannerly and more ornery over the years.

Of course, Will had told him that women had changed, along with most everything else. Even so, Alanna had taken him by surprise. A woman out here all on her own? What in tarnation kind of father did she have? And what about her brothers?

None of *his* sisters had ever been away from the family home for more than overnight until they'd married. And when his parents had moved to San Francisco, they'd expected his youngest sister, Emma, to go with them, even though she'd already been teaching school. They'd only let her stay behind because she'd agreed to live with him.

He reckoned families must have changed a lot, too. But women...well, he sure hadn't expected to encounter anyone like Alanna DeRain.

He *had* to leave so he wouldn't upset her damned ghosts! What did she think he'd do? Go looking for them so he could say "Boo" and scare them? And hellfire, they were all in her imagination, anyway.

He kicked another stone and told himself there was no point in saying any of that to her—nothing to be gained by *his* being as rude as she was.

Especially not since she'd offered to help him out. Even if she *was* only doing it because she wanted him gone.

"This is it," she said, turning in at a two-story brick building on their left.

He read the faded sign above the door. The Magnolia Lodging House.

"We chose it because it was in better shape than most of the buildings."

She opened the door and ushered him inside. Cold air hit him as he stepped through the doorway.

"It's freezing in here," he said in amazement. It felt like walking out of the August heat wave and into winter in the mountains.

"Surprising what a little portable air conditioner can do, isn't it?" Alanna gestured in the direction of a large metal box that was humming quietly in the corner. "And its battery only needs recharging once a week. Some of the other ones, I've got to charge every couple of days. It would be a lot easier if Chester City had electricity.''

He nodded. He knew some about batteries and electricity. Will had explained how they worked.

"I'll just get you that drink before I call Chris," Alanna was saying. "Friztee? Almondpear? Water? They're all cold. I've got a little fridge behind the bar."

"Uh . . . water, please." At least he recognized *one* of the choices.

Alanna started away and he looked around slowly.

When the Magnolia Lodging House had been operating, the single main floor room would have been a combination parlor and saloon. Now she had it organized as her office—and living quarters, he mentally added, spotting a bedroll stashed in one corner.

There'd be a few small bedrooms upstairs, but they'd be hot as blazes compared to down here. He was just about to comment on that when he heard something directly overhead.

A board creaked. Then a few more. It sounded as if someone was up there, hurrying across the floor.

Looking up, he saw there were wide cracks between the ceiling boards. He couldn't see anyone through them, though, and Alanna had distinctly said she was alone in town. He shot a questioning glance across the bar at her.

She shrugged. "I guess it's from running the air conditioner when the weather is so hot. With these old, dry boards . . ."

"Maybe." He had no idea how an air conditioner might affect old boards, so she could be right. It had sure sounded like someone was up there, though.

He smiled to himself, thinking it was a wonder she hadn't told him it was a ghost, then he resumed his visual inspection of the main floor.

The only window looked out onto the street. The far side wall was covered by a massive brick fireplace, the type with a hearth that extended, on one side, to house a bake oven.

The bar ran along in front of the wall opposite that, and the back wall was almost solidly lined with books. Shelves had been constructed of old bricks and boards that had probably come from one of the collapsed buildings.

Alanna had a big, rough-hewn table set up as a desk. It held more books, papers and several machines.

One, he knew, was a computer. He'd spent a lot of time tinkering with the tiny computer Will had brought along to 1887 with him. Another thing had to be the satellite communications unit she'd mentioned. An *SCU,* she'd called it. The rest he couldn't even guess at.

Wandering over to the shelves, he slowly scanned the books. Every single one seemed to be about ghosts, and the titles all sounded scientific as blazes.

Seeing an entire library on the subject, he almost began to wonder if this paranormalist profession was quite as crazy as he'd initially thought. Could time have shown that ghosts actually did exist?

Absently, he shook his head, certain Will would have thought to mention a major discovery like that.

"Here we are," Alanna said, crossing from the bar with a frosty glass.

After he'd downed the water in one gulp, she gave him a nervous little smile. "Should I get you another before I call Chris, or after?"

"After'd be fine."

She nodded, then took a few steps backward to the table and picked up a silver thing. It was about the size of a small, thin brick and he figured it must be the SCU.

When she began pressing buttons on it he turned back to the ghost books, not wanting to be obvious about listening.

His gaze caught on a separate little collection at one end of a shelf.

Theories of Time Travel was the first title he read. It started his heart thudding a little harder.

The one beside it, by an author named H. G. Wells, was called *The Time Machine.* Then there was *The Use of Quantum Theory in Predicting Time Warp Occurrences Related to Phases of the Moon.*

John stood staring at that one. Will had used the timing of full moons to figure out how to get from 2014 to 1887. In fact, it was the formulas for Will's moon calculations that John had relied on to travel today.

And while Will had said that few people in 2014 believed time travel was possible, *some* did. Was Alanna one of them?

Hellfire, he bet she was. If she believed in ghosts, she'd probably believe almost anything was possible.

He turned to ask her about it, but she'd just begun talking into the SCU.

"Chris, it's Alanna," she was saying. "I've got a little problem I need to speak to you about. As *soon* as possible. I'll wait right here until you call back."

Alanna put the SCU on the desk once more, looking anxiously over at John. His expression seemed strange. But maybe she was only imagining that.

So far, he'd behaved himself. But there was definitely something odd about him, and she'd desperately been hoping to reach Chris on the first try. The sooner she told him she needed help, the sooner he'd send it.

At least she was no longer defenseless, though. Thank heavens he'd insisted she should have *two* guns while she was alone here. Now that the Luger she normally kept behind the bar was snugged securely against the small of her back, she felt safe again.

"Why didn't you just tell him right away?" John asked.

"Excuse me?"

"Your... *research supervisor,* you called him?"

"Uh-huh. Chris."

"Well, why didn't you tell him about my needing a ride while you were talking to him? Why ask him to call back?"

She smiled uneasily. "That was his voice mail."

"What?"

"I got his voice mail. He wasn't in his office so... I wasn't speaking to *him,* John. I was just leaving a message," she added when he continued to look confused. But, Lord, if the man hadn't heard of voice mail, he must have been wandering around in those mountains for the past twenty-five years.

"Oh... so we wait and he calls back."

"Right."

John slowly nodded, although he still didn't look as if he understood. Then he gestured at the shelves, saying, "You've got books on time travel."

"Yes. You're interested in that?"

He gave her the most peculiar smile and nodded again. "Do you know much about it?"

"A fair bit. In fact, I did my thesis on it."

"Really?"

"Uh-huh. That's a copy of it, there." She pointed to a volume titled, *An Analysis of Theoretical Methods of Time Travel.* "I'm afraid it wasn't very original—mostly I just detailed the various theories of how people might manage to move along the time continuum, plus I did some number crunching. I wished I could have gotten information directly from a traveler... but I guess you don't believe *they* exist, either."

"Actually, I do."

"Oh." That was a surprise. Most people who didn't believe in ghosts certainly wouldn't believe time travel was possible. "Well, at any rate, I was never even able to meet anyone who'd actually traveled. There really aren't many people who've managed it. Or even dared to try."

Dared. John tried not to smile at the way she'd said that—as if it took the utmost bravery. But, hellfire, he *had* been brave, doing what most people would never even dream of trying.

He forced his attention back to Alanna, thinking that if she only knew...

"And those who *have* traveled," she was saying, "are so reluctant to talk about it that... well, one reason I ended up working with ghosts is that they're far easier to deal with."

"But you're still interested in time travelers?"

"*Fascinated* would be more accurate. As I was telling you earlier, though, if I want my career to go anywhere, I really do have to produce some significant work. And I'd probably have wasted years if I hadn't switched my focus to ghosts."

"Ah... but if you ever did have a chance to get information from a traveler...?"

"I'd give anything."

John pushed his hat back on his head a little, considering. She'd been uppity as hell earlier. But maybe that wasn't the way she normally acted. Since they'd left the saloon she'd actually been danged nice. And if she hadn't offered to help him get a ride out of here, he might have had a heap of trouble doing it.

Of course, there was Will's warning to keep in mind. But Will had meant telling people who weren't believers, people who'd take him for a madman if he said he was from the past.

Alanna *was* a believer, though. So what would it hurt to let her ask him a few questions? After all, he had nothing better to do until that Chris fellow got here, and he hadn't even called back yet.

"Alanna?"

"Yes?"

"I've got something to tell you that you'll find mighty interesting. Fascinating, even."

"Oh? What's that?"

"When I came into town earlier?"

"Yes?"

"Well, I'd just arrived from the past. I told you before, but I guess you were too upset to be listening. But I was born in 1853. And at the moment I belong back in 1887. I'm a time traveler."

He gave her a smile and waited to see what her reaction would be.

It was to pull a gun from behind her back and level it at the center of his chest.

"What are you doing?" he demanded, shocked that she had a second gun. And that she was pointing it at him.

"*Mr.* McCully, I still haven't figured out who you are or what you're doing in Chester City. But H. G. Wells didn't discover that it was possible to time travel until the 1890s. And nobody else knew a thing about the concept until he published *The Time Machine* in 1895.''

"I knew that," John lied.

"Oh? Well, then, since nobody but Mr. Wells knew anything about it before 1895, why on earth would I believe you could have come from 1887?''

CHAPTER THREE

JOHN STOOD GLARING at Alanna. More precisely, he stood glaring down the barrel of the gun she had trained on him.

Having been in this position once before, he wasn't worried that she had an itchy trigger finger. But she sure had an irritating way about her.

"I think it's time you explained a few things," she said in the same snippy tone she'd used earlier. "Let's start with what you're doing in Chester City."

He dragged his gaze from the gun and looked her in the eyes, thankful that at least she wasn't wearing those annoying goggles. "What would be the point in trying to explain anything when you don't believe a danged word I say?"

"I might believe you if you told me the truth."

"Tarnation, woman! You *don't* believe me when I tell you the truth. I told you I wasn't dead, didn't I? I told you I wasn't a ghost. And did you believe me?"

"That doesn't count. What were you doing in the mountains?"

"I'd just arrived from the past. I'd time traveled through the Broken Hill Mine."

"Stop being ridiculous," she snapped. "My patience is wearing thin."

"Well what do you want me to say? I should never have spoken up in the first place. But you were talking about how much you'd like to meet a time traveler and you didn't realize you had one standing right in front of your nose. So I thought I wouldn't mind helping you out a little and give you whatever information I could. And where did trying to help you out get me? Looking down the wrong end of a gun, that's where."

"Would you *please* knock it off? If you'd *really* just arrived from the past, how would you know anything about airports and planes and cars and—?"

"I have a friend who told me a lot about life in the future. He's from 2014."

"Oh? Well, since you just arrived, the two of you must have struck up a friendship awfully darned fast. Where did you meet him? Was he hanging around the Broken Hill Mine, just waiting for a time traveler to show up?"

"No, he was back in 1887. He still is, in fact. And *he's* the reason I was able to come here—even though people in 1887 don't know about traveling. He's an astrophysicist. And he figured out how to calculate the conditions when time travel is possible through Broken Hill. That's how he got to 1887 and I got here."

John's explanation took Alanna aback. If he *had* met someone who'd traveled to 1887...someone who could have told him how to get here...

Of course, chances were he'd fabricated his story entirely. But it had planted a tiny seed of doubt in her mind. She *was* a scientist, after all. She knew better than to ignore even the most remote possibility.

She let her eyes wander over those old-fashioned clothes of his and the seed began to germinate.

"What's your friend's name?" she asked at last.

"Will Lockhart."

"He's American?"

John nodded.

Keeping her gun pointed at him, she stepped across to the bookshelves and took down the first volume of her directory of American scientists. One eye on John, one on the book, she flipped through it.

Sure enough, under astrophysicists, there was an entry for William Lockhart—degrees from Harvard. But that hardly proved John knew him.

"Anyone could have checked and found the name of an astrophysicist," she said, flipping the book shut.

"Damnation! I reckon you're the most suspicious woman I've come across in my entire life. But I've got something I could show you. If you'll trust me to reach into my pocket."

That seed of doubt was quickly growing, so she nodded.

John stuck his hand into the pocket of his jeans and pulled out a couple of credit cards. "Will gave these to me," he said, holding them out to her. "So I could pay for my plane ticket to Boston and things. He said nobody ever asks if a credit card is really yours."

Taking them, she stepped back to check them over. They'd been issued to William Lockhart, with expiry dates in 2016. She turned them over and checked the signature—an almost illegible scrawl.

Was John McCully telling her the truth? Oh, Lord, if he was...

She ordered herself not to get *too* excited. Because John could still be lying about all of this. He might not be from the past any more than she was. And if he wasn't, she doubted Will Lockhart had *given* him those cards.

"At the risk of sounding even more suspicious," she finally said, "how do I know you didn't meet Will

Lockhart right here in 2014, conk him over the head and take his wallet?''

"Well . . . I reckon I could show you the letter."

"The letter?"

John reached into his shirt pocket and pulled out an envelope that had been folded in half.

He carefully unfolded it, then passed it to her, saying, "It's kind of worn, because I've been carrying it around for a month. Like I was trying to explain to you earlier, I went down the wrong mine tunnel—on my first try at getting here, I mean. I ended up in 1850, by mistake, and had to spend a month there."

Alanna could feel her heart beating faster. John had been in 1850 as well as coming here? Heavens, if he *was* telling the truth, she'd be able to write the most fascinating study of a time traveler ever.

She'd never before heard of anyone who'd run into trouble and ended up in the wrong year, and she couldn't help wondering whether John's experience was unique. If not, were there people who'd ended up in the wrong time and not known how to get out of it? People who'd been trapped in the wrong century for the rest of their lives?

Or maybe mishaps during time travels were normally fatal. Maybe John's having lived through one was highly unusual. She forced her attention from her speculations and focused on the envelope he'd given her.

It was made of the sort of fine, old, hand-laid paper that she'd only seen in archives. The writing on it, she realized, her breath catching, was the same almost-illegible scrawl as the signature on the credit cards.

"Will's penmanship is none too clear," John said. "But it's addressed to his parents. In Boston. You see, he explained to them that he was going to 1887 to keep me from getting killed, but—''

''He went back in time to keep you from getting killed?'' That raised her doubts again. Changing history was against the rules. All legitimate time travelers knew that. John was nodding emphatically, though.

''That's right,'' he went on. ''But it never occurred to Will that he might decide to stay in 1887. So this letter explains why he did, and I promised him I'd go to Boston and deliver it.''

She gazed at the envelope again. ''Yes... yes, I can make out what he's written now.'' The letter was to Hank and Erica Lockhart, with a street address in Boston. And over in the bottom left-hand corner was written, ''Care of John McCully.'' So, incredible as it might be...

''My Lord,'' she whispered, lowering her gun. ''You *are* the real thing.''

''ALL RIGHT,'' Alanna said, excitedly settling into a chair once she'd put a disk in the recorder. ''Start whenever you're ready. The machine is voice-activated.''

John finished off the last bite of the sandwiches she'd made him, then said, ''Where do I talk?''

''Just talk to me. It'll pick up your voice fine. And start at the beginning. Don't leave out a word.''

''There's not all that much worth telling,'' he said, leaning back. As I was saying earlier, Will came to 1887 and kind of saved my life.''

She wanted to stop him right there and find out how Will had known John's life needed saving, but she kept quiet. Better to let him tell the story his own way, then get him to fill in any gaps later.

"But while he was there," John continued, "he fell in love with my sister, Emma, and . . . this is a mite involved. Are you sure you want to hear the details?"

"Yes. Positive."

"Well, even after he fell in love with Emma, Will didn't intend to stay in 1887. He'd asked her to marry him, but he was going to bring her to the future and marry her here. Then our father suddenly took ill and she had to stay to nurse him. Will didn't want his parents thinking he was dead, though, so he felt he had to come back and see them. Then, just at the last minute, we decided I'd come and bring that letter from him. I'd been hankering for a little excitement, so it seemed a right fine idea all-around."

"But how did you meet Will in the first place?"

"Oh, Will and I were best friends when we were boys. In Mountainview, Nevada. It's a mining town over on the far side of Broken Hill. At least, it *was*."

"What?" Alanna could scarcely believe what she was hearing. "You mean your friend, Will, the astrophysicist, is actually from the past, too?"

John nodded. "But he left when we were both only nine—back in 1862. See, a woman arrived in Mountainview from the future. Of course, nobody knew where she was really from at the time, but Will's explained it all. Anyway, when Erica went back to 1989 Boston, where she'd come from, Will and his father went, too."

"My heavens," Alanna whispered. She'd known she was going to get something good, but this might be Nobel-prizewinning material. It would stand the scientific world on its ear.

"And then Will went to the past again," she prompted. "After all that time."

"Right. After twenty-five years. He'd been vacationing in the Sierra Nevadas and detoured to see what had become of Mountainview and . . . well, this part's a bit spooky, but he saw my tombstone. According to it, I got killed on July 25, 1887. So he came back in mid-July to warn me."

"Oh, my."

"Are you all right, Alanna? You're looking danged pale."

"No, I'm fine. Don't stop telling your story."

"Well . . . that's really about all there is to it."

She smiled, trying to keep her excitement under at least a modicum of control. John had absolutely no idea of the importance of his experience.

"You're underestimating how interesting your story is, John. Why, you could probably tell me so much I'd run out of disks. What about going down the wrong mine tunnel, for example? You said you had to spend a month in 1850."

"Right, I did. See, when Will came through Broken Hill he saw a shimmering blue light and got to 1887 by following it. But I saw *three* lights. It's a mite puzzling, but I reckon it had something to do with us starting out from different centuries. Anyway, I followed the wrong light the first time."

"Which led to 1850."

"Uh-huh. But there was no real harm done. Luckily, the moon was in the right phase when I ended up back there, so I could use Will's formula to figure out how to get myself a second try."

"*You* figured out how to try again? Oh, I hope that didn't sound insulting," she added quickly. "I just meant that the calculations have to be awfully complex."

John shrugged. "Way back, I studied to be an accountant. Turned out to be too boring, but I've always been good with numbers."

Good, Alanna thought, couldn't possibly cover it. John must have been born a mathematical genius, considering the kind of formulas astrophysicists worked with.

"At any rate," he was saying, "I had Will's formula to go on. We'd played around with it some when he was explaining how time travel was possible. Then I reckon I was just lucky to pick the right mine shaft this time."

"But you were in 1850?" she said, steering the conversation back to that. "What happened there?"

"Oh...well, I went off to Georgia and spent a couple of weeks on a plantation outside Savannah. Actually, it was the strangest coincidence you could ever imagine, but I came across another time traveler there. He was from 1993, and the plantation owner was plum determined to keep him in 1850."

"Oh, my," Alanna whispered again. Never mind just a Nobel prize, maybe what she wrote would be good enough for a Pulitzer in journalism as well.

The SCU beeped.

She ignored it, and smiled at John once more. "Did this other traveler tell you *his* story?"

"Uh-huh. We got to be pretty good friends while I was there. In fact, I helped him escape back to 1993."

Heavens, this just kept getting better and better!

The damned SCU beeped again.

John looked at it curiously. "Is that someone trying to reach you? Your Chris fellow calling back, maybe?"

"Could be." She reached over and grabbed the unit.

"You all right?" Chris's voice greeted her.

"Just fine."

"Well what's the problem? Your message sounded like you were scared spitless."

"Oh, it turned out to be nothing. Solved itself."

"Jeez, Alanna, I figured a serial killer had dropped in for lunch or something."

"No, nothing like that. Let me call you back, though, okay? I'm right in the middle of something."

"Yeah, well don't rush off too fast. If you've got anything that can't wait until after the weekend, we'd better get to it now. Sue and I are going camping. In fact, she's picking me up any minute. And she made me promise I wouldn't take my unit along, so you won't be able to reach me again until Tuesday."

Alanna hesitated, glancing at John, weighing her options. To get his entire story recorded would take days. But if Chris sent someone this afternoon, she'd have only a couple of hours. And once John was gone, he'd be gone forever.

She could practically see her Nobel prize and her Pulitzer sprouting wings and flying out the window. Besides, she really would be imposing on Chris when he was practically on his way...*and* imposing on whoever he made drive down here. And since it was a long weekend, all the planes would probably be full, anyway.

Heavens, why hadn't she thought about that before? If she sent John off, he'd undoubtedly spend the next few days stuck in some poky little airport eating vending machine food—a fate worse than death.

"Alanna?" Chris interrupted her thoughts. "Sue's just arrived. She's outside honking. You sure you're not desperate for something?"

"No...no, it'll wait. Have a good weekend."

Once she'd put down her SCU, Alanna shot John a guilty smile. She didn't meet his gaze, though, and he could tell something was amiss.

"Didn't sound like that was your Chris fellow, after all," he said at last.

"Well...actually, it was."

He tipped his chair back on two legs and waited, trying to suppress his suspicions. "I didn't hear you ask him about a ride," he finally pressed.

"No...well, I'm afraid I was forgetting about something. This is the Labor Day weekend."

"It's what?"

"It's the Labor Day weekend coming up...that's a *long* weekend."

"And just exactly what's a *long* weekend?" Will had told him people only worked five days a week in 2014, but what the hell was Alanna getting at?

"Well, Monday's a holiday, as well as Saturday and Sunday."

"So?"

"So a lot of people travel on long weekends. Especially this one, because children go back to school after Labor Day. So...well, I suddenly realized you wouldn't be able to get a flight. There won't be any empty seats on the planes until at least Tuesday."

He leaned forward, his chair thudding back down onto all four legs and his blood beginning to simmer—despite the air-conditioning. He might be from the past, but he wasn't a dunderhead. And he sure as blazes didn't cotton to being taken for one.

"Let me get this straight," he said slowly. "You just *decided* that there wouldn't be a single empty seat on any plane flying to Boston."

"Well...there won't be *all* that many flights from the airport nearest here. And I know there won't be any empty seats."

"You just *know*. Without checking."

Alanna shrugged.

"How about you make a few calls and see for sure?"

"It's too late."

"What?"

She shrugged again. "Chris was just leaving for the weekend. I won't be able to reach him again until next week."

"And he's the *only* person you could ask to drive me? What about your father? Or one of your brothers?" If they knew Alanna was talking about spending a few nights alone in town with a strange man, they'd be on their way with shotguns. So surely one of them would be *glad* to come get him out of here.

"John, my parents live in Oregon. That's where I grew up. And my brothers work in New York and Kansas City. There *really* isn't anyone else I could impose on. It would mean coming all the way out here, then driving all the way to the airport and...well, aside from that, everyone will have plans for the weekend."

He eyed her suspiciously. In 1887, people went out of their way to do for others. But now she was telling him there was *nobody* she could ask? The future wasn't looking like such a great place, after all.

"But I think I mentioned," she was going on, "that Frank Bronkowski, who brings my supplies, will be coming on Tuesday. And I'm sure we'll be able to arrange something with him. I'm *positive* we will. At least he'd take you back to Branchwater with him, and you could get another ride from there. So...well, you're *only* stuck here until then."

John could feel his blood quickly heating to a boil. This was Friday. And Friday to Tuesday was five whole danged days. Then he glanced at Alanna's recording machine and he knew. "You decided you *wanted* to keep me here, didn't you!"

"No, that's not it. I—"

"Oh, yes it is! You want to do some scientific probing, don't you?"

"No, I—"

"Oh, yes you do. An hour ago, you couldn't get rid of me fast enough. You were ordering me out of town like a danged sheriff. But that was before you found out where I was from, wasn't it? Before you realized I could offer you something you'd give *anything* for. The chance to pick the brain of a time traveler."

"No, it's just that I realized you're either going to be stuck here for the weekend or in some dumb airport. And you'll be far better off here. We can bring down a mattress from one of the bedrooms upstairs and you can sleep right here, where it's comfortable and—"

"Don't you try to hornswoggle me, Alanna DeRain! I *told* you I wanted to get to Boston and I trusted you to help me do it. Hell, I'm a month late delivering Will's letter already. His parents have got to be thinking he's dead."

"Oh...I didn't realize it was so important you get there fast, but if—"

"And you don't care, either, do you? No. All you care about is keeping me here so you can use me."

"I don't want to *use* you. I—"

"Yes you do. I haven't forgotten a word you said. When you were doing your thesis, you couldn't find a time traveler to talk to. And now that you've met one, you figure on holding me prisoner. Hellfire, you'd be as happy as a hound who'd treed a coon if I *did* tell you so much you ran out of disks."

"John, I really don't—"

"Oh, yes you do. To be a professor you've got to do some significant work. You've got to write an *important* paper. Well, it's danged well not going to be about me." He shoved himself up out of his chair and started for the door. "I'm not sitting here for a *long* weekend," he threw back over his shoulder, "so you can study me like some . . . some insect under a microscope. I'm a man, not a danged bug."

"Where do you think you're going?" Alanna demanded as he opened the door.

When he glanced back she was standing, hands on hips, glaring at him. *She* was glaring at *him!*

"John, it's a million degrees outside—and in every other building in town. And . . . well, maybe I made a slight error in judgment. If I did, I apologize."

"*Maybe* you made a *slight* error in judgment?"

"Yes. Slight. By not realizing how urgently you wanted to get to Boston. I was focusing so much on your story that I wasn't thinking about your friend and his parents. But I really didn't exaggerate about the planes being full. There probably wouldn't have been an empty seat. And . . . well, what's done is done and you're welcome to stay here in the Magnolia for a few days. And if—"

"I'd rather stay in hell," he snapped, slamming the door.

JOHN HADN'T WALKED far down Main Street before realizing Alanna had been right. The day was growing late, but it hadn't cooled down even a mite. It *was* a million degrees—and it seemed hotter than ever after coming out of the heavenly cold of the Magnolia.

Hot as blazes or not, though, he'd be hung for a horse thief before he'd stay under the same roof as that woman. She wanted to use him, plain and simple. And if her only interest in him was as a research subject...

But what was he thinking? He wouldn't want her having an interest in him at all—regardless of how good she looked and how enticing she smelled.

He wasn't quite sure when he'd first caught a whiff of her perfume, but it smelled good enough to practically start him drooling.

Still, it didn't matter. Not when she was an untrustworthy, conniving, underhanded...he couldn't come up with words bad enough. But what she was exactly didn't matter, either, because he'd never be setting foot near her again.

All he had to do was figure out how to get himself that two hundred miles to the airport without her help.

Except that, after a few seconds, it occurred to him that he didn't even know what direction the danged airport was. Which meant that he'd *have* to ask her, sooner or later. But it was damned well going to be later. He might be stuck here until Tuesday, but he sure wasn't going to be stuck with her.

Gazing ahead to where the mountains rose beyond the town, he decided the only sensible thing to do was go back up to the mine. Aside from the Magnolia, it was the only place he knew of that was cool. And he'd need shelter for the next few nights. Deserts were as cold at night as they were hot during the day.

He detoured down a side street and began checking inside the shacks. After he'd poked his head into half a dozen of them he found what he was looking for—an old bedroll someone had left behind.

Hoisting it over his shoulders, he started out of town, his load making him hotter yet. By the time he'd walked all the way up to the mine he was drenched in sweat.

"Danged woman will be the death of me," he muttered, stepping into the dim coolness of the main tunnel. "I'll end up with pneumonia."

Deciding he'd better just find a good place for the bedroll, then go back out and sit in the sun until his clothes dried, he walked a little farther, until the light from outside was so dim he could scarcely see. Then he tossed the roll down, untied it, and brushed away a few small rocks to make a smooth surface to spread it on.

Just as he was finishing up he heard a voice. The words were faint, but he could make out every one of them.

"'Bout time you showed up again," a man had snapped.

"Took the back trail," a second man was saying. "It was slower, but I figured she coulda looked up and seen me."

In the near darkness of the tunnel, John gazed slowly along its walls. The voices had to be coming from a secondary shaft, but how was the sound carrying?

He spotted something that looked like it might be a small opening near the ceiling and moved closer to it.

"So whatcha find out?" the first man asked.

"Well, all them books are 'bout ghosts. And all her notes and everythin', too. I think she's some kinda ghostbuster, or somethin'."

"Who the hell would wanna bust ghosts outta a ghost town?"

"I dunno, but that's what everything's about."

"You sure she ain't here after our gold?"

"Don't look like it. She's got a lotta stuff she wouldn't need for that."

"Maybe it's some kinda cover."

"Well . . . could be. But listen to this other problem. Before I got done checkin' through her things, I looked out and seen her comin' down the street. And there was some guy with her."

"What? Who?"

"I dunno. Some big guy—was wearin' a cowboy hat and a gun. And, hell, I sure wasn't stickin' around to ask who he was. I just charged upstairs. And I'll tell you, it was hotter 'an hell up there."

"But you could hear 'em?"

"Didn't get to hear much. A damned board creaked under my foot. I figured one of 'em'd come barreling up to check, so I got the hell out—went down that old fire escape out back just as fast as I could."

The first man swore, loud and long, then said, "You figure this guy was just droppin' somethin' off?"

"Uh-uh. More like somebody dropped *him* off. I couldn't see no car nowhere."

The first man swore loudly again, then muttered, "Damn the luck. We can't be hangin' around here forever. We gotta get rid of her fast. And it woulda been a helluva lot easier when she was alone."

John waited, but that was it. In the ensuing silence, he leaned against the wall of the tunnel and tried to figure out who the men could be. And what made them think there was gold in Chester City. That wasn't something people ever left behind when they moved on.

Whoever those guys were, though, they obviously meant to cause Alanna trouble . . . or did they have more than trouble in mind?

In 1887, getting rid of someone could refer to running them out of town, or it could mean killing them. But what exactly did it mean in 2014?

He pondered that question for a while, but he had no way of knowing the answer.

So what was he going to do? Leave that irritating, untrustworthy, conniving, underhanded woman down in Chester City on her own? To protect herself from whatever those characters had in mind?

That idea didn't set right with him, although he didn't know why. Maybe it was because Alanna reminded him a mite of his sister, Emma. He'd wager Alanna was the youngest in her family, just like Emma, and every bit as used to having her own way.

Not that Emma was as annoying as Alanna, but if she'd been in Alanna's shoes today, she'd probably have acted just the same. And he was right fond of Emma, despite the way she sometimes coaxed and cajoled and was as stubborn as a mule about getting what she wanted.

So, if Alanna *was* the baby of her family, it wasn't *entirely* her fault that she'd ruffled his feathers. It was just the way she'd learned to be, the same as an eldest son, like him, had learned to be responsible and dependable.

Finally, he wandered along to the tunnel's entrance and back out into the blistering heat.

There was no sign of the men he'd overheard, but he knew they were still around somewhere. Unless they were already on their way back to town.

John tilted his hat a little lower on his forehead and started off. Alanna might not be his kin, but if that was Emma down in Chester City, he'd want someone there to look after her.

CHAPTER FOUR

ALANNA EVENTUALLY GAVE UP trying to work and switched off her computer. Her concentration was totally shot. Every two seconds her thoughts wandered back to John McCully, and each time they did, she felt more like kicking herself.

Never, in all her life, had she mishandled a situation so badly. She'd had an honest-to-goodness time traveler willing to talk to her, and she'd blown it. And, she did have to admit that it had been extremely nice of him to offer.

She'd misread him entirely when she'd taken him for a lunatic. Actually, he was a very interesting man. What little he *had* told her had been absolutely fascinating.

But then she'd gone and blown the opportunity of a lifetime by not being entirely up-front with him. If only she'd thought about those darned planes being full sooner, she could have explained the situation *before* Chris had phoned back. Then John wouldn't have thought she was trying to... What had he said? *Hornswoggle* him, that's what he'd thought she'd been trying to do.

Guiltily, she admitted to herself that he'd been right. And now he was going to be spending the weekend out there in that heat, which made her feel even more guilty.

She'd sell her soul for a second chance with him. But given the way he'd stomped off to heaven knows where, her odds on ever seeing him again had to be lower than the odds on lightning striking the same place twice.

The only things that might make her feel a little better were loud music and double chocolate fudge ice cream. She grabbed the radio remote and clicked it on. Music blasted out as she headed for the fridge. She was halfway across the room when she thought she heard a knock on the door.

She stopped in her tracks, her heart suddenly beating triple time. As far as she knew, there was only one other person within fifty miles of Chester City. And every once in a blue moon, lightning *did* strike twice.

Praying that what she'd heard really had been a knock, not an erratic drummer on the radio, she hurried to the door, yanked it open...and there stood John McCully. It was all she could do to keep from jumping for joy.

"Come in out of the heat," she said, trying not to sound *too* thrilled to see him.

He didn't move an inch. "What's that noise?"

"The music, you mean?"

The look he gave her could have come from her grandfather. Obviously John didn't appreciate her music any more than he did.

"I'll turn it off." She hurried over to the worktable, grabbed the remote again and hit the Power button.

John stepped inside, staring at the radio, then at the remote.

"It's a radio remote control," she explained. "It lets me turn it on and off from over here. From anywhere within about a hundred feet away, actually. Even from another room, through a wall. But of course, here, I only need it for this one room."

She realized she was babbling, but couldn't help herself. John nodded, then shut the door.

She eyed it for a second. The old lock was broken, but if it hadn't been she'd have locked up behind him and swallowed the key for good measure. As things were, she was forced to make do with a smile. "I'm glad you came back, John. It gives me the chance to apologize for being so...pushy."

"Ah...well...that's all right. I reckon I should apologize, too. I wouldn't normally raise my voice to a woman. It's just that I've got a good idea how worried Will's parents must be."

"Then why don't you call them? I was going to suggest that earlier, but you left before I had the chance."

"Call them? You mean on that?" He glanced over at her SCU.

She nodded. "It's compatible with regular phones."

"And I can talk to somebody all the way in Boston?" He gave her a questioning smile. "Will told me how that worked, but I've never done anything like it before."

"Well, if you let me look at their address again, I can get the phone number for you."

John fished Will's letter out of his pocket, then followed her over to the SCU and watched her every move as she called Boston information.

Jotting down the number, she handed him both the slip of paper and the SCU. "Just press the button with number one on it, then six, one and seven, then these numbers."

Tentatively, he pushed the buttons, then looked startled. "It's making a noise."

"It's just ringing at their end." She tried not to smile, but he was as excited as an overgrown kid. A *very* overgrown kid, she silently amended, letting her gaze linger on his broad shoulders.

When she'd first laid eyes on him, she'd thought he was the most magnificent specimen of an apparition she'd ever seen. And now that she knew he wasn't an apparition...well, she couldn't deny he was an extremely attractive man, any more than she could deny being glad he'd come back.

But she was *only* glad because it meant she'd have another chance to ask about his time traveling. So why had merely gazing at him started a tiny curl of warmth in the pit of her stomach? Apparently, her hormones weren't entirely convinced of that *only reason* theory.

She let her gaze linger on him a little longer. Hot, sweaty and primordial, his shirt clung to his back the way a shirt would on a man who'd done a hard day's physical labor. But rather than being a turnoff, it gave him the kind of rough-and-ready appeal that had been almost entirely citified out of the twenty-first-century's male population.

Forcing her eyes from him and looking around the Magnolia, she recalled her offer to let him stay with her. Her rather *hasty* offer. If she'd considered the idea for more than three seconds, she doubted she'd have suggested it.

Of course, his staying here wouldn't *really* be a problem. She never let her hormones rule her head. And if John didn't look like a man who might show up in her wildest dreams, the prospect of spending the next few nights alone with him wouldn't be even a touch disconcerting.

He cleared his throat, breaking the silence, and she glanced back at him.

"Is that Mr. Lockhart?" he was asking into the SCU. "Mr. Hank Lockhart? Yes? Well, I expect you're going to find this mighty tough to believe, sir, but this is Will's friend, John McCully. Yes, sir, that's right. John McCully from Mountainview, Nevada. And I'm calling to talk to you about Will."

"I'LL DO THAT, SIR," John said, tucking the slip of paper with the Lockharts' number on it into his pocket. "I'll call again just as soon as I get to Boston. Definitely. Early next week. I gave Will my word I'd deliver his letter in person, and I'll be there just as soon as I can. Yes, goodbye for now." He put down the SCU and looked over at Alanna.

She was standing by the bookshelves, leafing through a volume, pretending she hadn't noticed that the conversation had ended. But he knew she'd been hanging on to every word he'd said to Will's father. Every word concerning how he'd gotten here from the past, at least.

He hadn't forgotten for a minute about that danged *important* paper she wanted to write. And he sure hadn't come back so that she could start picking his brain again. The last thing he was going to be was the subject of anyone's research.

She could try sweet-talking him all she wanted, but the only information he intended to give her was about those characters up in the mine. He just wasn't sure how to go about it without frightening the blazes out of her.

She glanced up from her book and smiled at him. It made him wonder how many women in 2014 were as beautiful as she was. He'd soon find out, though. Once he got away from here, he'd start to see what the future was really like.

"Did you get everything explained?" Alanna was asking. "Your friend's parents won't be worried about him now?"

"No, they were mighty surprised to hear he'd be staying in 1887 for a spell. And even more surprised that he was marrying my sister. But at least they know he's all right."

He could see Alanna had a million questions on the tip of her tongue. She just couldn't wait to get back to her scientific probing, so he gestured at her book collection and beat her to the punch. "All these books about ghosts. You never did tell me what makes you think there are ghosts in Chester City."

"I don't just think so, John, I *know* there are. I've been communicating with a lot of them. Two in particular."

She looked deadly serious about that, so he asked, "And what do ghosts *communicate*." Between the books and all her equipment...well, the more he thought about it, the less certain he was becoming that her ghosts were only figments of her imagination.

"Oh, mostly they talk about their own lives," she was saying. "And about the times and places they lived."

"So that's what you're doing here? Collecting historical information?"

"That's part of it."

"But why here? Aren't ghosts all over the place?"

His question made her smile. "No, they're not all over the place. Most people never appear as ghosts after they die. But you often find materializations in old mining towns."

"Why?"

"Because there were so many violent deaths. What with saloon brawls, claim jumping, and men stealing each other's gold, there were frequent killings in towns like this.''

"I know. Mountainview, where I grew up, *was* a town like this."

"Oh... of course. So you know precisely what I mean."

"No, not precisely. I know what Chester City would have been like in my time, but I don't know why violent deaths back then mean there are ghosts hanging around now."

"Well, let me try to explain. You see, ghosts are basically emotional images."

"I thought you said they were auras."

"No, I said they give off auras. That's what my digitizing glasses pick up, even when the ghost remains invisible to the naked eye. But the ghost itself is an emotional image."

"Which is?"

"It's kind of like a vibration in the air. And the reason there are an unusual number of ghosts in a town like this is because traumatic deaths are more difficult for spirits to cope with. So a victim often comes back to where he was killed, seeking peace."

"He comes back as a ghost."

"Yes, exactly. Because if a person dies suddenly— unexpectedly—he won't likely have experienced proper closure to his life."

"Proper closure to his life," John repeated. He didn't fancy sounding like a fool by asking too many questions, but he didn't understand half of what Alanna was saying. "And do they find this peace they're seeking?" he ventured.

"Some manage to. That's another part of what I do. I talk with them about their condition and try to help them come to terms with what happened to them. You see, they're here because they're still trying to cling to the living world. But if they come to terms with their death, they're able to pass on to where they'll be at peace. So, if I can, I help talk them through to the other side.''

John tipped his hat back thoughtfully, trying to get her explanation straight in his head. It sounded danged crazy, but maybe he just needed time to let it sink in.

In the meanwhile, he had to get around to warning her about those characters up in the mine. And he still hadn't thought of a way he could do it without scaring her, so he was just going to have to come straight out with it.

''Alanna, you didn't ask why I came back here.''

''No, I guess I didn't.''

''Well, it was because I overheard a conversation.''

''Oh?''

''Yes, I went back up to the Broken Hill Mine after I left here. I was planning on spending the night there. But when I got there . . . Alanna, there were a couple of fellows in the mine and they were talking about you.'' He paused because she was looking at him very strangely.

''Did you *see* these fellows, John?''

''No, they were in a different tunnel. I only heard them.''

''Oh.''

''Look, Alanna, I realize this is going to frighten you, but you've got to know about it. They don't want you in Chester City and they were talking about how they were going to get rid of you.''

''Yes, that's not surprising. It often happens.''

He eyed her uncertainly. She didn't look the least bit frightened. "What do you mean, it often happens?"

"Well, in a situation like this, there are often one or two ghosts who resent a paranormalist disturbing the status quo."

"The what?"

"The status quo... the existing state of affairs."

He nodded, then backed up a notch. "But these weren't ghosts. They were men."

"I thought you didn't see them."

"No, I told you, they were in a different tunnel."

"You're sure of that?"

"Of course. What other explanation could there be?"

"They could have been ghosts, John. Unless ghosts *want* to be seen, they're generally invisible. I'm surprised they let you hear them, though. Was it dark? The part of the mine you were in?"

"Yes, but—"

"That explains it then. They didn't notice you."

"Alanna, they *weren't* ghosts! They were men. I know what men sound like."

"And do you know what a ghost sounds like?"

"No, but—"

"Well, they can sound precisely like real people. Just think about it for a minute. Where would a couple of *men* have come from? And why would they be up in the mine talking about getting rid of me? Who would possibly care that I'm here?"

"The two guys I overheard, that's who! They're worried that you're here looking for some gold. *Their* gold, they said."

"John, nobody's been here looking for gold since before 1900. So, *obviously,* you heard ghosts."

"The hell I did! They said they had to get rid of you fast because they couldn't be hanging around here. And what important thing would a couple of ghosts have to go off and do? Go haunt another town? And they said something about not seeing any car here. How would ghosts know about cars?"

Alanna shook her head, smiling so smugly it infuriated him. "John, ghosts aren't blind, deaf and dumb. They're aware of what's been going on in the world. And there could be any number of reasons they don't want to stay here long. What you heard were *definitely* ghosts, still thinking in terms of when they were alive, back when there *was* gold here."

He simply glared at her. She thought she knew everything. That was something else that reminded him of his little sister. Maybe Emma only taught children, not university students, but there must be something about teaching . . . maybe when you added it up with being a youngest child. . . .

"Those brothers of yours," he said. "And your sister. They're all older than you, aren't they."

"Why . . . yes. What made you ask?"

"It's not important." What *was* important was that he couldn't talk to this woman for more than five minutes at a stretch, without her making him as touchy as a teased snake. Yet here he was, back in town, because he'd been worried about what might happen to her. All the time he'd spent in that danged hot sun today must have addled his brain.

"At any rate, then," Alanna went on, "getting back to the ghosts, there's really not much to worry about. Ghosts very seldom actually manage to harm people."

"Alanna, will you just listen to me for a minute? Just let me tell you exactly what they said, all right?"

"All right."

He repeated the conversation, as close to word for word as he could.

"So one of them," he concluded, "was right here inside the Magnolia, looking through your things. Now, why would a *ghost* do that?"

"Well, ghosts are no more psychic than people. So, if he wanted to know what I was up to, he'd have to come in and check."

"But he ran upstairs to hide when he saw us coming. Why would he hide? You just told me that ghosts are generally invisible."

"He was probably afraid I'd put on my digitizing glasses and be able to see him."

"Damnation! The guy made boards creak overhead. You heard that yourself. You're not going to tell me ghosts weigh anything, are you?"

"No, but they *can* cause noises. Either intentionally or by being clumsy. Would you like me to explain how that works? The scientific principles, I mean?"

John shook his head and decided not to even bother asking why a ghost would have used the backstairs to escape. What was the point when the woman thought she had answers to everything?

"You know," she was saying, "I think the problem is that you just don't realize how lifelike ghosts can be. But there's a way we can fix that. After dinner, I'd like you to go someplace with me."

BY THE TIME THEY LEFT the Magnolia Lodging House the sun had disappeared into a red haze behind the peaks of the Sierra Nevadas. The air had already grown cooler, and a purple gray dusk was rapidly blanketing

Chester City. Night fell so quickly in the desert that it would be dark in no time.

Alanna snuck a sidelong glance at John, trying to see if he was still annoyed with her. Yes, she decided, he was—unless, of course, he normally wandered around with his jaw clenched.

If she didn't so desperately want him to tell her about his time traveling, she'd just steer clear of him for the next few days. The two of them had turned out to be about as congenial as an alley cat and a pit bull.

And she had a feeling that no matter how badly she wanted to hear his stories, she might be out of luck. Once he'd told her about that conversation in the mine, he'd gone into a Silent Sam routine. Over dinner, getting him to say more than two words at a time had required a major effort.

He clearly didn't like her. In fact, every single thing she said or did seemed to bother him. He didn't even like her clothes. Her twenty-first-century shorts had obviously offended his nineteenth-century sensibilities.

He'd finally asked her what those *things* were called. And even after she'd explained that *everyone* wore shorts, he'd looked so disapproving that she'd changed into jeans and a T-shirt.

Of course, the two of them hadn't gotten off to the greatest start—her holding him at gunpoint and all. She could understand how that might have upset him a touch. But, after all, she'd had no idea who he was. For all she'd known, he might have been another Jack the Ripper.

But as for the rest, he'd simply overreacted. When she asked him to leave Chester City she clearly explained why she wanted him to go. But he'd still taken it as an insult.

Then, practically the very next second, he was having a fit because she wanted him to stay. The man had positively mercurial mood swings.

And her insistence that the voices he'd heard belonged to ghosts had really ticked him off, too—even though she was an expert on ghosts, while he knew absolutely nothing about them. That hadn't carried any weight at all with him.

Of course, he *was* from 1887. Which probably made him certain he knew more than any female possibly could. Lord, but she was glad she hadn't been born in the days of the Old West. The idea of being a woman back then was unthinkable.

The sound of quiet music suddenly broke the silence of the evening. Taken aback, John stopped in the middle of the street to listen. "Someone's playing a piano," he finally said, glancing uncertainly at Alanna.

"In the Miner's Saloon," she told him. She didn't seem as if she thought there was anything even a mite unusual about it.

He listened for another moment, then realized it was the same haunting melody that he'd heard when he first arrived in Chester City. Then, too, it had been coming from the Miner's Saloon. But when he'd met Alanna assumed *she* was the one he'd heard playing.

Gazing along the street, he could see there was faint light glowing inside the saloon. "You told me you were alone in town," he said, turning to her again.

"I am . . . except for the ghosts."

"The ghosts. You're saying there's a piano-playing ghost in there?"

Alanna merely gave him a little shrug, then began walking once more.

He started after her, drawing his Colt.

She glanced at it, then up at his face. "That's not necessary, John. And it wouldn't do you any good, anyway. Ghosts are already dead."

He stuck the gun back into its holster, feeling like a danged fool, and followed her through the squeaking doors.

Just as they had earlier in the day, the final notes of the song died as he stepped into the gloomy interior. And the saloon was every bit as empty as it had been the first time he'd been there.

Before he even turned toward the piano he knew what he'd see. And he was right. Undisturbed dust lay thickly on its surface. Its cover was pulled down over the keyboard and the piano stool sat empty.

"I don't understand this," he murmured to Alanna.

"Give me a minute." She looked over at the piano and said, "Mary? Roy? I've brought a friend I thought you'd like to meet. His name is John McCully and he's from 1887. He's traveled through time to come here. I know we've never talked about that being possible, but it is. And John really does live in 1887. He grew up in a town called Mountainview, just over on the other side of Broken Hill."

John glanced uneasily from the piano to Alanna. He'd started off thinking she was crazy, but she'd pretty well convinced him that she wasn't. Now, though, she sure started him wondering again. What kind of sane person talked to the air?

"Close your eyes for a minute, John," she whispered.

He closed his eyes. It was probably best to humor her.

"Now imagine you're in a saloon in the past. It'll make them feel more at ease with you."

He made a halfhearted attempt. Suddenly, he felt a rash of goose bumps crawling over his body. He could almost hear the murmuring of voices, could almost smell beer and perfume in the stale air.

"Mary? Roy?" Alanna was saying again. "I thought you'd *want* to talk with someone from your own time. I was so sure you'd materialize that I didn't even bring my glasses." She paused for a minute, then whispered to John, "Look."

He opened his eyes, looked across the room again, and his mouth went dry.

There was a vapory cloud floating in front of the piano. Gradually, it condensed into the shapes of two people.

A woman was sitting on the piano stool. The dust had vanished, and the cover was open. Her fingers rested on the now-exposed keys.

Behind her stood a man, one hand on her shoulder. They were both gazing steadily at Alanna and John.

He couldn't take his eyes off them. With each passing second they became lifelike.

The woman was in her early twenties, and had light brown hair pinned up the way his sisters always did theirs. She was pretty, in a frail, somehow melancholy way, and was wearing a gray dress that he thought was silk. It looked almost exactly like one Emma often wore to church.

The man was somewhere around thirty, with dark hair and a handlebar mustache. He looked like a prosperous businessman. His black suit had a long, well-styled jacket, and the detachable collar of his white shirt gleamed as if he wore a fresh one daily. Beneath his jacket, John could see a Colt, much like his own, strapped to the man's hip.

Both he and the woman were a mite fuzzy around the edges, but they were so close to looking real it was danged amazing.

"I'm glad you decided to join us," Alanna said, walking slowly across the room.

John followed her, half suspecting she'd somehow conjured up the images, half certain he was actually seeing ghosts.

Alanna stopped at the piano and glanced at him. "John, I'd like you to meet Mary Beckwith and Roy Hardin."

Roy extended his hand and John reached to shake it. His own hand went right through Roy's... or the image of Roy's... or whatever in blazes they were dealing with here. Whatever it was, it had the hairs on the back of John's neck standing on end.

"Sorry," Roy muttered. "I forget sometimes."

He rested his hand on Mary's shoulder once more. When it didn't go right through, John began trying to figure out how in tarnation things worked with ghosts. He could already see he was going to have a heap of questions for Alanna.

"Mountainview," Roy said. "Alanna said you were from Mountainview."

John merely nodded. He was still so surprised he wasn't sure his voice would work. Roy's voice, though, sounded just like a live man's. How in blazes could that be?

Mary looked up at Roy, and gave him a private little smile. "That's the town you almost settled in, isn't it? Before you decided on Chester City?"

"That's right." His eyes lingered on Mary for a second, then he looked at John again. "I almost bought a saloon in Mountainview a few years back. When my father died, I inherited some money, and decided to come west and invest in a business.''

John nodded again, wondering when *a few years back* was. "Uh...which saloon?" he managed to ask.

"The Dry Gulch."

"Really? Well so help me, Moses, that's the dangedest coincidence I've ever heard of. My father was the barkeep at the Dry Gulch for years. Bert. Bert McCully.''

"Did you meet him, love?" Mary asked.

"No, I don't believe I had the pleasure. It was back in 1889 that I was looking to buy, John.''

"Ahh...my parents moved to San Francisco a few years before that." John glanced at Alanna and she smiled serenely at him, as if all this talk of things happening so long ago didn't seem strange to her. But hellfire, it seemed mighty strange to him, and *he* was the time traveler here.

He desperately wanted to know what year Roy thought it was now...or, what year he'd died in was probably the proper question, but he had a feeling it might not be polite to ask.

"Well, I did seriously consider buying the Dry Gulch," Roy was saying, "but then I came to Chester City and decided to settle here and build the Magnolia, instead.''

"The Magnolia Lodging House? Where Alanna is staying?''

"Uh-huh. It was a good decision, too. A bed in a hotel room went for four dollars a night. Then I had the money from the bar, as well. The Magnolia's main floor was packed most every night, good whiskey was eight dollars a bottle, and those miners could down liquor faster than a mountain stream disappears into a sink-hole."

"You must have made a fortune," John said.

"I did right fine, John, and I didn't spend it as fast as I made it, like a lot of folks. Especially not after Mary came to town. I wanted to save for the future, then. For *our* future," he corrected himself, glancing at Mary and trailing his fingers gently across her shoulder.

She reached up and rested her hand on his.

"But things didn't work out," Roy continued quietly. "And saving did me no good, because the future . . . well, the future was suddenly taken away."

"Don't get yourself upset, love," Mary said gently.

"No, no I won't. I just want to say one more thing. You know," he continued, focusing on John, "I always hated folks who wanted to give advice, but I've told Alanna this and I'll tell you, too, because it's so important. Don't live your life giving too much concern to the future, because you can't count on having one."

"Oh, Roy," Mary murmured, patting his hand. "The past is past. Don't always be thinking of what might have been. Think of what we *did* have."

"If only we'd had it for longer," Roy murmured.

Mary gazed up at him, her eyes luminous, and even though she and Roy were ghosts—and strangers to him—John felt a lump in his throat.

Mary and Roy somehow made him think of his sister Emma and Will. Not in appearance. The couples didn't look alike at all. But Emma and Will had fallen so deeply in love that their feelings for each other seemed to surround them. They didn't go a minute without touching each other or smiling.

But where Emma and Will radiated happiness, the love surrounding Mary and Roy was clearly filled with melancholy.

"Forgive us," Mary said, glancing at Alanna. "I'm afraid we're not very good company tonight. Roy's been feeling a mite pensive today."

"We should leave, then. I didn't mean to impose."

"No, no, you didn't." Mary smiled at John. "We were honored to meet you, Mr. McCully. Alanna was right. It *is* nice to talk with someone from the old days. Sometimes, it almost seems as if they never really existed."

"Let's go, John." Alanna rested her hand on his arm and he could feel the heat of her touch through his shirt. He and Alanna were so warm and alive while Roy and Mary... Lord Almighty, but this visit had given him the spookiest feeling.

He tipped his hat to Mary, nodded at Roy and turned to leave with Alanna. And then he noticed something that set his heart pounding.

A man was standing outside, looking in at them. His face was clearly illuminated by the moonlight and his expression was one of pure menace.

CHAPTER FIVE

JOHN BOLTED OUT of the Miner's Saloon so suddenly that Alanna simply stood watching the doors swing for a moment. Then she gave Roy and Mary a final quick wave and hurried into the night after him.

He was gazing intently down the street. It was awash with the full moon's silvery light, but all she could make out were the shapes of buildings. "What?" she asked. "Do you see something?"

"Not anymore. There was a man staring in through the window at us—at *you* mostly, I think. But he'd disappeared by the time I got out here."

"John, it would have been a ghost, not a man."

"No, he looked too real."

"As real as Roy and Mary?"

John turned and glanced at her, his expression uncertain. "Alanna . . . I'm finding all this plumb hard to accept."

"I know. But there *are* a lot of ghosts here. I've talked to almost twenty so far. What did this one look like?"

"Big. Mean. I only got a quick look at him."

"Well, big and mean would describe half the ones I've seen." And now John had seen one of them, too—in addition to Roy and Mary, whom she'd known would cooperate by materializing for him. But why had this other one let John see him?

The only reason she could think of was that it had wanted to frighten him . . . or both of them. But why?

John shook his head, saying, "I don't know how you can have been staying in this place alone. There could be ghosts right in the same room with you and you wouldn't even know it. Just like I didn't know Roy and Mary were there at first."

"I've got my glasses."

"But you don't always have them on. And knowing there could be *things* watching us, anytime they like, makes me danged uneasy."

"They can't hurt us."

"Alanna, you don't know that for sure, do you? No, you *don't*," he went on when she said nothing. "You told me ghosts *seldom* manage to harm people. You didn't say *never*. And those guys I heard in the mine didn't sound like they'd think twice about hurting you. Maybe it was one of them who was out here. Or maybe there are *more* of them who don't want you disturbing their status quo."

"Well, whoever it was is gone now."

"You're certain about that?"

She shrugged, wishing she'd brought her glasses along so she *could* be certain there was nothing lurking. She hadn't felt anxious on the streets of Chester City other nights, but John's nervousness was contagious.

His presence, though, was reassuring, so that kind of balanced things out. She wasn't used to having a man worry about her, and she had to admit it made her feel a little special.

"Let's get back to the lodging house," he said, starting off.

She hurried a few steps to catch up. "You've decided to stay there with me, then?"

"That still all right with you?"

"Yes, of course."

"Good, because I don't fancy sleeping up in the mine with invisible company."

They continued along the street in silence, Alanna absently wondering what her parents would think if they knew she'd invited a strange man to stay with her. They both had pretty old-fashioned values when it came to their daughters.

Of course, by rights, John should have *really* old-fashioned values, so there was probably no reason for concern. And, just at the moment, she liked the idea of not being alone. It would be nice to have someone in the Magnolia with her. Someone *alive*. And big and strong and masculine . . . with protective instincts.

When they reached the lodging house, she opened the front door.

"Maybe you should start keeping that locked," John suggested.

She glanced back at him. "I would, but the lock's broken. I tried to fix it my first day here, but I couldn't."

"I'll have a shot at it."

"Well . . . if you like. There really isn't much point, though. There's no one to lock out. Until you arrived, I was the only one in town."

"Just you and the ghosts."

"That's right. And a lock wouldn't slow them down. They can go through walls as easily as doors."

"Well that's a comforting thought," he muttered.

Using the moonlight to see, Alanna lit the two oil lamps she generally used at night—to save on batteries.

"There," she said, putting one on the end of her worktable and the other on the bar. "Locked door or not, everything's just fine in here."

Then she realized it wasn't.

The room was unusually quiet. The air conditioner wasn't running, although she knew she'd left it on. She went over to the corner and flicked the On/Off switch a couple of times.

"Something wrong?" John asked.

"Yes. The air conditioner's stopped. And it can't be the battery because I just charged it yesterday. Do you know how these things work?"

He gave her a dim look. "I'd never even seen an air conditioner before today."

"Oh...of course. Well, I guess I can open it up and have a look, but I'm not much of a mechanic."

She pulled out her screwdrivers from behind the bar, put one of the oil lamps on the floor in front of the conditioner, then sank down and began unscrewing the front panel.

"Here, I've got it," John said when she started to pull it off.

He lifted it away and she sat staring at the unit's insides. Rather, she sat staring at the large space that shouldn't have been there.

"Can you tell what the problem is?" he asked.

She nodded, even though she couldn't quite believe her eyes. "The battery's gone. Somebody's taken it out."

NOTHING WAS MISSING from the Magnolia except the air conditioner's battery. Nothing, at least, that Alanna noticed during her quick search.

None of her papers or books had been disturbed and both the fridge and her computer, thank heavens, were still operating.

"That's it," she told John, switching the computer off again. "I might discover something else later, but it looks as if all they took was that one battery."

"Why in blazes would anyone take that?"

"Who knows? But I do know it's going to be awfully hot in here tomorrow."

"Can't you call someone? Get a replacement?"

"It's the long weekend, remember? Chris is gone. And Frank, who brings my groceries, was heading off someplace, too. And we'd never get a supplier to deliver way out here, so we're out of luck for the moment." She paused. "Do you think someone would actually have taken it just so we'd roast? I mean, there's the odd ghost with a warped sense of humor, but this would be *extremely* warped."

"Alanna, whoever the *someone* was...it couldn't really have been a ghost, could it?"

"Why not?"

"Well, mostly because when I went to shake Roy's hand there was nothing to shake. So if you don't have a real hand how could you get that thing apart and take out its battery?"

"Mental energy."

John closed his eyes and exhaled a long, slow breath. "What in tarnation," he finally said, looking at Alanna again, "is mental energy?"

"The power of mind over matter?" she tried. That obviously didn't make it any clearer.

"Okay...think of it this way. What ghosts lack in physical power, they can sometimes make up for in mental power. So they can often move something by thinking it to move. That's how Mary plays the piano. It isn't really her fingers pressing the keys."

"It's her mind?" John looked extremely dubious.

His expression didn't change, even after Alanna nodded. "Ghosts *think* things to move?" he said at last.

"Definitely. Poltergeists are the best example. They do it all the time."

"Poltergeists. I suppose you've proven they really exist, too, have you?"

"Well, not me personally. But, yes, it's been proven they exist. They're really nothing more than noisy, mischievous ghosts."

"You know what?" John said.

"What?"

"I don't want to hear another danged word about ghosts."

"All right." She gave him her best smile. "Why don't we talk about your time traveling, instead?"

"Maybe later." He took off his hat and put it on the bar. "Right now, why don't we go upstairs and find me one of those mattresses you mentioned earlier."

Telling herself they'd *definitely* have that talk later, she followed him across the room.

The heat from the day always remained trapped on the second floor and in the stairway. When they opened the door to the stairs it rushed to envelop them. They started up into it, each carrying a lamp.

Walking behind John, Alanna found it impossible not to think about what a tall, well-built man he was. There might not have been gyms back in the Old West, but people had certainly been in good shape.

At least, John McCully had been...*was,* she corrected herself. Every move he made revealed the outline of solid, lean muscle beneath his clothes.

By the time they reached the top of the stairs, she caught herself imagining what he'd look like without his shirt on.

Quickly, she assured herself the heat had to be affecting her. Her imagination would never normally run wild like that about a man.

She forced her attention to the task of finding a mattress for him—not much of a task when there were four beds in each of the stuffy bedrooms, all complete with old mattresses.

They eliminated the ones filled with straw. It had pretty well rotted over the years. But the ones stuffed with rags were still usable—assuming the user didn't mind lumps and mustiness.

Roy Hardin, she decided, hadn't been exaggerating about doing "right fine" with the Magnolia. Four dollars a night for a bed, four beds to a room, would have been an awful lot of money back in the 1890s. Or an awful lot of gold dust, as the case had been in Chester City.

They checked out the rag-filled mattresses and decided which was the least mouse eaten, then discovered some sheets and blankets in an old wardrobe.

"And what's in here?" John asked, poking his head into the bathroom at the end of the little hall. "Oh, a bathtub. All hooked up to a pipe."

Alanna nodded. "There's a big cistern full of water on the roof. And the tap still works. I tried it when I first got here. But the water that comes out is so rusty I haven't used any."

They turned back toward the bedrooms. Just outside the bathroom was a single hall window. Its glass long gone, it led out onto a rickety old staircase. In the little space between the bathroom and the window, a big old bucket still hung on the wall, the word Fire painted on it.

"Roy had a social conscience." Alanna gestured at the stairs. "This is the only building in town that had a fire escape—unless there were others that have rotted away."

"It needed a fire escape," John muttered. "It's a wonder there's never been spontaneous combustion up here with all those dust-dry mattresses."

For half a second, hearing John say "spontaneous combustion" seemed strange. Then she realized it was probably an old, old term. People had known for centuries that dry things could self-ignite in too much heat.

His pointing out that the mattresses were prime candidates, though, did nothing for her equanimity. Before he'd arrived, she'd felt completely at ease in Chester City. But one day here and he had her anxious about malevolent ghosts wanting to get rid of her. And now he'd started her worrying that the Magnolia might go up in flames—taking all her research data along with it.

"Would you like me to carry one of these downstairs for you, too?" he asked, yanking a mattress off its bed frame. "Be more comfortable than that bedroll I noticed you have."

"No, my sleeping bag is fine, thanks." She left it at that, but she wouldn't use one of the mattresses if her life depended on it. She suspected they had creatures living in them.

Since John's choice was between a mattress and the bare floor, though, he probably figured a mattress was the lesser of two evils.

"I can help you with that," she offered when he began to hoist it onto his back.

He gave her a look reminding her that women didn't do that sort of thing in his world. "Just go ahead and light the stairs so I don't fall down them."

She backed down ahead of him, holding the oil lamp up at shoulder level and praying he *wouldn't* fall. She'd rather not have six-foot-plus of solid muscle landing on top of her.

Once downstairs again, they set up his bed at the front of the Magnolia—the opposite side of the area from where she'd been spreading her sleeping bag.

It made the room seem far smaller. It also made the thought of going to bed a little unsettling. She wasn't used to sharing a room with anyone, let alone a strange man. She reminded herself he was a strange man with old-fashioned values. Then, as a delaying tactic, she asked if he'd like coffee.

He glanced over at the fireplace where an old wrought-iron kettle still hung in the hearth. "I'd have to bring in an awful lot of wood to get water boiling. You figure it's worth it?"

"No, no, I've got a microwave behind the bar."

"A what?"

"It's a kind of oven. Almost anything can run on batteries."

"Yeah? You mind if I look at the gadgets you've got back there?"

"No, of course not."

He followed her over and began examining the little bar fridge and microwave while she poured water into a couple of mugs.

The space behind the bar seemed to shrink once he was in it, and he was so close to her that she could feel his body heat and smell the faint scents of shaving soap and tantalizing maleness.

She concentrated on pouring water from the bottle, trying to ignore the way her pulse had begun racing, and silently swearing at her darned hormones. Why were they insisting on acting up around John McCully?

He might be a nice enough man...well, he might be a *very* nice man, but not for her. Not for *any* sane woman in 2014. His nineteenth-century attitudes were closer to Stone Age thinking than to the twenty-first century.

Besides, he obviously wasn't the least fond of her. Those protective instincts of his had only come into play because of the situation, not because of her, specifically. And even if he *had* liked her, he was merely passing through. Just a tourist, not only in her ghost town but in her entire century.

"I'd been hankering for a little excitement," he'd told her. So he'd decided to come to 2014 "for a spell" and take that letter to Will's parents.

After however long a *spell* was, though, he'd be going back to 1887. He was a drifter—in both time and space. Exactly the kind of man any intelligent woman would steer clear of. So why in heaven's name didn't her hormones seem to be taking that into account?

She put the mugs into the microwave and switched it on, then looked everywhere except at John until the timer pinged.

"That's how you make coffee now?" he asked when she spooned it into the mugs of boiling water.

"Sometimes. It's called instant and it's handy, but most people don't think it tastes as good as the real thing. Do you take milk or sugar?"

He shook his head, so she handed him a mug and waited for him to move.

He didn't, just stood looking at her. His eyes seemed even darker in the flickering light of the lamp, and she found his expression extremely unnerving.

Apparently, some of the ways men looked at women hadn't changed in the past hundred years. And whether John McCully liked her or not, he was obviously very much aware that she was a woman.

Maybe, she thought uneasily, she shouldn't be putting quite so much trust in his "old-fashioned" values.

When he finally raised the mug to his lips, she recalled that one of the first things she'd noticed about him was how sensuous his mouth was. It was undoubtedly something she should put out of her mind, but she couldn't quite manage to do that while she was looking at him.

"It tastes fine," he said, lowering the mug again. "Different, but fine."

"Glad you like it. But why don't we go and sit down...and talk," she added. Surely, over a relaxing cup of coffee she could get him talking about time travel.

"Good idea," he said. "I'm really curious about Mary and Roy. You can tell me about them."

DEEP DOWN, ALANNA KNEW that sitting on John's mattress with him wasn't a wise idea. He might not particularly like her, but now that she'd begun to have doubts about his intentions...well, she wasn't naive enough to think that lust had much to do with like.

But he'd walked straight over to the mattress, saying her wooden chairs weren't comfortable, so she had to choose between being companionable or standoffish. And he was far more likely to be forthcoming about his experiences if she was friendly. She just wouldn't be *too* friendly.

She sat down on one end of the mattress—so close to the edge that she'd be at risk of slipping off if she wasn't careful.

When John sank onto the far end and leaned back against the wall, she relaxed a little.

"So..." he said, taking a sip of coffee, "you were going to tell me about Mary and Roy."

"I thought you said you didn't want to hear another word about ghosts. I thought maybe you'd like to tell me—"

"I meant nasty ghosts," he interrupted. "Like the ones in Broken Hill and the one that took your battery."

"You're convinced they *were* ghosts, then?"

He shrugged. "Let's say half convinced. We're not talking about those ones, though, remember? It's Roy and Mary I'd like to hear about."

Alanna nodded slowly. She didn't mind telling him their story, but heavens he was a stubborn man. He was so obviously avoiding talking about his time traveling that she'd bet he was *still* thinking along that same ridiculous vein—that by writing about him she'd somehow be *using* him.

"Before you begin," he said just as she was about to, "first tell me how ghosts... I'm not quite sure how to put the question, but even though *my* hand went right through Roy's, he and Mary seemed to be touching each other."

"They were, in a way."

"In a way?"

"Yes, *you* couldn't touch him because he has no substance. But another ghost . . . in a limited sense, two ghosts can touch."

"Limited how?"

"Well, their senses aren't nearly as keen as living people's. Because the life force is so diminished, a ghost can't feel or smell or see things nearly as vividly. In fact, some people argue that ghosts don't *really* have any residual senses at all, that they simply recall how it felt to be alive."

"And what do you think is true?"

"I'm not sure. But even if they don't still have their senses, they believe they do. And they go on acting as they would have before they died. But they're aware of experiencing only shadows of what they once would have. It's quite . . . heartbreaking sometimes.

"Anyway," she continued quickly, before her emotions got the better of her, "as far as Roy and Mary are concerned, you already know the beginning of their story. Roy came to Nevada from back East to start a business. And he ended up settling in Chester City and building the Magnolia. That was in the spring of 1890."

"And Mary?"

"She didn't come here until near the end of 1894. She was from back East, too, but she came to Chester City to spend Christmas here that year. Her brother owned the Miner's Saloon and she was visiting him. Then, once she was here, she and Roy fell in love, so she stayed on."

"But what happened? Their last names are different, so they didn't get married, did they?"

"No. They intended to. In fact, the wedding was planned for July 7, the Sunday after Independence Day. Everyone in town was invited and Mary had a lace gown shipped all the way from New York City. It was so beautiful...*is* so beautiful. It's still in a trunk in the attic of the house her brother owned. She took me up to see it one day and...oh, it made me so sad. She cried, John. After all this time, she cried when she showed me that dress she'd never gotten to wear." Alanna paused, her throat growing tight.

"But what happened?" John prompted after a moment. "How did they come to die?"

"Roy was shot to death. In a brawl right in the Miner's Saloon. It was on the Fourth of July, 1895. The Independence Day celebrations got out of hand and people began shooting off their guns."

"They usually get out of hand.... I mean, back in my time, they usually do."

"Yes, well, they did that night. And the shooting led to some fighting and Roy was shot to death."

"So, he's an example of what you told me about. Someone who met a violent death, which means he didn't...how did you put it, exactly?"

"He didn't experience proper closure to his life. And coming to terms with his death has been particularly difficult for him because he was so happy at the time."

"That makes it worse?"

"Yes, when someone is really looking forward to the future, it makes their death even more traumatic. And his left him with too many residual emotions to work through. But until he manages to do that, he'll remain unable to pass over to the other side."

"Ah...and what about Mary? How did she die?"

"She literally died of a broken heart. She wanted to be with Roy again so badly that it killed her."

Alanna swallowed hard, then went on. "And now they're trapped in limbo—in that never-never land between life and death. Roy simply isn't able to pass over and Mary refuses to pass on and abandon him. She says she lost him in life and she isn't going to lose him again in death."

"But... isn't there something you can do to help them?"

"I've been trying to. I've been talking to Roy and trying to help him accept the fact that he's dead, that he just isn't going to get to live out the rest of the life he should have had."

"And it hasn't done any good?"

"Not so far. And the two of them... Oh, John, talking to them makes me feel like a grief counselor. They're so *real*. You saw that. It's as if they were both still alive but in mourning—for all the experiences they'll never share. And for the children they wanted but won't ever have."

As she finished speaking, Alanna gave John a sad little shrug. Even in the dim light he could see that her eyes were filled with tears. It gave him a crazy urge to take her in his arms and console her.

Instead, he put his hands behind his head and leaned back against the wall, wondering what in tarnation was the matter with him.

Maybe there was something in the air that was affecting him strangely. *Something* certainly was, because he realized he was beginning to feel things for Alanna that were plumb difficult to understand.

He'd come to the future for adventure, not to get... smitten, that was the word. He hadn't come to 2014 to get smitten the first day he was here—by the first pretty woman he laid eyes on.

Especially not a woman who'd tried to run him out of town. Especially not a woman who was ornery and argumentative and irritating as all get-out.

She had more faults than a dog had fleas. Despite that, though, there were things about her he couldn't help liking. The way she was so danged concerned about Roy and Mary, for one. And the fact that she didn't frighten off easily. Hellfire, most of the women he knew would have had the vapors at the thought of a ghost.

In fact, he was beginning to realize there were so many things he liked about Alanna that it wasn't smart to be staying here in the Magnolia with her.

But how could he leave her on her own tonight, having overheard that conversation in the mine? And after he'd seen that fellow—or ghost, if that's what it had been—staring menacingly into the saloon at her?

Not leaving her on her own, though, was an entirely different thing from taking her in his arms to console her. If he put his arms around her, he sure wouldn't want to stop with just consoling her. But he reckoned she'd be mighty fast about stopping him from doing anything more.

Then he'd feel like a danged fool again, and it wasn't a feeling he liked.

She picked that moment to smile at him, and her lips looked so soft he couldn't help imagining how they'd feel if he kissed her. Lord Almighty, those crazy feelings seemed to be coming faster and stronger by the minute.

"What are you thinking about?" she asked.

He shrugged and backed his thoughts up a mite. "I was thinking that I came to the future because I wanted an adventure. I wanted to see the big cities with their bright lights, to ride in a plane and try driving a car.

And here I am without even a horse to ride, sitting with a couple of oil lamps for light, in a town that doesn't look much different than what I'm used to—except that it's a danged sight more run-down and less lively."

"Ghosts are generally a quiet lot," Alanna told him with a small smile. "And Roy and Mary were particularly subdued tonight."

John nodded slowly. That Roy had looked sadder than a bloodhound's eyes. Surely there had to be *some* way of helping him, but if Alanna couldn't do it . . .

His gaze drifted to her bookshelves and he began thinking about his *own* problem. He still had to figure out a way to get back home. At least he'd be able to work on finding a solution while he was stuck here.

"Alanna?"

"Yes?"

"You wouldn't mind my looking at some of your books, would you?"

"The ones on ghosts, you mean?"

"Uh-uh, the ones on time traveling. I'd like to see what you scientists have to say about it."

"Well," she said slowly, "I don't mind your looking at them. But I'd like you to wait until after you've told me about your own experiences. Otherwise, your story is liable to get contaminated."

"Get contaminated?"

"What you read might color your memory . . . influence the purity of your recall."

"Ah," he said, wondering if she'd just *intentionally* hornswoggled him. If he wanted to read those books, he was apparently going to have to answer at least some of her danged questions.

He'd have to consider whether he was willing to do that or not. Even that smile of hers wasn't going to make him a mite more partial to being her research subject. And if he didn't look at *her* books on time travel, there'd be others he could look at once he got to Boston.

Glancing over at hers again, he tried to decide how badly he wanted a gander at them.

The sooner he could figure out the solution to his problem, the sooner he could stop worrying about it.

That was assuming, of course, he'd be *able* to figure out the solution.

He leaned back against the wall once more, knowing he *had* to. Because if he couldn't manage to come up with the answers he needed, he was going to be in a heap of trouble.

CHAPTER SIX

JOHN JOLTED AWAKE, rolling off the mattress and grabbing his gun belt from the floor beside him. He had his Colt half drawn before he realized where he was.

Alanna was across the room, sitting up in her bedroll. And she'd called his name—sounding frightened. That's what had wakened him.

"What?" he demanded, looking around in the morning light for whatever had scared her. He couldn't see a thing out of the ordinary, so he pushed his gun back into its holster.

"What?" he repeated, trying to ignore the fact that she was nearly naked. He'd slept in his clothes, but she had on some sleeveless thing that was clinging to her like a second skin.

"I saw a man outside the window," she whispered. "Not a ghost, but a man. There wasn't even a hint of fuzziness."

"He was looking in?"

"I'm not sure. He might have been, then ducked out of sight, but he could have been just walking by. I only caught a glimpse."

"Just walking by?" John muttered, reaching for his boots and yanking them on. "That doesn't sound too danged likely. It was probably the same guy I saw last night. I told you he wasn't any ghost."

Shoving himself up, he started for the door, strapping his gun on.

"John? Where are you going?"

He reached for the door handle with his left hand and the butt of his Colt with his right. "To find him, of course."

Before Alanna could say another word, he opened the door, stepped out onto Main Street, then yanked the door shut again.

Slowly, he scanned the street, watching for movement. There wasn't any, but the guy couldn't have gone far.

He started cautiously along the front of the Magnolia, his gun at the ready, but he'd only taken a few steps before he heard the door open behind him.

"John?" Alanna whispered.

He looked back as she hurried along to where he was standing. She'd thrown on a blouse and those little yellow shorts she'd been wearing yesterday, and was heading after him—her gun stuck in her waistband again, after he'd *told* her that wasn't a safe way to carry it.

He took the time to remind her of that, then told her to get back inside. After all, she wasn't even fully dressed—at least in his opinion. But he might as well have saved his breath, because she completely ignored his order.

"Just exactly what do you think you're doing with that gun?" she demanded.

"I told you what I'm doing. I'm going to find out who that guy is and what he's up to."

"And you really figure you need your gun drawn?"

"Until I find out who I'm dealing with, yes. Now get back inside."

"Don't be ridiculous," she snapped. "I want to know who we're dealing with, too."

Her glare told him arguing was pointless, so he pushed her in against the wall behind him and started off again.

They crept along Main Street, hugging the fronts of the buildings, and John was just beginning to think they'd headed in the wrong direction when he heard a man's voice. He swore silently. Unless the guy was talking to himself, there were at least two of them.

"Wait right here," he whispered to Alanna, then started forward again. As ornery as usual, she followed along on his heels.

The voice had come from inside the old bakery. The building no longer had a door, and John paused for a moment beside the opening, gesturing Alanna not to move. Then he stepped quickly into the doorway, cocking his Colt and saying, "Get your hands in the air."

Three very startled people threw up their hands and stood staring at him.

Feeling a mite foolish, he lowered his gun. Whoever this guy was, he looked as timid as a mouse. He certainly wasn't the big mean character who'd been peering into the Miner's Saloon last night.

And the other two were probably his children. A boy of about twelve and a girl who was maybe sixteen. At least her face looked about sixteen. Her body looked like . . . well, he hadn't seen anything like it since he'd visited Maisie's saloon in Dodge City, known for its dancing girls.

He tried to drag his eyes off her but it was tough. He'd thought Alanna's clothes were revealing, but this girl was wearing shorts that he doubted could be legal and a top so tight he didn't see how she could breathe without ripping the seams.

She smiled at him. For some reason, it made him uncomfortable—the way he'd feel if a rattlesnake smiled at him.

"Uhhh...we didn't mean any harm," the man said nervously. "We were just looking around."

"John?" Alanna said.

He glanced at her. She'd come in without him noticing.

"John, they're just tourists. Every now and then, someone detours off the main highway to see the town."

"That's exactly what we did," the man said quickly. "Our car's parked down a side street."

"So you can put away your gun, John," Alanna added pointedly.

"I *know* that," he muttered, shoving it into its holster. Lord Almighty, she was a bossy woman. He just couldn't understand how the things he'd started to like about her kept making him forget that.

"Sorry to scare you," he said, looking back at the man. "We had a mite of trouble last night, and I thought you could have been—"

"No problem. Mistakes happen. Look, I'm Roger Tanner." The man extended his hand. "And this is my son, Mark, and my daughter, Libby. But we weren't around last night. We're just passing through this morning—on our way to Reno. Made an early start so we could stop and have a look around here. The kids have never seen a ghost town before. But I guess we've seen enough, right, kids?"

Neither of them answered him.

"You a real cowboy, mister?" Mark asked, staring at John's gun.

He nodded.

"You two live here?" Libby asked.

"No," Alanna told her. "I've been here for the summer, doing some research, and John is just passing through."

"I kind of got stranded here for the long weekend," he elaborated.

"Oh . . . then you aren't like . . . a couple?"

When John shook his head, Libby gave him another smile. This one made him even more uncomfortable than the first.

"Where were you heading?" she asked. "When you got stranded?"

"No place in particular. I was just looking to find an airport."

"Reno has an airport. We could give you a ride, couldn't we, Daddy?" She glanced at her father.

Roger Tanner looked at John's gun. "Well . . ." he said slowly.

"I'd be glad to pay you," John offered. "Tell him I'm not a criminal or anything," he added, glancing at Alanna.

"He's not a criminal or anything," she said.

John squared his shoulders and tried to look as honest and upstanding as possible. The prospect of a ride, coming straight out of the blue like this had to be fate at work. Then he glanced at Alanna once more and couldn't help wondering if fate knew what it was doing.

He *did* want to get on his way. But if it meant leaving her on her own here . . . with those characters from the mine still around someplace. . . .

"Daddy?" Libby said. "Just last Sunday the minister was talking about doing unto others, remember?"

Her father eyed her with a trapped expression. "Well," he finally said again, "I guess we could help you out, John."

"Why, that'd be right kind of you. If you'll just give me a minute to get my hat, I'll be ready to leave whenever you are."

He turned and headed back to the Magnolia, grabbed his hat, then paused, thinking about that face he'd seen in the window last night.

Nothing had actually *happened,* though. Not the whole time he'd been in town. Well, there'd been the thing with the air conditioner, but Alanna figured that had just been a ghostly practical joke.

And if those guys he'd overheard in the mine *did* try anything, she had two guns. Besides, she wasn't his responsibility. And leaving her on her own here would only be leaving her the way he'd found her.

Of course, if there were no empty seats on the planes to Boston, he'd be stuck in Reno. But spending the weekend in a real city would be a danged sight more exciting than sitting around a ghost town. So, he'd just be on his way and—

"Well," Alanna said from behind him, "I guess this is goodbye."

He turned toward the door.

She gave him a forced smile. "Have a good trip to Boston. And I hope you enjoy the rest of your time in 2014. It was...it was very interesting meeting you, John."

"It was very interesting meeting you, too."

She nodded, then stepped out of the doorway so he could leave.

ALANNA HEARD A CAR drive down Main Street but didn't bother going to look out. She knew it was Roger Tanner and his kids—taking John off to Reno. What had she expected? That he'd change his mind and stay?

She sank into one of the chairs beside her worktable and gazed across at her recorder, unable to keep from wishing he hadn't left...and not only because she wanted to hear the rest of his story.

But that was the *main* reason, she told herself firmly. Besides, there was no point in wishing for things that couldn't be. She was never going to see John McCully again, so she'd better just forget about him and make do with what he'd told her yesterday. If she was lucky, it would be enough to let her write a half-decent article.

She was composing an opening sentence in her head when someone knocked on the door.

Before she could get up, it opened and John stood looking at her. "I hope you don't mind too much," he said, "but I didn't go with them."

Mind too much? She didn't mind *at all*. In fact, seeing him standing there was making her absurdly happy.

John *could* be annoying, but she'd been very glad of his company last night. Having him with her had made her feel far less nervous than she would have—given all the strange things that had happened yesterday.

And this morning, if Roger Tanner *hadn't* turned out to be a harmless tourist...well, she might not like the idea of John brandishing his gun so freely, but he wasn't a bad man to have around. Not bad at all.

"I got so excited at the prospect of getting a ride," he said, "that I *completely* forgot you'd said there'd be no seats available, that I'd just end up spending the rest of the weekend in the airport. But when I remembered—''

''I didn't think you believed me.''

''Well . . . I asked the Tanners what they figured.''

''And they said?''

''Well, Libby seemed positive there'd be the odd seat free. She really thought I should go with them.''

''Mmm, that's a big surprise.''

''What do you mean?''

Alanna eyed John curiously, realizing he really didn't know. Maybe there weren't many women in his century as precocious as the Tanner girl.

''What?'' he pressed.

''I meant, I think Lolita was interested in you.''

''Her name's Libby.''

''Oh . . . right, Libby.''

''And what do you mean by interested in me?''

''Interested in you as a *man*.''

''Really?''

''Yes, really.''

''Oh, I don't think so, Alanna.''

She eyed him again. He honestly *didn't* think so. She found that extremely refreshing. Most men she knew assumed every woman under eighty was interested in them.

''Hellfire,'' John was saying, ''I must be close to twenty years older than Libby.''

Alanna merely shrugged. When a man looked like John, a lot of women wouldn't let a minor thing like age bother them.

''And anyway, Roger Tanner said exactly what you'd told me. That I probably wouldn't get out of the airport until Tuesday. Which meant there didn't seem much point in going. So, since I'm still here, what do you usually do with your days?''

"With my days," she said slowly, buying a minute to think. As glad as she was that John hadn't left, she still had work to do. And it was work she had to do on her own, so she hoped his staying wasn't going to cause complications.

"Usually," she finally told him, "I wander around and see if I can find any new ghosts to interview. But there's no point in doing that today."

"No?"

She shook her head. "They'll have gone into hiding. It's like I told you yesterday, living people make them nervous, so—"

"I thought you were just saying that. Trying to convince me to leave."

"No...no, it's true. I wasn't just saying it." Not that she *hadn't* been trying to convince him to leave, but that had been yesterday. It was amazing what a difference a day had made.

"Anyway," she went on, "Roger Tanner and his kids will have sent the ghosts into hiding, so I guess I'll—" Her gaze flickered to the recorder again, but she bit her tongue.

As much as she wanted to hear all of John's story, she had *some* pride. She wasn't going to beg him. She'd made it clear how important it was to her, and if he was bound and determined not to tell her anything more, she'd darned well live with that.

"You guess you'll do what?" he prompted.

"I guess I'll go down to the Miner's Saloon and see Roy and Mary. They're always willing to spend time with me, so I'll have another go at trying to help Roy work through his feelings."

"Oh...well, I don't reckon I'd be any help there. But that's *all* you'll do? Just spend some time with them, then come straight back here?"

She nodded, wondering why he was so interested.

"Well, maybe I'll wander on down with you. I could do with a walk. But then I'll just find something to do here. I wonder..."

"Yes?"

"Would you mind if I played around on your computer a mite?"

"Oh, John, I hate to say no, but you don't know anything about computers and—"

"Sure I do. I know a lot about them. My friend, Will, brought one with him when he came to 1887. It was a little one he called a pocket computer."

She nodded, imagining how astonished John must have been when he first saw a computer.

"But even though it was little," he continued, "it could do really amazing things."

"Yes, I guess an astrophysicist would have the most advanced technology."

"That's exactly what Will said it was. And he showed me how to use it to figure out all kinds of things."

"You must be a natural-born hacker."

"A what?"

"A natural computer genius. And in that case, I don't mind your using mine at all."

"You're sure?"

"Sure. If your friend trusted you with his, I can't imagine you could do any harm to my old thing."

ALANNA WIPED her forehead, thinking she'd kill to have the air conditioner working again.

The Magnolia had gotten incredibly hot during the day, and it hadn't cooled down much since sunset. She was tempted to open the door and let some air in, but the lamplight would attract insects . . . and possibly lizards and snakes.

Deciding she'd rather be hot than risk playing hostess to an assortment of wildlife, she glanced over at John.

The heat didn't seem to be bothering him—probably because he wasn't used to air-conditioning. In fact, she doubted he was even aware of how hot it really was. He didn't seem conscious of anything except whatever he was playing at on her computer.

She'd asked him what he was doing, but he'd given her a vague, meaningless answer. Whatever it was, though, he was utterly engrossed in it.

He'd been working away when she'd gotten back from seeing Roy and Mary, and he was still going strong—so involved that he'd barely taken time to eat dinner.

"John," she finally said, dragging his attention from the screen. "I wonder if you'd mind going outside for a couple of minutes? So I can get ready for bed?"

"Sure." He glanced at the computer's clock, surprised to see how late it had gotten. "Don't rush," he added. "I want to stretch my legs a mite."

Pushing himself up, he headed out into the night and started down Main Street. He figured he'd just walk to the end and back—making sure he didn't see anything worrisome.

Of course, if there were ghosts around, they could be standing three feet away and he wouldn't see them. That, in itself, was worrisome.

But when it came to those two characters in the mine, he still wasn't convinced they were ghosts at all. Whoever they were, though, they'd said they wanted to get rid of Alanna *fast*. So if they came up with a plan, they'd be trying it soon. Maybe he'd be wise to stay awake tonight and keep an eye out.

Nearing the Miner's Saloon, he could hear Mary playing the same sad song as last night. It started him thinking about her and Roy's predicament.

Earlier in the evening, Alanna had said she still hadn't managed to get anywhere with helping Roy. John shook his head, considering the problem. He'd always thought people were either alive or dead and it just didn't seem right for folks to be caught in between like that.

Alanna knew all about ghosts, though, so if she wasn't able to help Roy out, there couldn't be much *he* could do.

Or could there?

He hit the end of the street and turned to start back, thinking on an idea. He hadn't quite solved his own problem yet, but once he did...

Of course, he'd have a far easier time solving it if he could study those books of Alanna's.

But to do that, he'd have to tell her more about time travel, and he still hadn't decided if he was going to.

He considered it again while he walked. Just the thought of it really did make him feel as if he'd be a bug under her microscope. And there *would* be other books on time travel he could look at in Boston. And other computers he'd be able to use.

It was just that he'd feel a whole lot better once he got things sorted out. And if he could manage to do that while he was still in Chester City, he might be able to help Mary and Roy, too.

Walking on a little farther, he started thinking how Alanna seemed so certain that writing about him would help her career.

"What the blazes," he finally muttered. It wouldn't kill him to tell her a few things—especially if it was the only way he could get at those books.

When he reached the Magnolia again, he gave a quick knock on the door, then opened it. He'd expected to find her already tucked into her bedroll—the way she'd been last night when he'd come back after giving her time to change.

Tonight, though, she was standing across the room in a lacy white robe. He couldn't exactly see right through it, but he could see enough to start both his imagination and his heart pumping like crazy.

Beneath the robe, she was wearing that little white sleeveless thing she'd had on when he'd woken up this morning. He had to assume it was some sort of nightdress, since she wore it to bed. But it didn't bear the slightest resemblance to anything he'd seen his sisters wearing.

Their nightdresses were shapeless cotton or flannel things that reached their wrists and ankles. Alanna's, though . . . well, he could see enough through that lace to tell hers didn't even reach her knees.

Thinking on how little she slept in almost made him forget about needing to use her books. Then she smiled at him, making him almost forget his own name.

With considerable effort, he managed to remind himself that he hadn't come to 2014 to fall for the first pretty woman he laid eyes on. And maybe he'd passed up his chance to go to Reno because he was concerned about her, but he danged well wasn't intending to get *too* concerned.

He still had a lot of places to go and things to see. In the meantime, though, if he could give Roy and Mary a helping hand, he'd like to. And . . . well, he *would* like to help out Alanna, too.

"How tired are you?" he asked her.

"Well . . . why are you asking?"

He gestured at the recording machine. "I was thinking this might be a good time to tell you about my traveling."

CHAPTER SEVEN

ALANNA WOKE UP, in the middle of dreaming that she was naked in a sauna. Naked but not alone. She was with John McCully.

Even in her semiasleep state that shocked her. She simply wasn't the type who dreamed about being naked with men.

Groggily, she realized she was actually in her sleeping bag—her hair and nightshirt plastered to her and her body temperature so high she had to be at serious risk of heatstroke.

She tried to force her brain awake and remembered the air conditioner was out of commission. That explained the heat. That, plus the sun streaming in through the Magnolia's windows. It was so strong it had to be at least noon.

Actually a little past, she discovered, checking her watch. Recollections of the night before began surfacing as she crawled out of the sleeping bag.

She and John had stayed up until dawn while he'd told her...unless... Oh, heavens, it wasn't possible she'd only dreamed everything, was it?

When she sat up and looked across the room at the recorder, relief washed over her. Neatly stacked beside it were the disks they'd recorded. John really *had* told her all the details of his adventures.

Not quite *all,* she corrected herself. He hadn't shown her Will Lockhart's formula for traveling. But she could hardly complain about that when he'd given her more information than she'd ever hoped for.

And now he was quietly working at her computer again, concentrating so hard that he hadn't even noticed she was awake. He was a slow, two-finger typist, and was giving the keyboard all his attention.

She watched him for a minute. His dark growth of beard made him seem even more masculine. She wouldn't have imagined *anything* could do that, but he looked so darned sexy that...

Quickly, she put the brakes on her train of thought. Dreaming steamy scenes with him as her leading man was bad enough. But being wide-awake and thinking about him *that* way was bordering on ridiculous. Especially when, in reality, he'd never laid a finger on her—a fact of which she was disconcertingly aware.

And that awareness, in itself, was insane.

The heat really *was* making her lose her grip. That had to be the explanation. She'd certainly never had these kinds of reactions to a man before.

Or maybe she was suffering the effects of having spent most of the summer alone. The only men she'd been seeing were her research supervisor, who was very married, and her deliveryman, who was very old. To put it in scientific terms, by the time John had appeared on the scene, she'd been in a state of severe deprivation. That could be another reason she was so acutely conscious of his presence.

Yes, it had to be strictly some sort of reaction to either the temperature or her isolation. After all, even though having John around had proved reassuring, she really didn't like him all *that* much.

Although, after he'd been so darned nice last night . . . well, it was hardly surprising that sharing his story with her had made her feel more positive toward him.

She reminded herself that there was a limit to how positive she dared let herself feel.

John would be leaving on Tuesday—the day after tomorrow. And she wasn't into playing kiss and run. Not with men who belonged in her century, and definitely not with one who didn't.

So, under the circumstances, things were exactly as they should be. Their platonic little relationship, if it even qualified as that, was perfect just the way it was.

If the circumstances had been different, though . . .

After a second sharp application of her mental brakes, she tugged her nightshirt down as far as she could, self-conscious about the way it was sticking to her in the heat. If she had anything less revealing to sleep in, she'd certainly be wearing it. But she hadn't been expecting company.

Reaching for her lace robe, she pulled it on, wishing it was velour or something—regardless of the heat. It was all she had in the robe department, though, and she certainly wasn't going to get dressed in front of John.

Once adequately covered, given what she had to work with, she sat looking over at that little pile of disks again. Visions of Nobels and Pulitzers began dancing in her head once more—so vividly she couldn't keep from smiling.

John's story was absolutely incredible, and she had every last detail recorded. Just as soon as she finished her paper about the ghosts of Chester City, she'd begin spending all her spare time working on a book about

John. *Surely,* that would be enough to earn her an assistant professorship.

The thought made her so happy she felt like hugging herself. Then John realized she was awake and said good morning, shooting her a smile that made her feel like hugging *him.*

He turned back to the computer and she reminded herself again that the circumstances demanded *platonic.* But telling her about his traveling had been the most wonderful thing he could have done. So for the rest of the time he was here, she simply wasn't going to let herself get annoyed at him—no matter how many of his Stone Age attitudes he trotted out. It was the least she could do in appreciation.

"You weren't playing with that computer the entire time I was sleeping, were you?" she asked, pushing herself up off her sleeping bag.

"Pretty well. Except when I was looking through your books on time travel."

Until he said that, she hadn't noticed he had a stack of them on the table.

"It was all right to read them, wasn't it? You said I could, once I'd told you about my traveling."

"Sure. It was fine. Would you like some coffee?"

He nodded. "You know, these books are plumb fascinating," he said while she headed for the makeshift kitchen. "Especially the one *you* wrote."

Glancing across from behind the bar, she realized her thesis was sitting on top of the stack.

"Oh…you thought it was interesting?" She couldn't help smiling again. As far as she could recall, that was the only compliment he'd ever given her.

"Plumb fascinating," he repeated as she poured water into two mugs. "I read every word of it. All those different methods people have figured out to time travel—it's astonishing. But you know, it got me wondering about something.''

"Yes?''

"Well, if scientists have time travel all figured out, how come most people still don't believe it's possible? And why isn't everyone doing it? I remember Will saying it would be disastrous if that happened, but why hasn't it?''

"Because everything you've got there is still basically theory. Only a handful of people we know about have *really* figured out ways of traveling. Ways that have actually been put to the test and worked, I mean. And they never talk about them except in the vaguest of generalities. As I was telling you when we were first talking about time travelers, they seem to have an impenetrable code of silence.''

John nodded. "Will mentioned something like that—he warned me off saying anything about it. But your thesis... you made the particulars sound so clear.''

"They're particulars of *theories,* though. And there's nothing, anywhere, that lays out, step by concrete step, how Joe Public could go about traveling. So most people are still skeptical that it's really possible.''

"But Will and I both did it. And others have, too.''

"I know. But Will won't come back and talk openly about it, will he?''

"No... no, he says he'd never do that.''

"And he won't give anyone his formula, either, will he? I mean, aside from you, and you refused to give it to me.''

"He made me swear I'd never share it with anyone.''

"Exactly. That's the party line.'' She waited to see if the discussion was over. When John didn't pursue it further, she began rummaging around in the fridge, deciding she'd make a quick brunch, as well as coffee. She was in a decidedly good mood this morning.

ALANNA JUST ABOUT HAD the food ready when John looked up from the keyboard and asked if the coffee was done yet.

"No, not quite. I left it for a minute. I thought I'd make us something to eat, too, before I go out."

"Go out where?"

"To see if I can find a new ghost to interview. I told you yesterday, that's how I normally spend my days."

"But I'm just in the middle of puzzling through something. I'd really rather stay here and work on your computer."

"That's fine."

"But you can't go wandering around town on your own."

"Excuse me?"

"Well you can't."

"What on earth are you talking about? I was gone for most of yesterday and you didn't say a word about it."

"But you were with Roy and Mary—not on your own. And you were in the saloon, not wandering around all over the place."

"John, I—"

"Tarnation, Alanna, you know there are at least two or three of those... *whatevers* who don't want you here."

"So what?"

"So what? So you can't go wandering around town on your own, that's what. Why in blazes do you think I stayed here, instead of leaving with the Tanners?"

She simply stared at him while his words sank in. As they did, she felt a little fluttering sensation around her heart. But maybe she'd misunderstood.

"I thought you stayed because it beat out being stuck in the Reno airport," she said at last.

"Well, that too," he muttered. "But it was partly because of those guys—or ghosts, whatever the tarnation they are. You need someone to look out for you."

"Oh, John, I really don't."

"You certainly do!"

"John, I've been wandering around here on my own for weeks, and I've been just fine."

"That was before those guys showed up."

"No, that was only before we *knew* they were here. Look, if they're ghosts, it's really not likely they could manage to hurt me. And if they aren't ghosts," she added, only because John seemed so convinced it was a possibility, "I *always* carry my Glock. Just in case."

He didn't seem to appreciate her setting him straight, but that seemed perfectly fair. *She* didn't like *him* telling her what to do. But the idea that he'd stayed because he was worried about her…she couldn't *honestly* say she didn't like that.

The microwave pinged and switched off, so she took out the mugs and spooned coffee into the water. If John had really stayed in Chester City because of her…

But she wasn't entirely sure how the nineteenth-century-male mind worked. Maybe his staying didn't actually mean he cared anything about what happened to *her,* personally. She'd already realized he had protective instincts, so maybe he just figured it was a man's duty to protect any woman on her own.

He shoved himself up from his chair and took his mug off the bar, giving her a distinctly unfriendly look.

It certainly didn't make her think he cared anything about what happened to her personally. And neither did the next words that came out of his mouth.

"You can be a danged stubborn woman," he muttered after a sip of coffee.

"*I* can be stubborn? What do you think you were being your first two days here? Before you decided to relent and tell me about your time traveling? Now, you *do* want some lunch before I go, don't you?"

"Before *we* go, you mean. If you're going, I'm going with you."

She reminded herself that she'd decided not to get annoyed at John, but she just couldn't keep from giving him a dirty look. He was being extremely difficult.

"Don't you look at me like that, Alanna," he snapped, sounding as if he had every right to dictate how she should look at him. "You just listen to me and—"

"No. You just listen to *me*. You are *not* going with me. In the first place, I don't need a bodyguard. And in the second place, as I've already told you more than once, living people make ghosts nervous. When I'm alone, their curiosity sometimes outweighs that. But if you were along, the only ones who'd talk to me would be Mary and Roy."

"Well, I'm not planning on tagging along forever, you know. Just until those fellows...or ghosts," he amended quickly when she shot another dagger or two in his direction, "try whatever it is they're going to try. Then I'll take care of them for you and you'll be safe here when I *do* leave for Boston."

"You'll *take care* of them for me? Just like that? Regardless of how many there are?" Lord, the man had an ego the size of Texas.

"Yes, just like that and however many. Hellfire, back in 1887, me, Will and General William Tecumseh Sherman took care of the Apache Kid and his whole gang of renegades. Just the three of us. And after ambushing the Apache Kid, taking care of those characters out to get you will be like shooting fish in a barrel."

Alanna counted to ten. It didn't help.

"John," she said as evenly as she could, "I have to wrap up my research here next weekend and go back to Elko. Come Saturday, there'll be a moving van here to cart me and all my equipment away. So I have to spend every minute I've got left trying to interview more ghosts. I simply don't have any time to waste while you *take care* of things for me. So let's just drop this discussion, okay?"

He glared at her for a moment. Then he slapped his mug down so hard half the coffee splashed onto the bar. Without another word, he turned on his heel and marched toward the door.

"Thank you," she called sarcastically after him. "I need some privacy to get dressed."

JOHN STOMPED ALONG to the Miner's Saloon, his boots hitting the street so hard they were raising clouds of dust with each step. Alanna had made him as mad as a hornet someone was swatting at.

Didn't she know how dangerous it could be in a town like this? Maybe Roy Hardin had been a fine, upstanding citizen in life, but most of the men who were ghosts here would have been the dregs of the West—rough-and-tumble polecats who'd gotten themselves killed by one of the other skunks who populated towns like Chester City.

"Why do I care?" he muttered to himself. And why did he? Every single time he decided Alanna might not actually be the *most* infuriating and ornery woman he'd ever met, she did something new to demonstrate that she was. So if she wanted to go and get herself into trouble, why didn't he just let her?

He danged well should have gone to Reno when he'd had the chance. Because Alanna certainly didn't appreciate him trying to look out for her.

Didn't she realize a woman alone should be *grateful* for a decent man's protection?

He kicked a rock out of his way. She didn't appreciate his concern a whit. And for all he knew, she might not even think of him as a man.

Maybe she thought he was a freak. A being from another time who was only of interest for what she could pry out of him.

Well, she'd gotten what she wanted. He'd told her his story and he couldn't take it back. But he was so mad that he wished he could.

He hesitated outside the saloon, feeling more than a little peculiar about the idea of talking to Roy. If anyone had told him a few days ago that he'd be coming to a ghost for advice about a woman...and a ghost he barely knew, to boot...

But there was no one else around, so he stepped into the saloon and glared over at the dusty piano. "Roy? Roy, you here?"

The room was silent. Which might mean Roy wasn't here or might just mean he didn't feel like talking. Tarnation, but trying to deal with ghosts was irritating. About the only thing *more* irritating was trying to deal with Alanna.

"Roy?" he tried again. "Roy, I need your help. *Alanna* needs your help."

That worked, he saw with grim satisfaction. Just as it had the other night, a vapory cloud began floating in front of the piano, then gradually condensed into two human forms.

Roy was standing with his arm around Mary's waist and both of them were gazing expectantly across the room. They were dressed exactly as they'd been the first time he'd seen them, making him suspect that ghosts didn't have to bother with things like changing underwear.

"What's wrong?" Mary asked. "Is Alanna sick?"

"No, but she's liable to end up a heap worse than sick. There are some...well, she says they're ghosts, but I'm not too sure they aren't live men. And they're out to get her."

Quickly, he told Roy and Mary about hearing the voices in Broken Hill, seeing the face at the window, and about the air conditioner's battery vanishing.

"None of the other ghosts have mentioned anything about not wanting Alanna here," Mary said when he'd finished. "And I can't understand why we wouldn't have heard something about it."

"But from what John said those two were new in town," Roy pointed out. "And just passing through...do I have that right, John?"

"That's what it sounded like, all right. They said something about not wanting to hang around."

"So maybe we haven't heard anything because nobody knows they're here," Roy said to Mary.

"Maybe they've been staying invisible," John ventured.

Roy shook his head. "Ghosts aren't invisible to other ghosts. But they might have been keeping out of sight— until they do whatever they came to do."

"I got the impression they came to get some gold that's around here someplace."

"Why would ghosts care about getting gold?" Mary asked Roy.

He shook his head. "It does sound kinda strange. So maybe they *aren't* ghosts. I could drift on up to the mine and have a look," he suggested to John. "If they're still up there I'd see them, whether they're men or ghosts."

"Well whatever they are," John muttered, "they want to get rid of Alanna. And they might not be up in the mine anymore. For all we know they're right down here in town. But she's so danged stubborn she won't stop wandering around, looking for ghosts to talk to. Ghosts other than you two, I mean."

"Well," Mary said, "that *is* why she came here."

"But it's not safe! And she's insisting I can't go with her 'cuz I'd make the ghosts nervous."

"She's right about that," Roy told him.

"So what in tarnation am I supposed to do? Let her go off alone and get herself killed?"

Mary quietly cleared her throat, then said, "May I speak plainly to you, John?"

He nodded. *He'd* already been speaking more plainly than he would to most *people.* Certainly more than he would to people he'd scarcely met. Maybe there was something about ghosts that made them easy to confide in.

"The way you're thinking is wrong," Mary said. "I mean about *letting* Alanna do something. She isn't like women from our time, John. Things have changed in the world—between men and women."

"I know that. A friend told me all about it." Not that he'd been able to believe all the stories Will had told him, but he did know things had changed.

"Then you must know," Mary went on, "that Alana will do whatever she wants. Women are like men now."

John shook his head, picturing Alanna in her little yellow shorts . . . then in that silky nightdress that clung to every luscious curve of her body.

She'd practically had him drooling last night, so he sure couldn't agree that she was like a man. But he *would* admit she wasn't like any other woman he'd ever met.

"All right," he said at last. "If I can't make her let me go with her, what in thunder do I do? No, wait a minute . . . what about you, Roy? If you stuck with her, would *you* make other ghosts nervous?"

"No," he admitted slowly.

"Well, there's the solution, then. How about if you go along with her? She couldn't say you'd be causing her problems. And you *can* shoot, can't you?" he asked, glancing at Roy's revolver.

Roy looked at Mary, then back at John.

"Well, can't you?" he repeated impatiently. "That gun's real, isn't it? Or is it? The way it disappeared when you did last night made me wonder."

"It's real. Our things just come and go when we do because . . . well, that's just how it works."

"We don't quite understand all of the *hows*," Mary elaborated. "But Roy's gun still shoots, and our clothes never wear out. Alanna tried to explain it all to us a few times, and she says it's because we're in what she calls a state of suspension. But your question about *using* the gun . . . well, it's not quite that straightforward. If those fellows *are* ghosts, shooting them wouldn't make any difference.''

"Yeah, they're already dead," John muttered, remembering Alanna had made that point the other night.

"And if they're live men," Roy said, "well, for me to use my gun is more than middling hard.''

"What about mental energy?"

Roy shrugged. "Sometimes that works. But it's not too plumb reliable.''

"Well what in blazes do I do, then? Just sit in the Magnolia and worry?"

"I still think," Roy said, "that the first thing to do is find out whether those two you overheard are men or ghosts. So let me go try to get a look at them. If they're not up at the mine, I'll scout around town a bit.''

"But what about Alanna? What if they're one step ahead of you? And they make their move while you're scouting around?"

"Do you think you could keep an eye on Alanna, Mary?" Roy asked. "And let John know if anything troublesome happens?"

"It would take her too long to get to me," John objected.

"No. Mary could materialize in the Magnolia just like that." Roy snapped his fingers. When there wasn't the slightest sound, he looked dismayed, as if he'd actually expected there to be one.

"I *could* keep an eye on her," Mary was saying, "but she wouldn't like it. She'd take it as my siding with you," she added, glancing at John.

"But she wouldn't know you were watching her. Not if you didn't materialize.''

"She *would* know. She always wears her glasses when she's looking for ghosts, so she'd know I was there. But maybe..."

"Maybe what?"

"Well, she has to leave Chester City soon, you know."

"Next weekend, she told me."

"Well, then, maybe I could say I wanted to help her because she's running out of time. And that I thought my being with her might encourage some of the other ghosts to talk to her. Ones that haven't, so far."

"You know," Roy said, "I reckon that could work."

His words made John feel a bit less worried. "And if there was any trouble, you really could get to me fast, Mary?"

"In a second."

He tilted his hat back on his head and thought the situation through. Alanna obviously wasn't going to listen to reason and do what was sensible. And having Mary watch out for her might not be as good as his doing it, but it would be a danged sight better than nothing.

CHAPTER EIGHT

BY THE TIME John arrived back at the Magnolia, Alanna had dressed and eaten. She tensed when he opened the door, sure he'd pick up where he'd left off. Or, at the very least, give her shorts a thoroughly disapproving glare.

He surprised her though. He looked pleased about something.

"On your way?" he asked casually.

She nodded, trying to figure out what game he was playing.

"Well, have a nice afternoon. Hope you find some ghosts to talk to."

She picked up her digitizing glasses and notebook, then tucked her Glock into her waistband, expecting him to tell her again that she shouldn't carry it that way—despite the fact that she obviously had nowhere else to put it.

He didn't say a word. Merely walked over to the computer and sat down in front of it.

It had to be the nineteenth-century version of reverse psychology, she decided after a moment's consideration. That's what he was up to with his abrupt about-face. Well, it wasn't going to work on a twenty-first-century woman.

"I put your lunch in the fridge," she told him.

"Great. Thanks. I'll just do a little more puzzling on your computer, then eat."

"Yes . . . well, I'll see you later."

"Mmm," he said absently as she started for the door, already engrossed in whatever he'd called up on the screen.

Giving him a final suspicious glance, Alanna opened the door and stepped out onto Main Street.

The interior of the Magnolia was so hot that there was barely a noticeable difference in the temperature outside. But the sun beating down was doing all it could to make it *seem* far hotter on the street.

She'd barely begun walking when Mary materialized at her side. Alone.

"Hi. What's up?" Alanna smiled curiously. Mary and Roy were rarely apart.

"Oh, I just thought some of the other ghosts might feel more at ease about talking to you if I was around. And if not, at least I can keep you company for a while."

"Keep me company," Alanna repeated, her curiosity growing. "Where's Roy?" she asked.

"Oh . . . he had some things to do."

They continued down the street, Alanna more certain with each step that she knew exactly what was happening. And the more certain she grew, the more angry she became. No wonder John had looked so darned smug.

"John asked you to come with me, didn't he?" she finally said, stopping and looking Mary straight in the eyes.

She gave a little shrug.

Alanna muttered a few choice words under her breath. "And what's he got Roy doing?" she demanded out loud.

"Oh...just looking around a mite. He told us about the voices in the mine. And the face at the window. So Roy thought he'd see what he could find out."

"Lord," Alanna snapped. "I specifically told John to butt out. That man is the most obnoxious, impossible, bossy—"

"That man is in love with you," Mary said quietly.

For a second, Alanna thought Mary was trying to be funny, but the expression on her face was serious.

"Alanna, don't look at me that way. You should have heard him talking to Roy and me. He was ever so worried that something might happen to you. Why do you think he enlisted us to help make sure you'd be safe? It's because he's fallen in love with you, that's why."

"No, it isn't. It just has something to do with his old-fashioned idea that women need looking out for. It certainly has nothing to do with love. Good grief, Mary, John McCully only met me three days ago."

"That's plenty of time to fall in love. I fell in love with Roy the first moment I saw him."

"Well that's not the way it works with most people. And John is definitely *not* in love with me. He doesn't even like me. We can barely go for two seconds without annoying the hell out of each other. We're oil and water, fire and ice."

Mary gave her a knowing smile. "The hotter the fire, the more sparks it throws."

"Oh..." Alanna couldn't even think of a response to that. The whole idea of John... It was utterly preposterous.

"I suppose you're going to tell me you don't feel anything at all for him," Mary said after a minute.

"I certainly do. I feel anger. Frequently."

"Ah," Mary said, laughing quietly. "But what did you feel the first moment you saw him?"

"Surprised."

"No, I mean what did you think about him. What was your first impression."

"I didn't think anything. I mean, I thought he was a ghost."

"An ugly ghost?"

"No, of course not. I thought he was... rather attractive. But what has that got to do with anything?"

"Oh, I was just wondering. You probably don't believe people can fall in love at first sight, do you."

"Well...I don't exactly believe it's impossible. Love usually needs time to develop though. I mean, I could never fall in love with somebody until I got to know him. Very well. Over a long period of time."

"Ahh."

Alanna waited, but Mary didn't go on. "Ahh, what?" she finally pressed.

"Well, that's one of the things that's changed a lot over the years. I don't think it's just you. From the few people who come through town, I've gotten the sense that people don't trust their instincts the way they used to. Back in the 1800s, if a man and a woman met and felt... attracted, that was that."

"That was what?"

"Love. The start of love, at least. And people simply recognized that and... well, they didn't waste time analyzing their feelings. They simply felt."

"Mary, I'm a scientist. I've been trained to analyze *everything*."

"I suppose you have. But John hasn't. He just feels. And whether you believe in love at first sight or not, what he's feeling for you is love. I could see it written all over his face. Plain as day."

Mary lapsed into silence as they walked on, which was just as well. Alanna's mind had begun spinning so fast she couldn't have concentrated on any more conversation.

She couldn't believe John McCully was in love with her. So why on earth *was* he so worried that something might happen to her? Because of his old-fashioned attitudes? Or was there really something more to it?

"BYE FOR NOW," Mary said, fading to mist, then into nothingness.

"Bye," Alanna replied. "And thanks again for convincing that ghost to talk to me," she called as the last wisps vanished.

She turned toward the Magnolia, but rather than opening the door she just stood and worried a little more. She'd begun worrying the moment Mary had dropped her bombshell, and hadn't stopped all afternoon.

In fact, she'd been so preoccupied that when she'd interviewed the new ghost she'd forgotten half the questions she normally asked.

Of course, in all likelihood, Mary had been totally off base. But if by any chance she'd been right, it could make spending another couple of nights under the same roof with John extremely awkward.

Before going inside, Alanna tried to fluff some fullness into her hair—a futile effort, since the heat had it almost soaking wet. Then she procrastinated a little longer by carefully reclipping her pen to the cover of her notebook.

It was absurd to be feeling anxious about facing the man again. She couldn't *really* believe he'd fallen in love with her any more than she'd fallen in love with him. And she'd certainly been at no risk of doing that...had she?

As physically attractive as she'd admit finding him, she'd never let herself fall in love with a man who belonged in the past. Not *any* man, let alone one as difficult as John McCully. It would be utterly foolish. There couldn't be the slightest possibility of a future together.

She couldn't imagine never seeing her family again. Or her friends. And even if she *could* consider leaving her entire life behind, she'd hate living in 1887. She wouldn't have a prayer of coping with life in the nineteenth century.

And looking at things from John's point of view, a man from 1887 could never live in her world. In addition to all the culture-shock problems he'd face, his occupational skills would be seriously outdated.

But John was an intelligent man. So those obvious facts would have occurred to him. Except, according to Mary, men from the nineteenth century didn't tend to think about what they were feeling.

With a few butterflies in her stomach, Alanna opened the door and stepped into the heat of the Magnolia.

John looked over from the computer and positively beamed at her.

Instantly, the butterflies seemed to multiply at an alarming rate. Was that the smile of a man in love? Oh, Lord, she hoped not.

"Guess what," he said.

"What?"

"I've figured out the solution to Roy and Mary's problem."

That came at her from left field and she just continued to look at him.

"Their *problem*," he repeated, enunciating slowly, as if she were feebleminded. "You know, their being stuck in limbo because Roy can't accept he's dead."

"And...you've figured out how to make him accept it?" She tried to keep the skepticism out of her voice but couldn't quite manage it. John might be an intelligent man, but *she* was the one with the doctorate in paranormalism. And if she hadn't been able to help Roy, then—

"Not exactly how to make him accept it. More like how to change things so he doesn't have to accept it."

She waited.

John's smile slowly faded. "I thought you'd be excited."

"I'm restraining myself. Until you tell me the details."

"Oh. Well, it's simple. You said that Roy was killed on July fourth, 1895."

Alanna nodded.

"So I've figured out how to send him back to July third."

That took a minute to register. "You mean," she said slowly, "July third, 1895?"

"Of course that's what I mean."

She glanced at the books on time travel, still stacked on the table, noting that her thesis was lying open. At the moment, she didn't feel the slightest bit flattered that he'd used it in his studies.

"That's what you've been doing on my computer all this time? And with those books? Trying to figure out how to send Roy back to 1895?"

"Uh-huh. Partly, at least. I had a problem of my own to solve, too."

"Oh?" She glanced at the computer, then back at John's face, feeling rather dazed. She knew some hackers could do incredible things with computers but—

"Remember I mentioned," he went on, "that I decided to leave 1887 quite suddenly?"

She nodded once more.

"Well, it was actually *very* suddenly. In fact, I had only a couple of minutes to think about coming in Will's place."

"Oh?" she said again. She knew she was sounding inane, but it was the only word that came to mind.

"See, like I told you, Will felt he had to make a trip home and let his family know he was all right. But there was a problem with that. According to his calculations, once he returned to 2014 he wouldn't be able to get back to my sister for three years."

"Three years?" Better. She'd managed two words that time.

"Uh-huh. His formula calculated the next possible travel date to Emma's time as three years in the future. But . . . is this getting boring?"

She shook her head. Confusing, yes. Boring, no.

"See, the basic formula only works for very specific times—when blue moons warp the space-time continuum and create stasis points. And Will didn't want to be away from Emma for three years. So . . . well, that's why we decided at the last minute that I'd come instead."

"I see," she managed to say, although she didn't understand half of what he'd said.

"But I didn't have time to think through the fact that if Will wouldn't be able to get back for three years, then neither would I."

"So you're stuck here? But I thought you said—"

"No, no. I'm not stuck. Not anymore. But that's the problem I had to solve. See, as soon as I had a chance to think, I realized I had to figure out a way of getting back a lot sooner than the date Will had come up with. I can't stay in 2014 for three months, let alone three years. I've only got the money he had with him. Just that and his credit cards."

"So... you figured out how to get back sooner than Will thought was possible?"

"Uh-huh. As I said, he'd just put together a *basic* formula. It was all he originally needed. But I needed more, so... well, your books helped a lot. And once I got going, it wasn't much more trouble to figure out how to get Roy back in time as well. And Mary, too, of course."

"I... I don't believe this. Those are things most scientists wouldn't be able to figure out if they had years. And you're saying you've done it this fast?"

John shrugged. "I had a big head start. I already knew that travel is possible through Broken Hill, so I didn't have to worry about determining a site. I gather," he added, gesturing at the books, "that's a major problem scientists have. But between knowing about Broken Hill and having Will's formula... well, the only part that was a mite tricky was modifying it."

"You modified it," Alanna murmured, still not quite believing her ears. Had this cowboy really taken an astrophysicist's formula, one she imagined would cover six blackboards, and adapted it to fit a different situation?

"I *had* to modify it," he was explaining blithely. "Oh, I'm sure Will could have managed it far more easily than I did, but he didn't put his mind to trying. He was so upset about having to leave Emma that I reckon he wasn't thinking right straight. At any rate, the way I've got things figured for Roy and Mary, there's going to be what Will would call a window of opportunity this coming week."

"A window of opportunity...you mean a time when they'd be able to travel?"

"Right. It'll just be a small window, but the alignment between now and July third, 1895, will be perfect for about five minutes next Wednesday morning. And that's long enough to let them sneak on back to 1895. Then, once they're there, all they'll have to do is hightail it out of Chester City until July fourth is over. If Roy's not in the Miner's Saloon on Independence Day, he can't get killed there."

Her brain whirling, Alanna wandered over and sank onto the chair across the table from John. She put down her glasses, set her notebook beside them, then looked over at him.

He smiled expectantly, but she wasn't quite up to speaking yet. If he'd figured things out right, he'd done something absolutely amazing. And he was so clearly pleased with himself that she just hated to burst his balloon.

"Well, Alanna? Aren't you going to say something?"

She nodded. "John...Roy and Mary can't go back in time."

"You think I've calculated wrong? Well, I haven't. But I reckon you'll just have to take my word for that because it's still basically Will's formula I used—the one I swore I'd never let anyone see. But I'm danged sure that I've—"

"No, John, wait. I'm sure your calculations are fine. It's just that . . . we can't send them back."

"Sure we can. Oh, I know I'll be leaving for Boston on Tuesday, before that little window opens up, but I'll tell them exactly what to do before I go."

"No, you don't understand what I'm saying. We can't change history."

"That's just not true, Alanna. Don't you remember what I told you about the reason Will came back to 1887? He'd seen my tombstone, knew that I got killed on July twenty-fifth. So he came back to warn me and we prevented it from happening. And what we'll be doing for Roy is more or less the same thing. He can change what happened just by getting out of Chester City for a spell."

"John . . . look, I realize you're trying to help, but I can't go along with this."

"Why in tarnation not? I'll bet Roy and Mary will be thrilled."

"No, you can't tell them it's possible. Knowing that would only make Roy feel worse, so—"

"Alanna, what in blazes is wrong with you? I thought you wanted to help them."

"I do. I'd give anything to help them. But I can't do it the way you're suggesting. It's against all the rules of paranormalism."

"What?"

"I—it would be completely unethical. I can try to help ghosts work through their emotional problems, but

I'm not allowed to rewrite history. If I did, they'd drum me out of the profession so fast my head would spin."

John eyed her with undisguised annoyance for a minute, then said, "Fine. There's no reason you have to be involved. I just thought you'd want to be. But I'll explain everything to Roy and Mary myself. I can give them step-by-step instructions before I leave."

"John, you can't! Doing anything to change history is against the rules for time travelers, too."

"Oh?" His expression clearly said he didn't believe her. "I didn't read that in any of your books. And Will never said a word about it. Whose rules are they?"

"They're *the* rules. There are councils that . . . John, the details don't matter. Just trust me on this, all right? There *are* rules. And changing history is against them."

"You're saying Will broke these rules, then? By changing history for me?"

"Yes, that's exactly what I'm saying. I guess he took a chance because you were such good friends. And he probably didn't want you to know he shouldn't be helping you, so he kept quiet about it. But you told me yourself that Will said time travelers could potentially cause disasters."

"Well . . . yes, but—"

"What he meant was, there'd be disasters if people start changing this, that and the other thing after they've already happened. I mean, what if Roy didn't get killed, and then he went on to murder the president or something?"

"Roy? He'd never do anything like that."

"I know he wouldn't, but you're missing my point."

"What in tarnation *is* your point?"

She ignored his sarcastic tone. This issue was too important to let herself get sidetracked. "John, Will took a chance by helping save your life. He shouldn't have but he did, and what's done is done. But the more chances people take, the more changes time travelers make to history, the higher the risk that something terrible will result from one of them."

"But neither Roy nor Mary would ever—"

"I know. Neither of them would ever *intentionally* do anything awful. But somehow, through a quirk of fate, they might end up responsible for something horrendous happening. Or maybe they'd have a child who grew up to be... I don't know, maybe Hitler or somebody."

"Who's Hitler?"

"Oh, he was this man who— John, it's not important. The point is that he was pure evil. And that Roy and Mary could conceivably have a child who grew up to be pure evil."

"Alanna—"

"I didn't say likely, John. I said conceivably. And it's because of that kind of possibility that it's unethical to change anything that's already happened."

John merely sat glaring across the table at her.

"I know you want to help them," she said softly. "But you just can't do it. Not that way."

MARY AND ROY WAITED on tenterhooks for John and Alanna to continue their argument, but neither uttered another word.

Eventually, Alanna rose and headed to the bar, quietly saying, "Why don't I make us some ice tea."

Not wanting Roy to see the tears in her eyes, Mary merely nudged him.

"No," he whispered beneath the quiet hum of the computer. "Let's wait a few more minutes."

Still not looking at him, she shook her head and drifted back out through the wall. After a second, Roy followed her to the street.

"I want to hear the rest of what they say," he told her with a touch of annoyance.

"They're done talking about it for the moment. And we shouldn't have heard as much as we did. We're completely forgetting our manners, Roy. Being invisible eavesdroppers is terribly rude. We should have materialized and knocked on the door, instead of just drifting in like that."

"If we hadn't just drifted in, we wouldn't have heard a thing. But now that we have... Mary, it's the answer to our prayers. We can have a whole lifetime together, after all."

"Only if John tells us how to travel," she murmured.

"He will," Roy said, wrapping his arms around her and drawing her close. "He will."

"Unless Alanna stops him."

"Well, we'll just have to figure out how to convince her it's the right thing."

Mary rested her cheek against Roy's chest, no longer able to hold back her tears. Even by calling up her most precious memories, even by using her imagination to the fullest, she could no longer quite recapture many of the sensations of being alive.

Their life forces, already vastly diminished, were continually wasting away. The process was so gradual it might take forever. But every now and then, she'd realize they'd faded a tad more.

She closed her eyes and tried harder to feel what she'd once felt with no effort at all. Tried to feel Roy as the warm, solid man who'd held her when she'd been alive—held her as if he'd love her until they were old and gray.

Back then, they'd never given a thought to their own mortality, nor to the possibility that death would rip their happiness from them.

Slowly, Roy's arms began to seem stronger around her. Finally, she started to feel his heart beating against her cheek, began to hear its even, reassuring rhythm. A faint scent of the bay rum he'd always worn began to tickle her nose.

"Oh, Roy, I love you so," she whispered, slipping her hand behind his neck and drawing his mouth to hers.

His kiss was like a cool, gentle breeze, so faint she could barely taste his lips against hers or feel the soft brush of his mustache against her skin.

It almost broke her heart to recall how his kisses had once started her blood racing. How he'd turned her to jelly with his touch.

And now they lived in a shadowland of memories, facing the almost imperceptibly slow deterioration of what little remained of them.

"We'll convince Alanna," Roy whispered against her ear, his breath as cool as his kiss. "Why don't we knock on the door and start talking to her about it right now? I know she'll come around."

"I'm not so sure of that, love. I . . . I'm not even sure we should try to make her."

"What?" Roy drew back and gazed down at Mary. "Of course we should try. And we *will* make her. Darling, we can have everything back. And more. We can raise a family and—"

"We might have a child who grew up to be pure evil."

"That's nonsense. We'd have wonderful children. And we'd—"

"Shh," Mary murmured, resting her fingers against his lips. She couldn't bear to start really believing that might happen, then have her hopes dashed. "Roy, I don't think it can be. Not when Alanna said it's against all the rules."

"To hell with the rules! John will help us. I know he will, whether Alanna likes it or not. Come on. We're going to talk to him about it right now."

Roy took Mary's hand but she resisted.

"Come on," he repeated. "I have to talk to him, anyway. That's the whole reason we dropped by, remember. To tell him I couldn't find any trace of those two guys."

"Roy, that's not really important news. It would have been if you *had* seen them but...look, love, we're both upset now. So let's not go rushing in there and start putting pressure on Alanna without thinking about it first."

"Hellfire, Mary, what's to think about?"

"Well...if we *did* go back in time...Alanna said she'd be drummed out of her profession. We might ruin her life."

Roy stroked his mustache thoughtfully. "She was probably exaggerating," he said at last. "Who would ever find out she'd been involved?"

"I don't know. But somebody might. Maybe they have ways of finding out and...Roy, our going back isn't natural. And maybe...I'm just not sure I could unless Alanna decides she wants us to."

"You'd give up our only chance at happiness?"

Mary gazed at him, a hollow feeling where her heart should be. "No," she finally said. "No, I want a second chance at life, a second chance with you, more than anything. But I'd just feel so much better knowing our happiness wouldn't destroy someone else's life. I'd like Alanna to decide it's worth the risk that it might cause her trouble.''

"So what do you want to do?''

"I . . . let's wait for a bit. Wait and see what happens before we say anything. Maybe John will convince her it's a good idea.''

"And if he doesn't?''

"Let's just be patient, Roy. We haven't been the way we are for 120 years without learning patience. And John said he's not leaving until Tuesday, so we have a while before we need to find out how to get back.''

CHAPTER NINE

ALANNA GAZED across the room to where John was sitting on his mattress, reading one of her books by lamplight. Except for his gun belt and hat, he was still fully dressed—wearing some of his newly acquired clothes.

While they'd been together during the afternoon, Mary had suggested to Alanna that he look through the trunks in the attic of what had been her brother's house and take anything he could use. So when they'd gone for a walk after dinner, he'd done just that. At least now he had fresh clothes and shaving gear.

Cleaned up and shaved, he didn't look as rough around the edges as he had before, but he did look decidedly tired. It was a wonder he could even see to read, after working through last night and most of today on the computer.

"Good night, John," she finally said when he still hadn't noticed her watching him.

"'Night." He glanced over and smiled.

"You're going to get some sleep tonight, aren't you?"

"Sure. Just want to read for a while, first."

She blew out her lamp, then took off her robe and crawled into the sleeping bag. Her thoughts returned to what they'd spent most of the evening talking about—Roy and Mary's situation.

Amazingly, the discussion hadn't disintegrated into an argument. For once, she and John had been able to see each other's point of view.

She had to admit that what he was proposing would be wonderful for Roy and Mary. But sending them back would be changing history. And once John had thought it over, he'd realized the importance of having rules against that.

Still, he definitely wanted to offer them the chance to break those rules, while she felt utterly torn.

As badly as she wanted to help the couple, John's plan was so unethical that just considering it made her feel guilty. And it seemed that the longer they'd talked, the more potential problems they'd foreseen. And the most frustrating part was that they'd come up with far more questions than answers about how the travelers being ghosts would affect a time-travel attempt.

Alanna turned onto her side, trying to quiet her mind so she could get to sleep, but her thoughts continued racing.

She'd sworn a professional oath that she'd prevent exactly what John was proposing. But she had less than a week left in Chester City. Less than one more week to help Roy come to terms with his death.

What if she couldn't do it in the time remaining? If that turned out to be the case, could she really just walk away and leave him and Mary in limbo?

But what if she went along with John's plan and it resulted in disaster?

Across the room, John closed his book and stretched wearily. It looked as if he was going to have to stay awake all night again, in case trouble arrived.

He'd been hoping Roy would come by to say he'd found those characters from the mine, but there'd been no sign of him. So it was still a matter of waiting and watching until they made their move.

He stretched a second time. Another night without sleep wasn't going to kill him, but he was too tired to read anymore. He blew out his lamp and sat gazing through the moonlight. Across the room, he could just make out Alanna's shape in the darkness. It was enough, though, to make him wish he was over there lying beside her.

If she'd let him, he'd be sticking to her like glue, making sure she was safe—even though he knew he was a danged fool to be feeling so protective of her. But hellfire, he was a danged fool to be feeling all of the things he was feeling about her.

He had only one more day in Chester City. Come Tuesday, he'd be leaving. And she'd be glad to see him gone. But he couldn't help what he felt. No more than he could stop worrying about what in tarnation he was going to do if those fellows hadn't made their move by Tuesday.

His eyes felt so heavy he let them close, deciding it wouldn't hurt to rest for a spell. As long as he didn't take off his boots, there wasn't a chance he'd fall asleep.

HE THOUGHT IT WAS a nightmare at first. Then he jolted fully awake and knew it wasn't. The Magnolia was afire.

He couldn't see any flames, but he could sure smell smoke—so acrid it had his eyes watering.

"Alanna?" he called.

She didn't answer, and between the darkness and the smoke he couldn't see a danged thing. He shoved himself up from the mattress and started blindly across the room.

"Damnation," he muttered, running smack into the table. He hobbled on by it in the direction of Alanna's bedroll.

He was trying not to breathe, but his lungs were hurting and his throat was raw by the time he reached her.

"Alanna, wake up," he said loudly, bending down and shaking her.

She mumbled something that sounded like "Leave me alone."

He swore again. There was no time to waste, so he hauled her up and heaved her over his shoulder.

Before he'd taken a single step she started yelling, pounding and kicking at him. But she broke into a coughing fit before she could do any damage and he lurched back across the room with her, hoping to Moses he didn't hit the table again.

Reaching the door, he burst out into the chill night air and set her on her feet. Then he turned back to look at the Magnolia.

With the building illuminated by the moonlight, the smoke was clearly visible—a gray fog drifting out into the street. It was coming through both the open door and one of the broken second-story windows—the one that belonged to the bedroom at the far end of the hall from the bathroom, the bedroom directly over Alanna's bedroll.

So that was where the fire had to be, and all the cracks between the ceiling boards had let the smoke seep right down into the main floor.

He glanced at Alanna, trying to ignore the way she looked in that short little nightdress. "It's probably one of those old mattresses on fire up there," he told her, "but I can't see any flames, can you?"

She just stared at the building for a minute, then said, "Maybe the fire's only smoldering. And my whole summer's research is in there. And the disks you recorded. I've got to go back in, John. I have to save as much as I can."

She started for the door but he grabbed her by the wrist. "Are you crazy?"

"No. I'd be crazy if I just stood here and let everything be destroyed."

"Well you're not going back in there. You stay right where you are and..."

He paused, realizing that if he let her out of his sight he couldn't trust her to do a danged thing he'd told her. "Can you walk in those bare feet?"

"Of course."

"Then come on. We'll try something else." He raced for the old fire stairs at the back of the building, surprised that she managed to stay with him.

There was no smoke coming out the hall window at the top of the stairs, even though he remembered the glass was gone from it, so the fire hadn't spread into the hall.

"You wait down here," he ordered, heading up the steps. "You'd get slivers from these stairs."

He hadn't even finished speaking before she was starting up after him. Tarnation but she was an ornery woman.

Miraculously, they reached the second story without the old staircase collapsing beneath them. John climbed in through the window frame, then gave Alanna a hand.

"You stay right here and try not to breathe," he told her, although the smoke wasn't too bad in the hallway. Then he felt along the wall for the fire bucket.

He couldn't see in the darkness, but he knew exactly where it was hanging . . . except it wasn't there.

He took a few steps along the hall and kicked something with his boot. The bucket.

Scooping it up, he hurried into the bathroom and filled it from the old tap, then started for the end bedroom.

"The door handle," Alanna said, right behind him. "Don't touch the door handle. It might be hot."

He put the bucket down, ripped his shirt off and wrapped it around his hand.

When he opened the door, thick hot smoke poured out, stinging his eyes while he looked around for the flames. Even with all the smoke he should have been able to see the fire, but he couldn't.

"There," Alanna said, right beside him now.

He was barely able to see the finger she was holding out, but when he looked in the direction she was pointing he spotted a tiny orange glow—just the right height to be a smoldering mattress.

Closing the distance to it in two steps, he poured the bucket of water over the glow, producing steam and a loud hissing noise.

He raced back down the hall, refilled the bucket, then ran to the bedroom again.

Three more trips and he couldn't see a trace of any lingering glow. But the smoke was still thick and the stench of wet ashes hung heavily in the air.

"I think we got it," he said, his throat so sore he could barely speak. "Let's get the hell out of here."

In the darkness, he couldn't find where he'd tossed his shirt, so he just left it and they climbed back through the hall window into the desert night.

The outside air was an abrupt contrast to the heat of the fire. By the time they reached the bottom of the stairs John's teeth were chattering.

"We make a great pair," he muttered. "Both half dressed in the cold. I'll run inside and grab us some clothes, but we'll have to stay out of there until the smoke clears some."

When he started away, Alanna said, "No, wait."

He turned back. In the moonlight, wearing almost nothing, her hair tousled and her skin flushed, she looked like a woman who'd just been well and properly made love to.

That thought went straight to his groin, and he didn't have his hat to hide the way it was affecting him.

Then she gave him a tentative little smile that started his fingers itching to touch her. All those feelings he was a danged fool to have about her began flooding through him at once.

Alanna tried to find the right words for what she was feeling, but couldn't because it all seemed too confusing.

Despite the cold, a warm, tingly feeling had spread through her entire body. It had to be her blasted hormones at work again, spurred on to record activity by the sight of John naked to the waist.

And either the excitement of the fire had left her weak in the knees or he was the source of that problem, too.

She strongly suspected it was him. All lean muscle and dark chest hair, he looked as if he belonged in a male pinup calendar.

January, she decided. He'd be perfect for January, when a woman most wanted to be kept warm at night.

But her hormones weren't responsible for *everything* she was feeling. She couldn't imagine any other man she knew doing what John had just done. And he had no reason to care whether the Magnolia burned to the ground, so she knew he'd done it entirely for her.

"Alanna? Did you want to say something? I really should go grab us some clothes before we freeze."

"I just wanted to say thank you," she murmured. "I thought I was going to lose everything I'd worked on all summer."

"Yeah . . . well, I know your work's the most important thing in the world to you."

She started to nod, then didn't. Only a few hours ago, she would have agreed with that remark. But right at this moment, she wasn't so sure. Her work would never keep her warm on a January night.

"Hellfire, you're already freezing," John muttered when a shiver seized her. He took a step closer and began briskly rubbing his hands back and forth on her bare shoulders.

Then *she* took a step closer and was in his arms.

He whispered her name, the warmth of his breath fanning her cheek. Then he drew her even closer against him, slowly but firmly moving his hands down her back. With only the thin silk of her nightshirt between them, she might as well have been naked to the waist, just as he was.

His nearness sent delicious shivers up her spine. *Hot*, delicious shivers. As she'd suspected, his arms were absolutely perfect for keeping a woman warm on a cold night—regardless of the month.

For keeping *her* warm on a cold night, she corrected herself. It might be totally irrational, but the instant he'd wrapped his arms around her she'd decided the idea of his holding any other woman was unthinkable.

She rested her cheek against his bare chest, drinking in his essence. He smelled of smoke, but there was an underlying scent of primordial male that had her senses reeling.

He molded her to him by resting his hands on her behind and pulling her lower body tightly to his. Feeling his hardness against her started a dull throbbing deep inside her and made her knees weaker yet.

Her bones didn't feel too solid, either. If he released her, she'd likely melt into a pool of desire at his feet.

But she knew he had no intention of releasing her. The way he was holding her felt as if he'd *never* let her go.

John murmured Alanna's name again, shifting one hand to brush her hair away from her neck. Then he bent and kissed the hollow at the base of her throat. She felt and tasted so incredible he thought he was dreaming.

He wasn't, though. Alanna was really in his arms, and she felt so perfect there he wanted her with him forever. Crazy as all this might be, he wasn't merely smitten with her. He'd fallen in love with her, fallen so hard he couldn't imagine ever being without her again. Somehow, someway, they had to stay together for eternity.

Alanna's pulse leapt at the moist warmth of John's lips and she smoothed her hands over his back, loving the feel of him, trying to press her body even closer to his.

By the time he'd kissed his way from her neck to her mouth, the dull throbbing within her had become a burning, aching need. And when his lips met hers she was certain she'd been waiting for his kiss her entire life.

It was a rough-but-tender kiss—hard, searing and proprietary, as if his lips were branding her as *his* woman.

Possessively, he explored her mouth with his tongue and her body with his hands. He slid them under the hem of her nightshirt, over her panties, the heat of his touch burning her skin.

She vaguely wondered at a man from 1887 not being more tentative. Then his hands reached her breasts and he cupped them, beginning to gently caress her nipples with his thumbs, and she stopped wondering about anything.

The fire in the Magnolia had been nothing compared to the fire inside her. John was making her so hot her blood began to boil.

She pressed even closer to him, moaning with arousal.

"My, God, Alanna," he whispered against her throat. "I love you so much I can't believe it."

He loved her. Loved her *so much*. Even after Mary had told her, Alanna still felt stunned by the words. Unbelievable as it seemed, John *had* fallen in love with her. And even more unbelievably, she thought she'd...

Lord, her feelings were so mixed up she didn't know *what* she thought.

John slid his hands slowly back down her body, memorizing her with his fingers, then he dropped his hands to his sides. She reached out and took them in her own, certain she'd die if she wasn't touching him.

He smiled at her in the moonlight. "I'll be right back. I'm just going to go get those things now. Some clothes and blankets, before we really do freeze."

"I'll come with you," she whispered, unable to let go of him.

His arm wrapped securely around her shoulders, they headed along to the Magnolia's front door. Once inside, John lit a lamp and Alanna quickly inspected things, relieved at what she saw.

No water or charred chunks of debris had come through the ceiling, so her work was safe. Only the smoke still hanging in the air said there'd almost been a catastrophe.

"Put on the warmest things you've got," John said, pulling on a flannel shirt. "I'll open the windows down here and we can leave the door open all night. That way, it might not be too bad by morning."

Alanna tugged on socks and jeans, then began wiggling into a sweater and out of her nightshirt at the same time.

Realizing what she was doing made her smile to herself. After what had gone on outside, her modesty hardly seemed warranted.

But she and John…it had happened so suddenly that she hadn't had a second to think about it first. And now that she had time, her facility for thought seemed totally out of whack.

John had said he loved her. That was clear enough in her head. In fact, she suspected it was indelibly burned into her brain. But everything else was all muddled up.

She could recall thinking she'd never fall in love with a man who belonged in the past. And that keeping their relationship platonic was the only way to go. But for the life of her she couldn't remember the reasons. Only by trying really hard could she make a few bits and pieces of them come to her.

There wasn't the slightest possibility of a future with a man who'd soon be going back to 1887. And she wasn't into one-night stands.

She gazed at John anxiously. He was wrestling one of the old windows open, his back and arm muscles clearly defined beneath his shirt.

The man was an absolute hunk. She'd been intensely aware of that right from the start, so was it merely lust she felt for him, even now? Maybe mixed with over-whelming gratitude that he'd kept the Magnolia from burning down?

It was impossible to be sure *what* it was when she'd never felt anything even half as powerful before. But whatever she was feeling, she'd better put her brain back in charge and find some internal cupboard to lock her emotions up in. Because no matter what she felt, John McCully was definitely not the right man for her.

She just hoped having thought that he might be, even briefly, wasn't a harbinger of incipient insanity.

TOTING THREE PILLOWS, while John carried her sleep-ing bag and one of the oil lamps, Alanna followed him across the street to Chester City's barber shop.

It consisted of one tiny room, almost filled by an an-cient padded shaving chair. But it hadn't lost its roof or front door over the years, so he'd decided it would do fine for the remainder of the night.

He spread the sleeping bag out below the front win-dow, then took the pillows and lined them up along it as cushions, making a passable couch.

Or a passable bed, Alanna reflected nervously. She imagined John was thinking more along that line, and she certainly couldn't blame him. Not after she'd been ready to make passionate love with him in the middle of Main Street.

Now that her brain was working again she was going to have to do some fast explaining.

He took off his hat and gun belt, sat down on one of the pillows, and smiled at her so sexily her knees felt weak again. Then he patted the pillow beside him. She sat on the third one, at the far end of their "couch."

It proved not nearly far enough away to make her feel safe. Her brain might be working again, but her body was still having thoughts of its own, and just looking at the man, without touching him, was stretching her willpower to the limit.

He reached for her hands but she clasped them under her chin, saying, "We've got to talk about what happened . . . happened between us, I mean."

"Ah." He let his hands casually drop and gave her another devastating smile. "It's all right, Alanna. I understand."

"You do?" *She* didn't really understand, so how on earth could he?

"Perfectly," he assured her.

"Oh...good." Now what did she do? Ask *him* to tell *her* why she could barely keep her hands off him?

"Will explained it to me."

"Will?"

"My friend . . . Will Lockhart . . . the astrophysicist, remember?"

"Yes, of course I remember." But unless Will Lockhart was clairvoyant, he couldn't have said a word to John about her.

"Just exactly how did he explain it?" she asked.

"Well, he told me how things had changed between men and women over the years. How men have learned to be more considerate . . . lovers."

The way he mumbled the word "lovers," she barely caught it. But she heard it well enough to begin wondering just how much locker-room coaching Will Lockhart had done with John.

If the way he'd held her earlier was a fair example, Will must have been pretty explicit about what women in his era wanted in the lovemaking department. And John must have been an extremely good listener.

That possibility almost made her wish she hadn't been so quick to put her brain back in charge.

"And how, because men had gotten more considerate," John was elaborating, "women had actually come to enjoy..." He paused and cleared his throat. "To enjoy...that sort of thing as much as men. Decent women, I mean."

"Oh. I see." Thank heavens. At least he hadn't decided she was indecent.

"I found it plumb hard to believe. I thought Will had to be exaggerating more than a mite. But the way you...well, I sure do believe him now. He said women made it clear when they'd like...and I could see what he meant. I knew you didn't want me to be a perfect gentleman."

Which certainly explained, Alanna thought ruefully, why he hadn't been more tentative. She could feel her face flushing and was glad there was only the dim light of the lamp.

John cleared his throat a second time. "Will also said that most decent women only enjoyed it with men they were in love with."

Certain her face was beet red by now, she nodded. "Yes, that's usually the case."

John shot her yet another smile, this one a mile wide. "Well, when you made it plain you were enjoying it, I thought it only right to declare myself. Tell you how I felt. And I reckon, even though you didn't say the words to me . . ." He waited for her to rectify that small omission.

"John . . . I wouldn't even try to deny that I feel very attracted to you but . . ."

His smile faded as she searched for a way to explain. "I . . . look," she said at last, "this whole situation is just so unreal. And . . . well, what Will told you was right. Things have definitely changed. But *some* things— John, a lot of women still don't take intimate relationships casually. *I* don't, for one. And you're leaving on Tuesday and we'll never see each other again so . . . so regardless of what I feel . . ."

She hesitated, suddenly near tears and not certain why. Whatever she was feeling for him, it couldn't possibly be love. Falling in love in a matter of days wasn't like her at all. And it wouldn't be the least bit rational. So why was the thought of never seeing him again so incredibly upsetting?

"What *do* you feel, Alanna?" he asked quietly.

"I . . . I don't know exactly. And even if I *did,* no matter what I feel or we both feel . . . John, do you understand what I'm trying to say?"

"No! What in tarnation *are* you trying to say?"

"That . . . that what happened was . . . Oh, John, it doesn't really matter what it was. The point is that the two of us are from different worlds. And I'm just not the type of woman to get involved with a man who's merely passing through her life."

"What are you talking about? You're already involved with me. Hellfire, we've been spending all our time together. We've even been sleeping in the same room, so—"

"John?" she interrupted. Embarrassing as it might be, she had to explain exactly what she was trying to tell him.

"What?"

"When I said *get involved,* I meant... I guess Will didn't happen to mention the term, but what it generally means these days, if you're talking about a man and a woman, is getting *physically* involved."

His expression remained blank, so she was forced to go on. "As in *making love,* John. And I just wouldn't do that casually with a man I know is going to move on soon. No matter how I felt about him."

He simply sat looking at her at first, then shoved himself to his feet and strode across the room. It took him all of three steps to reach the far wall.

He stood facing it for a minute, then turned and rested his hands on the back of the shaving chair. "Alanna, I told you I love you. Does that sound like I mean to merely pass through your life?"

"Well what *do* you mean to do?"

"Hellfire, I don't have any idea! I came to the future for an adventure, not to fall in love. This just snuck up on me. I didn't much like you at first, you know, but all of a sudden I realized I had these feelings and... well, I just haven't had time to think what to do about them."

"There's nothing *to* do about them. Once you've had your adventure you'll be going back to 1887. You even modified Will's formula, so you could figure out how to travel back just as soon as you want."

"Well...1887 *is* where I live, Alanna."

"Exactly. And, in the meantime, you're going to Boston on Tuesday and I'm staying here and—"

"Don't be ridiculous," he snapped.

"Pardon?"

"You can't stay here. You've got to leave just as soon as someone can come and get you."

She sat gazing blankly at him. Either she'd missed something or he'd completely jumped tracks.

"Alanna, haven't you realized what's going on?"

"What do you mean, going on?"

"That fire didn't start itself. Somebody set it."

"How can you leap to a conclusion like that? *You* were the one talking about spontaneous combustion the other night. And without the air conditioner going downstairs it probably got even hotter up there and—"

"The fire started in the middle of the night. Not in the heat of the day. Besides, somebody had been upstairs. They used the bucket."

"What?"

"The fire bucket. Didn't you notice? When we were up there getting my mattress, the bucket was hanging on the wall. But tonight it was lying on the floor. I only found it by accident, when I kicked it in the dark."

"It must have fallen off the wall, then."

"After hanging there for more than a hundred years?"

"Well . . . maybe we banged it when we were up there the first time." She was certain, though, that they hadn't.

The way John was shaking his head said he was certain, too. "Those guys who want to get rid of you set that fire, Alanna. And you can forget about them being ghosts. Roy told me that mental energy stuff isn't very reliable. That it was hard for him even to manage using a gun. So a couple of ghosts haven't managed everything that's been happening. Those guys I heard in the mine are as alive as we are."

She didn't argue this time because, if John was right about the fire being set, she suspected he was also right about the arsonists.

Using mental energy *was* tricky. Besides, she had trouble with the idea of even an extremely malevolent ghost starting a fire in Chester City. A lot of ghosts called it home, and a fire could destroy the entire town.

"But you can't be one hundred percent sure the fire was set," she finally said.

"I'm ninety-nine-percent sure. We can go back up there in the daylight and see if there are any clues besides the bucket being moved. But while we were getting things organized to bring over here, I was thinking everything through."

"And?"

"And the way I figure it, I've been waiting for those characters to make their move without realizing they'd already made it. And tonight was their second try."

"I'm not following you."

"The air conditioner battery. They were the ones who took it. It's been so danged hot in the Magnolia the last couple of days...Alanna, *think*. They were hoping you'd decide it was too hot to stay here. But when they didn't see any sign of your leaving, they started the fire."

John took his hands off the back of the barber's chair, walked around and sank into it, then simply sat gazing at her.

"But what about the bucket?" she asked after a minute. "If somebody was starting a fire, why on earth would they need to use a bucket?"

"That puzzled me, too. Then I got to thinking how dry all those mattresses were. And wondering why that one didn't go right up in flames instead of just smoldering.''

"Of course. It should have burned like crazy, shouldn't it. And the fire should have spread, too.''

"But it didn't—maybe because whoever set it didn't want the place to burn down so fast you wouldn't have a chance to get out. I guess they didn't want to kill you—just scare you enough to make you leave. And if only a bit of the mattress was dry, only enough to start a fire, but the rest of it was damp...''

"It would just smolder," Alanna concluded, realizing what he was getting at. Someone had used the bucket to wet down most of that mattress.

"So, like I told you at the start," John said, "you have to get out of Chester City. Because if they can't drive you out by making you uncomfortable or scaring you, maybe next time they won't worry about killing you.''

CHAPTER TEN

WHEN THE MORNING LIGHT woke John, he had such a crick in his neck he could barely move.

He glared over at Alanna. It was entirely her fault he'd slept in the danged barber's chair.

All he'd done, last night, was point out that her life would be in danger if she didn't get out of Chester City right away. But after he'd made his case—very calmly and logically—the next thing he knew they were fighting again.

By the time they'd finished, he was so mad he wouldn't have shared that bed with her if she'd begged him to. Of course, there hadn't been any chance of that.

He sat watching her sleep for a minute—on the bed he'd made before she'd told him she wasn't going to *get involved* with him because he was just passing through her life.

Then, when he'd said that just passing through wasn't what he had in mind, and she'd asked what he *did* have in mind...well, admitting he had no idea might not have been the smartest thing to say.

It had been the truth, though. Since the first moment he'd realized he was smitten with her he'd known how crazy he'd been to let that happen. But he'd just gone ahead and let his feelings multiply, anyway—without thinking at all on what he was going to do about them.

He'd sure thought on it before he'd gone to sleep, though. Once his anger had cooled down some, he'd thought on it long and hard. And he'd finally realized what he'd do about things if they were in 1887.

He'd ask Alanna to marry him, that's what he'd do.

She might be an impossible woman who made him furious half the time, but the other half more than made up for that. So much so, he'd started wondering how he was going to live without her once he left.

Because she'd been right. After he'd spent a little time in 2014, he'd be going back to where he belonged, while she'd stay here. That meant he really *was* just passing through her life, and whether he liked the fact or not, he couldn't see any way around it.

He knew danged well she'd never consider giving up her precious research to live in 1887. And the only way he could stay in 2014 for very long would be to find work here—which would be more than a mite tricky.

Will had talked about everyone needing *credentials* to get a job. And he wouldn't just need a job, he'd need a danged good job. He could hardly expect a university professor like Alanna to marry a man who...

Of course, she might not even want to marry him. Not even if he *could* manage to get a good job. Will had said that was another way women had changed. They'd gotten so independent that a lot of them refused to get married. Even if they were in love.

Well, he'd sure have to put his boot down about that. If he was going to stay here...

But he knew those were insane thoughts. He wasn't going to stay in 2014 and he wasn't going to marry Alanna. Hell, he probably wasn't even going to kiss her again—because she wasn't going to let him.

He gazed over at her again, and it made him feel as if there were steel bars pressing in on his heart. She was the most beautiful woman he'd ever seen, the only woman he'd ever wanted to marry, and he couldn't have her. All he could do was try to keep her from harm. So he still had to convince her to leave town *now*. Which would be tough as all get-out when she was as stubborn as twenty mules.

"I just *can't* go," she'd kept insisting last night. "I have to have this final week here. I still want to try and help Roy—*my* way. And I've got to talk to another ghost or two. Every extra one adds to the value of my research."

Hellfire, he'd tried to understand her thinking, but he just couldn't. She figured her danged research was so important she was ready to risk her life over it. And to his mind, that was plumb crazy.

He swore silently at himself. Just looking at her lying there, even though she was fully dressed, make him hard with wanting her. He wished to blazes it didn't, though.

Since he couldn't have her, he shouldn't be letting himself want her even a little. But when he'd held her in his arms, she'd felt so good that the thought of making love to her was enough to drive him mad.

She stirred in her sleep, then opened her eyes and glanced warily over at him, as if trying to decide whether he was still angry.

"'Morning," he said, forcing a smile. Now that she'd had some sleep, maybe she'd discuss things more sensibly.

She sat up and eyed him curiously. "What's wrong with you?"

"Wrong?"

"You're holding your head funny."

"Oh, that. It's nothing. I've just got a crick in my neck."

"From sleeping in that chair." She gave him a guilty look, then pushed herself up. "Let me see if I can help."

When she began massaging his neck, he tried his hardest not to react to her touch. It was impossible. He wanted her so badly that—

He *had* to stop dwelling on it, though, and concentrate on talking some sense into her. But this time he wasn't going to jump in with both boots. This time he'd ease into the subject real slow, maybe even pretend he thought she had a point, so she'd see how reasonable he was being in the face of her pigheadedness.

"Better?" she finally asked.

"Much...thanks." His neck did feel a whole lot better—she had the touch of an angel. He stood up, unable to keep from thinking how he'd love to feel those clever hands of hers a lot further south than his neck.

He opened the door, saying, "Let's go back over to the Magnolia and check things out. See if we can find any clues about our fire setters."

"All right." Alanna followed John out of the barber shop, feeling more suspicious with each passing second. She'd expected the first words out of his mouth this morning would be about her leaving. But he hadn't even mentioned it yet. Was he trying his reverse psychology again?

She trailed across Main Street after him, trying to keep her eyes off his broad shoulders. Looking at them made her recall how hard and muscular his body felt pressed against hers. And that was a dangerous train of thought.

She *wasn't* going to have a brief affair with John, no matter how much she wanted to make love with him. Her brain still realized it was a bad idea.

But even giving him that little neck rub had started her pulse racing and her heart pounding, so the further away from him she stayed, the better.

There was only today left to get through. Tomorrow, Frank Bronkowski would arrive with the groceries and take John McCully out of her life.

That prospect started sudden tears stinging her eyes. She told herself the reaction was absurd. She was *not* in love with John. And he probably wasn't *really* in love with her, either.

Maybe he honestly believed he was. He was so forthright that she didn't suspect him of lying. But despite what he believed, or what Mary claimed she could see written all over his face— Well, it was critical to keep reminding herself that pure and simple lust could account for what both she and John were feeling.

And logic told her that that's what *was* accounting for it. Love couldn't be real if it was just for the moment. And that's all they had. Just a few brief moments in time, when their lives should never have intersected in the first place.

"Not too bad in here now," John said as they stepped inside the lodging house.

He was right. The smoky smell wasn't entirely gone, but it wasn't nearly as bad as it had been.

"Let's head upstairs, see what we've got," he suggested, starting up.

Alanna followed him, unable to stop thinking that the two of them should never have met. It had been against the cosmic laws of the universe. And how could people fall in love against the dictates of cosmic laws?

They couldn't, she told herself. And they hadn't. Not *really*. Aside from anything else—aside from *everything* else, to be more accurate—she couldn't possibly have fallen in love with a man who believed he had a God-given right to tell her what to do.

Not that ordering her around was doing him any good. She wasn't going to leave Chester City until she absolutely had to. Nervous as she might be about staying, it was exactly what she intended to do.

She just hoped she'd finally made that clear to John last night. She'd had more than enough of his arguing.

By the time they reached the the second floor, the smoky stench was stronger, but still not awful enough to keep them from poking around.

"What's this?" John asked after a minute, picking something up off the floor and holding it out to her.

It was a very soggy matchbook, and its being there left no doubt in her mind that the fire had been deliberately set.

The print on the cover had run, but she could make it out. Happy's Bar and Grill, it read. Fine Dining in Las Vegas, Since 2010.

"What is it?" John asked again.

"A matchbook, of course."

"A what?"

"Oh...oh, I guess they hadn't been invented by 1887."

"No, I guess they hadn't. So what in tarnation is it?"

She reached for it and peeled back the soggy cover. "Matches. For lighting the mattress on fire."

"Yeah?" He took the matchbook back and looked at it with more interest. "I'm used to matches in boxes. But is this...*matchbook* something a ghost might have used?"

"I doubt it. These matches can't be from earlier than 2010, which would make for a very young ghost. And it would take decades for one to get good enough with mental energy to use a matchbook."

"So I was right. We're dealing with live men."

Alanna nodded, uncertain whether that made her feel better or worse.

John flipped the matchbook over in his hand, thinking. It had occurred to him, long before now, that even in this barren area of Nevada there had to be a lawman in charge. But he hadn't reckoned it would be a good idea to contact the fellow—not with Alanna insisting those voices he'd heard had belonged to ghosts.

He'd taken her for a crazy woman when he'd first met her. And from things she'd said since, he knew that there were still a lot of people who didn't believe in what she referred to as the paranormal. So he hadn't reckoned that calling a lawman out here, then telling him that ghosts were causing problems, would be a right good idea.

But now that she'd decided the troublemakers were flesh and blood... Hell, if he couldn't make her leave town, getting the law here before he headed for Boston had to be the next best thing.

"Well," he said, sticking the wet matchbook in his shirt pocket. "I guess now that these guys have done something as serious as setting a fire, we should call... what would he be out here these days? A marshal?"

Alanna looked at him blankly.

"The law... who's responsible for the law in these parts?"

"The state police."

"Oh, well, then that's who we'd better call."

"Call to do what?"

"Why, to come here, of course. To find out where those guys are holed up and cart them off to the nearest jail."

"You mean come here and search through the buildings?"

"I reckon that's how they'd go about finding them, all right."

"John, don't be ridiculous. I've told you a hundred times that I've got only this last week to find more ghosts to talk to."

"So?"

"So, there's absolutely no way we're having the police come here."

"Alanna, don't be—"

"*Absolutely* no way. How often do I have to remind you that living people make ghosts nervous?"

"But I—"

"And the state police would be far worse than regular people. A lot of Chester City's ghosts weren't exactly fond of sheriffs when they were alive. And if the police showed up here and started searching through buildings like a herd of storm troopers, every last ghost in town would be out of here—so fast you'd feel the air moving as they left."

John half wanted to ask what in tarnation a storm trooper was, but she was making him so danged mad again that he refused to give her the satisfaction of knowing something *else* that he didn't.

JOHN PACED THE WIDTH of the Miner's Saloon once more, so frustrated he couldn't stand still. He hadn't really wanted to leave Alanna alone in the Magnolia, not even knowing she had those two guns of hers, but he needed help again. And besides that, if he'd stayed there any longer he just might have murdered her.

"If I had a horse," he muttered, turning back toward Mary and Roy, "I'd hog-tie her, throw her across my saddle and ride out of town with her—right this minute."

"You know she'd never pardon you for doing something like that," Mary said quietly.

"But at least she wouldn't end up dead, would she."

"She's not going to end up dead," Roy assured him. "You and I can handle those guys, John. I'll bet we can handle them easy."

"First we've got to find them."

"We'll find them. And when we do, we'll make them sorry they ever set foot in Chester City. Fellows who would come sneaking in the night, and set a fire in *my* lodging house, can't be nothing but yellow-livered skunks, right?"

John agreed, realizing it had slipped his mind that Roy had built the Magnolia.

"And there are two of them and two of us," Roy was going on. "Even odds."

"Better than even," Mary put in. "I can help, too. Maybe Roy and I can't do everything as well as we could when we were alive, but in some ways we can be *more* helpful."

"How's that?" John did his best to conceal his doubts.

"Well, it's easier for us to drift up and check Broken Hill than for you to walk all the way up there," Mary explained. "And if they aren't in the mine, we'll search every building in town if we have to. Roy only had time to check the most likely ones yesterday. But today we can look everywhere until we find them. And they won't even know they've been found, because we won't materialize."

"And if you did find them," John said, starting to feel a bit better, "then we *could* take care of them. The only problem would be if they caught up with Alanna before you two caught up with them. If that happened, and I wasn't with her... well, damnation, I'm just going to *have* to tag along with her. No matter how much she hates the idea."

"Compromise with her, John," Mary said.

"Compromise how?"

"Alanna's only worried about you frightening off ghosts. So why not suggest going with her, but waiting on the street when she goes into buildings?"

"But what if something happens while she's inside?"

"Well, if you'd like, I could spend the afternoon with her again."

"She'd probably object to that, too," he muttered. "I swear, I've never met another woman like her."

Mary smiled at that, making him wonder what she thought was funny. He couldn't see a danged thing.

"John," she said after a moment, "Alanna wouldn't object at all. Not after I convinced a new ghost to talk to her yesterday. She'll be thrilled if I offer to go with her again. And if we ran into any trouble, you'd be right outside."

"Sure," Roy put in. "Mary can go with Alanna while I do the snooping around."

"Just be certain you don't exhaust yourself," Mary told him.

Roy waved off her remark, but she glanced at John with a concerned expression, saying, "He has to be careful. Our life forces aren't as strong as they used to be."

John nodded. He wasn't certain what she meant, but Alanna could explain it to him—if she was speaking to him when he got back to the lodging house.

"So?" Mary pressed. "Will you suggest my going with her?"

"I reckon it's worth a try. But Alanna never seems right partial to my suggestions."

"Uh...do you think that might be because they seem more like orders to her?"

"You're saying I should sound like I'm *asking* her, not telling her?"

"I think she'd take more kindly to it."

"All right," he said slowly. "I'll go give it a shot."

"John?" Roy said as he started for the door.

He turned back in time to catch the questioning glance Mary was giving Roy.

"It's come time to say my piece," Roy told her. "If John had already decided he was going to tell us without Alanna's okay, he'd have done it now, while she wasn't here."

"Tell you what?" John asked.

"We were in the Magnolia yesterday," Roy said. "We decided to drop in and tell you I hadn't found any trace of those fellows—just after Mary came back from her afternoon with Alanna."

"But then you changed your minds?" John asked uncertainly.

Roy shook his head. "Like I said, we were there."

"We just drifted in through the wall," Mary offered quietly. "Instead of knocking on the door. And before we could materialize, we overheard enough of what you were telling Alanna that we couldn't resist staying invisible and listening. We're sorry...it wasn't at all mannerly. And we've agreed that we won't do it again. From now on, we promise we'll be visible when we're around you and Alanna.''

It took a second for John to realize what Mary and Roy had overheard. When he did, he got a mighty anxious feeling.

He knew Alanna had been right about not mentioning his calculations for the moment. Until they came to a decision about helping Roy and Mary time travel, he shouldn't say a word.

Apparently, though, it was a little too late to be thinking about that.

"You heard me saying I'd been fooling with my friend's time travel formula," he finally ventured, trying not to give away anything they didn't already know. Hopefully, they hadn't overheard very much.

"We heard *everything*," Roy said, dashing his hopes. "We heard you say there'll be five minutes on Wednesday when we can get back to 1895. And we want to go."

"We *desperately* want to go," Mary put in.

"If you tell us how to do it," Roy went on, "we sure in blazes won't be anywhere near Chester City on Independence Day. And when I don't get killed, we'll get married on the seventh, just like we planned."

"I have the most beautiful gown," Mary murmured. "It came all the way from New York City."

John glanced at her, then quickly looked away when he saw her eyes were glistening. He recalled Alanna telling him how Mary had cried showing her that dress. Hearing the story had made him feel badly for her, but seeing tears in her eyes made him feel even worse.

"We know you want to help us, John," Roy pressed.

"Yes...I do...but if you heard *everything*, you heard why Alanna's against the idea. She wants to help you, too, but sending you back would be against the rules."

"Rules," Roy muttered. "What do rules matter when we're talking about life and death? Mary's life. My life. The life together that was stolen from us. John, you can give us the chance to get back everything we lost."

"But—"

"And you're like us. You come from a time when people didn't make up rules against every little thing. When decent folks just did whatever they felt was right."

Roy's voice quavered on the final words. Just a little, but enough to make John want to promise he'd help them. Regardless of what Alanna thought.

He caught himself, though, and said, "Roy, it's not *just* the rules. There are...you weren't in the Magnolia later, too, were you? In the evening?"

The idea of people listening in, when he couldn't see them, gave him a very spooky feeling. Of course, Roy and Mary weren't exactly people, no matter how alive they seemed. But still, it was no wonder Alanna wore those ghost-seeing goggles so much of the time.

"No, we weren't there in the evening," Roy was saying.

"Well, Alanna and I talked about the possibility some more, then. And as I said, it's not just the rules. There's also what she calls the *downside* of your attempting the trip back."

"Downside?" Roy repeated.

John nodded. "It means there'd be some risk involved."

Neither Mary nor Roy said a word; they simply gazed at him until he explained.

"See, first of all, to figure out when you might be able to travel, I had to modify my friend's formula."

"We heard that part," Roy told him.

"Well, what you didn't hear, later on, was us talking about the chance I could have made an error in adjusting it."

"How much of a chance?" Mary asked quietly.

"That's impossible to say. I don't *think* I made any mistakes, but the only way to be sure is to try it out. Trouble is, if I've done anything wrong, you wouldn't reach 1895. You could end up in any year."

Roy took Mary's hand and gave it a pat before turning back to John. "Is that the only risk? That you made an error and we'd end up in a different year?"

"No... I'm afraid there are a few others."

The couple's expressions grew even more somber, making John feel worse yet. They'd probably been in seventh heaven, ever since they'd heard there was the possibility they'd have a second chance.

"Another thing," he continued, "is that time travel through Broken Hill isn't entirely reliable. Even if the formula is fine, the tunnels are confusing and... well, the first time I tried to come here, I ended up in 1850."

Mary gave Roy an anxious glance. "We weren't even born in 1850."

John wished he didn't have to say anything more. But now that he'd gone this far, he should tell them everything. Assuming Alanna finally went along with the idea, Roy and Mary would have a tough decision to make, so the longer they had to think about it, the better.

"And if you *did* end up in the wrong time," he pressed on, "well, the more Alanna and I talked about it, the more we realized that your being ghosts adds extra complications."

"Go on," Roy said, not quite evenly.

"It's confusing, because we're not really sure how everything would work. But when I found myself in 1850, I managed to figure when I'd be able to travel out of that year, then just lived there until the time was right."

"But we wouldn't be able to figure it out," Mary said.

"No, you wouldn't."

"So we'd be stuck wherever we ended up," Roy said. "But we'd still be together, darling," he added, giving Mary a reassuring smile. "That's all that really matters."

John cleared his throat uneasily and they both looked at him again.

"There's still the complication of your being ghosts," he told them. "See, we figure that if you didn't make it all the way back to 1895, you'd *still* be ghosts—just in a different year."

"But as long as we made it back to before I was killed?" Roy said. "Then everything would be fine, wouldn't it?"

"Well...unless you went back too far. It's like Mary mentioned a minute ago—1850 is before you were born. Before I was born, too. But even though I went back without any problem, Alanna's afraid you might not be as lucky. She's worried that, since you've already died, if you ended up back too far you'd be...."

"We'd be what?" Mary whispered.

"Nonexistent. Ever," John forced himself to say. "I don't understand exactly how, but *somehow* it would be that you'd never existed at all."

"Then we'd never have met...never have fallen in love," Mary murmured, looking at Roy. "And, oh, love, how could I ever give up my memories of that?"

She glanced at John. "It must be difficult for you to understand, but ghosts have so little. And I treasure my memories of being in love with Roy more than anything." A single tear trickled down her cheek.

"We'll have to think on this a spell, John," Roy was saying. "But you'll talk to Alanna again? Try to convince her? So that if we do decide we want to take the chance...?"

"Yes, I'll talk to her again."

"Right away?" Mary said. "When you go back to the Magnolia? Yesterday, it sounded as if it would take time to persuade her, and if she doesn't agree...

"Because I want Alanna to agree more than ever, now," she added, looking at Roy. "Between knowing that we could cause serious trouble for her *and* the risks to us...well, she's the scientist, and I really need her to say she thinks it's worth whatever chances we'd all be taking."

"John?" Roy said, patting Mary's hand but looking straight at him.

"I'll talk to her about it. And I'll try to convince her to go along with whatever you decide. You have my word on that."

"And if she still won't agree?" Roy asked. "Will you tell us how to travel back, anyway?"

John slowly shook his head, saying, "I just don't know." And he truly didn't.

CHAPTER ELEVEN

THE FIRST THING John did when he got back to the Magnolia was tell Alanna that Mary had offered to spend another afternoon with her. Then he asked about going along with them—if he didn't go into the buildings.

But even though he tried danged hard to make it sound as if he was only *suggesting* the plan, he knew she probably wasn't going to agree to it.

She did, though. "I think that's a really good idea," she said without a moment's hesitation. "And...well, thank you for still wanting to keep an eye out for me. To tell you the truth, I wasn't too concerned when I thought those fellows were ghosts. But now that we know they aren't, I'd feel a lot better knowing you were nearby."

When she finished speaking, she gave him a smile that made him feel ten feet tall. He suddenly wanted to hold her so badly he was aching with need, but she quickly backed away and said, "I'll make some lunch before we go, okay?"

John merely nodded. If he told her what he *really* wanted her to do, she'd start in again about how she wasn't going to get involved with him. Those weren't words he particularly wanted to hear.

He was mighty partial to the words she'd just spoken, though. She'd feel better knowing he was nearby.

A lot better. Damnation, that was more like the way a woman was supposed to feel about her man.

Of course, he wasn't her man. But he sure as blazes had to do something about that, because he couldn't go more than two minutes without remembering how incredible it had been to stand in the moonlight with her last night... his arms around her... kissing her and touching her.

And the way she'd reacted to his touch, her body telling him how much she wanted more... and that urgent sound she'd made deep in her throat....

Lord Almighty, he was straining the buttons on his jeans again, just thinking about her body pressed to his, about how soft and warm her lips had been, about the way she'd moved against him, driving him crazy.

If he could only figure out what to do about that *merely passing through* problem.... Well, he was just going to have to figure something out, because he'd never before met a woman he wanted to spend the rest of his life with.

Of course, there was still that other little problem he had to worry about. What if Roy and Mary decided they wanted to try getting back to 1895, and Alanna continued to argue against it?

For all the possible risks, he really believed he could get the couple there safely. And if they were willing to take the chance, he wanted to help them go.

But if he helped them without Alanna's agreeing to it, he knew she'd never forgive him. Of course, then there'd be no point in even trying to think of a solution to the *merely passing through* problem. If he crossed Alanna about Roy and Mary, it would ruin his chance at having a future with her.

He glanced over at her. She was setting one corner of the worktable for lunch, and just watching her took his mind off Roy and Mary.

Instead, he let himself think a little more about how good Alanna had felt in his arms. So good that there had to be some way to keep her in his life.

He waited until they finished lunch to tell her about Roy and Mary overhearing their conversation.

"*All* of it?" she asked, clearly upset.

"As far as I could tell. So I didn't see I had any choice but to tell them everything else—about the risks there might be."

"What did they say?"

"They wanted to think about it. They wanted me to talk to you again, too—about agreeing to let them go, if that's the way they decide."

Alanna pushed herself up from the chair and wandered over to the front window. She knew she shouldn't agree. It was against all she believed in. But what if they decided they wanted to go, and John still felt he should help them?

Should she just keep quiet and hope nothing went wrong? Hope that nobody ever found out what she'd been a party to?

Odds were, she could get away with it. But *she'd* always know she'd done something unethical. She stood looking at the heat waves shimmering in the air outside, trying to determine right from wrong.

"What are you thinking?" John asked.

She turned back to face him. "That I want to help them as much as you do. But I'm not sure you're doing the right thing. I think . . . I think I could go along with it more easily if I felt sure they'd be fine. But what if they did end up in the wrong year? If they remained ghosts and nothing improved for them?''

''Would it be any worse?''

''I don't know. But what if they ended up back too far and ceased to exist? Surely, that would be worse.''

John shrugged slowly. ''Mary thought it would be, too. She said she treasured her memories of being in love with Roy more than anything and couldn't bear to risk giving them up.''

''That's all they have, John. There's nothing for them but memories. It's so sad.''

''I know. Just hearing them talk about it made me appreciate being alive. But they aren't even certain they want to chance going back. They just want to know you'll go along with them if that's what they decide. Mary in particular. She really seems to need your approval. So... what should I tell them?''

Lord, if only she knew. ''Let me think about it for a little longer, okay?''

''It's already Monday,'' John reminded her. ''And I'll be leaving.... What time will your delivery fellow be coming tomorrow?''

''Early. He always comes in the morning.''

''Then we don't have much more time left to think about it, do we?''

She shook her head. They didn't have nearly enough time left to think about Roy and Mary, and they didn't have nearly enough time to be together.

Taking a deep breath, she tried to calm herself. ''John, I just can't make a snap decision. You're all asking me to say I'll agree to something when I know I shouldn't. Yet, if I don't... Oh, I really hate this. I feel as if we're holding their fate in our hands.''

"I reckon that's because we are," John said quietly. "And I don't see how we can choose someone else's fate for them. Seems to me, we should abide by whatever they decide."

Alanna pushed her hair back from her face, wishing John had never said a word about modifying Will's formula.

She didn't want to play God. She didn't want to break the rules. And she didn't want to see Roy and Mary suffer any more than they already had. But she couldn't get everything she wanted.

"Look, how about this?" she finally suggested. "We'll go out with Mary, now, while Roy checks around for those guys. Then, later, the four of us can sit down together and discuss the situation. I'd really still like to have another try at talking Roy over to the other side. That would be the safest solution."

"But they'd still be dead. That isn't what they want."

"At least they'd be at peace. Roy wouldn't be torn up inside, and Mary wouldn't be worried about him all the time."

John didn't say another word, just sat watching her, his dark eyes solemn.

She turned away and stared out the window once more. All it took was looking at him to remind her of how soon he'd be gone. And the more she thought about it, the more certain she became that she didn't want him to leave her. Not ever. But there was no way he'd stay.

Come morning, he'd be heading off to see his bright lights and big cities, and then he'd be going home. And she'd be left to face the cold January nights alone.

Slowly, she rubbed her hands up and down her bare arms, feeling suddenly cool, despite the oppressive heat of the day. Then Mary materialized outside the Magnolia and it was time to go.

ROY COULD HEAR TWO MEN talking, but he couldn't see them. That puzzled him until he recalled John saying he'd thought they were holed up in a secondary tunnel.

At first, because of the strange way sounds travel in mines, he couldn't figure out exactly where that shaft was. And not being able to close in on them was annoying the devil out of him.

They seemed to be in the midst of an argument, but their words weren't clear. Unfortunately, his hearing wasn't nearly as good as it had been.

Of course, nothing was what it once had been. And for all he tried to keep Mary from knowing, he was deteriorating so quickly it terrified him.

His memory had faded a lot. He had trouble remembering even details that had once been really important to him. And most of the time, his mental energy was so low he couldn't be sure of managing anything physical.

He made a more concerted effort at listening and finally pinpointed where the sound was coming from.

When he drifted through the wall toward it, he ended up practically on top of the two men. That made him feel a little better, and he settled in to listen.

"I still say we should kill both of 'em and be done with it," one of them was saying.

"Just shut the hell up about that, will you, Chilli?" the other one snapped. "I'm sicka listening to you mouth off about it."

"But we've been here since Thursday. How the hell long we gonna hav'ta wait?"

"Long as it takes."

"We're gonna starve."

"We ain't gonna starve. We gotta ton more supplies than we shoulda needed. And if that guy wasn't here, we'd of scared her off by now for sure."

"Yeah, well he is here, ain't he. But if we was to kill 'em—"

"You's a lunatic, you know that? You wanna end up in the pen again? On death row this time?"

"We wouldn't. We could kill 'em and nobody'd ever know it was us. We'd never get caught."

"No? Well, if you's so smart, how come you's done two stretches in jail? You figured nobody'd ever know it was you broke into them houses, neither."

"That was different."

"Yeah, you got that one right, little brother. The cops work a lot harder at catchin' killers than at catchin' two-bit burglars."

"Dammit, Artie, we're in the middle o' nowhere. Who's gonna know we was even here?"

"How 'bout the guy in the grocery store? That Branchwater place was only fifty miles away. And how 'bout the guy in the gas station? He's even got my name on the credit card slip. *Plus,* you hadda go and ask him howta get here. You's a lunatic *and* an idiot. I can read a map, even if you can't."

"I thought maybe there was a shortcut. And stop talkin' to me like I was three years old."

"Then stop *thinking* like you was three years old. We don't hav'ta kill them. We just gotta get them outta the Magnolia so we can find where old Roy hid the damned gold."

Hearing that took Roy so aback he actually felt the jolt of surprise. How in tarnation did these two galoots know he'd hidden gold in the Magnolia? For that matter, how in tarnation did they know his name?

"So let's stop talkin' and start thinkin'," the one named Artie was saying. "We gotta think of some way that'll finally get rid of them."

The one called Chilli glared at Artie but didn't say another word. He just stretched his legs out in front of him, then pulled a gun out from under his bedroll and began aiming shots at imaginary targets.

He put Roy in mind of someone, but he couldn't think who. That fellow sure had a volatile temper, though. That much he was sure of. And he couldn't help wondering how long Artie would be able to keep the reins on Chilli.

He eyed the two men closely once they'd fallen silent, memorizing details to report to John.

Both were big, about John's size, but were only in their middle to late twenties. Both had dark, greased-back hair and sallow complexions. Artie was a tad heavier and a couple of years older. "Little brother" he'd called Chilli.

Like Chilli, Artie was sitting on a bedroll. Behind them, a few feet down the tunnel, was a small stack of cans and bottled water. Garbage was piled against the other wall.

One of them had said they'd arrived Thursday. And from the amount of garbage, Roy guessed they'd settled into Broken Hill right away.

They didn't seem any too smart, but they had enough brains to realize a mine would be the coolest place around.

Waiting for them to start talking again, he let his thoughts return to the question of how they knew about his gold.

The banks had been none too secure in mining towns, so when the Magnolia was being built he'd rigged a secret hiding place in it. And that was where he'd stashed most of the gold dust his customers had paid him over the years.

But he'd never told that to a soul. In fact, he'd made sure nobody would ever suspect he kept gold in the lodging house by going to the bank regularly, just like all the other businessmen in Chester City.

He'd never deposited more than a quarter of what he actually took in, though. And by the time he'd been killed there must have been—

That familiar feeling of frustration began seeping through him. It had been a long, long time since he'd thought about the gold he'd put aside for his future with Mary.

Once you were dead, there was no point in thinking about the material things of life. And now, try as he might, he couldn't remember how much there'd been hidden away in the Magnolia when he'd been killed.

Of course, he'd only had a rough idea of the total, even back then. Keeping a written record would have been right foolish. Someone might have come across it. So he'd just kept adding little bags of gold dust to the ones already in his secret hiding place.

He'd planned to surprise Mary by showing it all to her after the wedding. She'd have been plumb amazed that she'd married such a rich man. He'd easily had enough to ensure a secure future for them and—

And it would *still* be enough. Mary and he could have a wonderful life together with all that gold, just like he'd planned long ago.

He hadn't been thinking about that. Tarnation, he hadn't been thinking a minute beyond them actually getting back to 1895 and being alive again.

Learning that was possible had been so danged overwhelming . . . and it had been so many years since he'd had any thoughts of a future. . . .

He hadn't actually *forgotten* about the gold, but he'd had a lot of other things to worry about, what with being a ghost and all. Now that he had a chance to live again, though . . .

A feeling of excitement rushed through him. Excitement and anticipation.

It had been so long since he'd felt optimistic he could scarcely believe that's what he was feeling now. But all those risks involved in trying to travel back . . . why, he could practically see his concerns over them fading away.

No matter how worried Mary was about taking the chance, he knew for certain now what their decision was going to be. A second shot at a future just had to be worth *any* risk. And then he'd still be able to surprise her with the gold—just like he'd planned so many years ago.

But he was going to have to tell John and Alanna why these guys wanted them out of the Magnolia so badly. And that would spoil the surprise for Mary. Unless . . .

Maybe he could tell them there was just a little gold hidden away. And that Artie and Chilli must figure there to be a lot more than there really was.

Considering the idea for a minute, he decided it would work. Then he'd still be able to surprise Mary, because she wouldn't be expecting much when they got back . . . *if* they got back.

No, *when* they got back. He had a right good feeling about that now, and it seemed to be getting stronger by the minute. All they needed was John's help, and come

Wednesday they were going to make it safely back to July third, 1895.

And Wednesday was the day after tomorrow. That meant, he realized, his excitement growing even stronger, that they'd only be ghosts for one more day. Then they'd be Roy Hardin and Mary Beckwith again— not mere shadows of themselves.

The exhilaration he felt was beginning to grow unbearable, so he focused on Chilli, trying to stop thinking about the prospect of being alive once more.

Chilli was still playing games with his gun, and Roy suddenly realized who the man reminded him of.

The thought tempered his excitement with anxiety. Chilli looked a whole lot like Billy the Kid.

Young Bill Bonney had been killed before Roy came West, but folks had still been talking about him and there'd still been Wanted posters around. And the picture on those posters had looked a whole lot like Chilli.

And the way Chilli'd been going on about killing John and Alanna, he was probably as mean a little sidewinder as the Kid had been.

Roy took a deep breath, willing himself strength. John would go along with helping him and Mary. He just knew that was going to work out. But in the meantime, he'd better do all he could to help John.

He decided Artie and Chilli weren't likely to come up with any brilliant ideas very fast. So instead of waiting here, maybe he'd be wiser to go scout around and see what else he could learn.

WHEN ALANNA arrived back at the Magnolia with Mary and John, the only thing she wanted to do was collapse onto her sleeping bag. The afternoon had been a total washout as far as finding ghosts to interview, and the heat had all but done her in.

Then Roy opened the front door and stepped out onto Main Street, wearing an enormous grin that went a long way to reviving her.

Opening the door, rather than just drifting through the wall, meant he was feeling stronger than he often did. And he looked so pleased with himself that he must have found the creeps who were trying to drive her out of town. Maybe now they could do something about them.

Roy eased the lapels of his suit jacket back a little and laced his thumbs under his suspenders, looking proud as punch.

"Roy?" Mary said, hurrying over to him. "Roy, what is it? What's happened?"

"You found those guys, didn't you," John said.

"Yup, I sure did." He wrapped his arm around Mary's waist and smiled at her, then looked back at John. "Artie and Chilli, their names are."

"Those names mean anything to you?" John asked Alanna.

When she shook her head, he turned to Roy again.

"They're brothers," Roy went on. "And it's just like John thought from the first. They're holed up in one of Broken Hill's side tunnels. I reckon they were off someplace when I checked the mine yesterday, or I'd have spotted them then."

"And what are they doing here?" John asked. "Why do they want to get rid of Alanna? Did you find out?"

Roy nodded. "You were right about why they're here, too. When you said you heard them talking about coming to get some gold, it didn't make any sense to me. But it does now. It's *my* gold they're after."

"*Your* gold?" Mary said.

"I had a little gold dust stashed away in the Magnolia."

"You never told me that."

"I never told anybody. It was only a little, darling, not even worth mentioning. But they seem to think they're going to find a whole lot."

"But how do they know there's *any*, love?"

Roy shook his head. "I have no idea. Somehow they do, though. And that's why they want John and Alanna out. So they can have as long as they need to search for it."

"That explains," Alanna said, "why they just started the mattress smoldering. They didn't want to set a fire that would burn the whole place down."

John swore quietly. "I thought they wanted to scare Alanna off without really harming her," he explained to Roy and Mary. "But they weren't worrying about her safety at all. They were only worrying about the gold."

Having realized that did nothing to improve Alanna's mood. Neither did the serious expression on John's face. Roy might have discovered where this Artie and Chilli were, but that didn't mean she was anywhere near safe from them yet.

"I'd better head right up to Broken Hill," John muttered. "The faster I get rid of those guys, the better."

He turned toward the mountains, but Roy said, "Just a minute. You can't go marching up there in broad daylight. They've both got guns. Besides, I haven't finished telling you all I learned."

John turned back and Alanna relaxed a little. Deep down, she knew they'd have guns, but she'd been doing her best to keep the thought buried in her subconscious.

Now that she had to face facts, though, she certainly didn't want John going up there alone and playing hero. If those guys started taking potshots at him... Oh, Lord, she didn't want to think about anything happening to him.

Roy began speaking again, and she dragged her gaze from John.

"They've been here since Thursday," Roy was saying. "Just drove into town, bold as you please, and made themselves right at home up there in the mine."

"Drove?" Alanna said. "But I didn't hear a car."

John gave her a wry look. "Were you playing that so-called music of yours on Thursday? Loud enough to raise the dead? Oh... sorry," he said quickly, glancing at Roy and Mary.

"It's okay," Roy told him. "But yes, they definitely drove. Not only did I find *them,* I found their car."

"Really?" Mary said. "Why, Roy, even after a hundred and twenty years you can surprise me with how wonderful you are."

Roy gave an aw-shucks kind of shrug and said, "Well, it wasn't too hard. I'd overheard enough to know they'd driven here, so all I had to do was check the places that were big enough to hide a car in. They've got an ancient big Cadillac. Pink. With a V-8 engine."

"How do you know anything about cars?" John asked. "The only one I've ever seen was the one those tourists were driving the other day."

"We try to keep up with what's going on in the world," Mary explained. "Even before Alanna came, we were pretty up-to-date on things. Those weren't the only tourists who've ever come to look around Chester

City. And whenever any arrive, we do a little looking, too. And listening.''

"Did you check out the Cadillac?" Alanna asked Roy. "Inside it, I mean?"

"Not yet. By the time I found it, I was a mite tuckered out, so—"

"Oh, Roy," Mary murmured. "I told you not to overexert yourself. You know how easily you tire."

"I'm fine, Mary. Right fine. But I figured I'd just come back here and rest up a bit until you three were done. So we could all have a look-see at it together. It's down in Miller's stable."

"Let's go, then," John said, starting off with Roy at his side.

"Alanna?" Mary said. "Wait just a second."

Alanna gazed after the two men, anxious not to miss anything, then turned to Mary.

"Roy isn't well," Mary said quietly. "I know he looked fine just now. And he tries to hide it from me...and I've been going along with him, just doing my best to deny what's happening. But he's...Alanna, I realize ghosts gradually lose their life forces, but it's supposed to take almost forever, isn't it?"

Alanna nodded uneasily. Mary looked close to tears.

"Well it's not taking very long at all for Roy. It's happening so fast I can almost see him failing more each day. He has trouble with his memory. And..."

"And?" Alanna prompted gently.

"And sometimes he can't manage to do even the simplest things. I think the real reason he didn't look through the car was because he couldn't. Because he didn't have the energy to materialize inside it. Alanna, he's been getting worse and worse. And I have to know...what will happen if it keeps up? If we don't try to travel back in time, and you can't talk him over to the other side, what will happen?''

A few tears trickled down Mary's cheeks and she quickly wiped at them.

Alanna felt like crying herself, but that would only make things worse. If Mary realized exactly how serious Roy's decline was, it would just upset her more.

"Ghosts can maintain their life forces for centuries and centuries, Mary. There's a church in Sussex, England—St. Nicholas, it's called. And people are still seeing two ghosts there who are dressed in the period of Henry VIII. And—"

"Alanna, I don't care about two ghosts in Sussex, England. I only care about Roy. And just because ghosts *can* maintain their life forces for centuries doesn't mean they all do, does it.''

"Well...no. It seems to depend on their emotional state.''

"And if their emotional state is poor? Like Roy's has been?''

Alanna looked away, not certain what to say. Ghosts couldn't die when they were already dead. But they couldn't exist in limbo forever, either. Eventually, if they never found peace, they faded away into oblivion. And the length of time it took to reach that point could vary greatly.

"Alanna? Tell me the truth. Could Roy waste away to nothing? Is that what finally happens?''

Oh, Lord, but she wished Mary hadn't asked that. "Well...if he never managed to find peace...then sooner or later..."

"That is what would happen," Mary murmured. "But we can't let it. We've got to do something to help him, Alanna. We've just got to.''

She tried to smile. "Let me talk to him again, okay? After we've checked out the car?"

Mary nodded. She didn't look at all reassured, but she started off in the direction of Miller's stable without another word.

Alanna walked along silently at her side, wishing there was something she could say to make Mary feel better. But there wasn't.

If Roy continued deteriorating, Mary was going to lose him.

CHAPTER TWELVE

WHEN ALANNA AND MARY reached the stable, John had the car's hood up and was leaning halfway under it. The way his jeans were pulled tightly across his behind took Alanna's thoughts away from Roy's problem for a moment.

Since that little neck massage she'd given John first thing in the morning, she *had* been managing to keep her hands to herself. But her eyes had been a different story. And now they suddenly seemed glued to him.

"This is amazing," he said, straightening up and glancing back at her. "Will talked some about engines," he added, shoving the hood back down. "But I didn't realize there were so many parts. It's plumb astonishing. I sure do wish we had the keys, so I could try my hand at driving."

As Roy had told them, the car was a very old Caddy. A two-door model, painted hot pink and decorated with a large pair of purple plush dice hanging from the rearview mirror. Artie and Chilli, Alanna decided, were not a class act.

"I still haven't unlocked it," Roy said. "I saved the honors for you, Mary."

She smiled at him, then glanced at Alanna—the message in her expression crystal clear. Just as she'd hypothesized earlier, Roy wasn't sure he could handle a simple ghostly task like getting inside the car and flicking the locks.

"Here goes, then," she said brightly. She vanished into mist, reappearing a moment later in the front seat.

"Locks . . . there," she murmured, reaching forward to the dashboard.

The locks popped up and John opened the driver's door.

"You and Alanna take over," Mary said, climbing out. "I'm feeling a tad tired . . . must be the heat. Roy, come and sit with me while I rest, all right?" She took his hand and led him over to a large bale of straw.

The top of it was about waist high, and Roy seemed to have difficulty maneuvering himself up onto it.

Mary shot Alanna another meaningful glance.

Alanna nodded that she'd seen the problem. But what on earth was she going to do about it? Nothing she'd tried so far had helped at all. And now that he knew recovering the lives they'd never had might be possible, she suspected he'd be even more resistant to the idea of passing over.

"Alanna?" John said. "Are you going to help me? All there seem to be back here are dirty clothes and empty beer cans."

He was hanging over the front seat and rummaging around in the back, and her eyes settled on his behind again. This time, she forced them away and looked into the back seat. A quick glance told her John was right. Full of dirty clothes and beer cans. *Definitely* not a class act.

"Try the glove compartment," she suggested.

"The what?"

"Over there." She pointed it out, then slid in under the wheel when he moved over to open it.

"Garbage," he muttered. "Just bits of old paper and stuff."

"Let's see."

He dumped everything onto the seat between them and she picked up the gas receipt that landed on top. "Arthur Fechner."

"What?" John said.

"Our friend, Artie. His full name is Arthur Fechner. This is a credit card receipt," she explained when John looked puzzled.

"Really?" He took it from her and examined it.

She rummaged further and found what she was looking for. "Arthur Fechner lives on Marston Street in Las Vegas. Car registration," she added, handing it to John.

He shook his head. "A man sure doesn't have many secrets in this century, does he?"

"And look at these," she said, discovering a book of matches near the bottom of the pile. "From Happy's Bar and Grill in Vegas, the same as the ones we found in the Magnolia. Just in case we had any lingering doubts about who started the fire."

John grinned at her. "You'd make a good detective."

"If I was good, I'd be able to figure out how Artie and his brother know about Roy hiding gold more than a century ago. But let's have a look in the trunk. Maybe there'll be something in there." Pushing the release, she slid back out of the car.

When she opened the trunk, her first glimpse of its contents was disappointing. Just the usual stuff. A spare tire, thrown in loose instead of neatly stowed, a jack, jumper cables, a couple of old towels . . . But there was one thing that didn't fit with the others.

Alanna reached in, tossed aside the ratty towel that was almost hiding the old book and lifted it out. Its faded cover, a pattern of pink cabbage roses on a pale green background, looked like a wallpaper design from a hundred years ago.

"A scrapbook?" John said, peering over her shoulder.

His breath fanned her neck with warmth, sending a tiny rush through her. She did her best to ignore it. "Maybe Artie's the sentimental type."

"Let's have a look." John took the book from her and opened it. "Letters," he said, flipping through a few of the pages. "Look, it's full of old letters."

Alanna looked. Sure enough, each page had three yellowed envelopes neatly glued onto it, address side out. And each envelope contained a letter.

She quickly scanned a few of the addresses. "They're all in the same handwriting. And all to the same person. A Mrs. Herbert Robinson, on Hyde Street in San Francisco."

"What?" Roy said.

Alanna glanced over to where he was still sitting on the bale of straw with Mary. He looked far more alert than he had a few minutes ago.

"Mrs. Herbert Robinson?" he said.

"Yes . . . you know the name?"

"Know the name? Tarnation, Alanna, Mrs. Herbert Robinson of San Francisco, *Lydia* Robinson, was my sister."

Nobody uttered another word for a moment. The expression on Roy's face said he wanted to look at the book, but he didn't move.

Then Alanna realized he was worried his mental energy wasn't up to letting him hold it. "John?" she said.

"The letters were written to Roy's sister. Give them to him."

When John carried the scrapbook over and handed it to Roy, who quickly put it down on the straw beside him and flipped open the front cover. "Why, they're letters *I* wrote to her," he murmured. "Just let me look through them for a minute, huh?" he said to Mary.

Mary nodded, then wandered over to the car and feigned interest in the contents of the trunk—all the while keeping one eye on Roy.

"What does this mean?" she finally whispered to Alanna.

"I'm sure Roy will figure it out," she whispered back. It looked as if it might take him a while, though. He seemed to be reading several of the letters in their entirety.

WHEN HE WAS FINALLY DONE, Roy looked over to where the other three were still poking around the Cadillac, glad they'd given him some privacy.

The letters had brought so many bittersweet memories flooding back that he'd been overwhelmed.

He'd written to Lydia about the first time he'd seen Mary. Then, later, he'd talked about how in love they were. And his final letter had invited his sister to the wedding.

She'd written back, he recalled, saying she was so sorry she couldn't come—she couldn't leave Herbert and the children for long enough to make the trip. As things had turned out, of course, that had been just as well.

He glanced back down at the open scrapbook. The last letter pasted into it wasn't from him. It was one that Mary had written to Lydia, informing her of his death.

And reading it had left his eyes feeling a mite damp and his throat aching. If he'd ever doubted just how much Mary had loved him, he wouldn't doubt it now.

That made him even more determined that they get their lives back. They had to regain the years together that they'd been meant to share.

He flipped slowly back through the pages, back to the letters he'd written before Mary had ever come to Chester City. So many things had happened in his early days here—so many things that he'd completely forgotten about.

He'd also forgotten about telling Lydia he was keeping most of his gold in the Magnolia. He'd thought he hadn't confided that to a soul. But here was the proof, written in his own hand. He'd mentioned that danged gold to her on several different occasions. He glanced again at the one letter he hadn't yet put back in its envelope.

. . . I'm making so much money that it amazes me. And most men pay in gold dust, too, even though some of the mining in these parts is for silver.

I don't have much faith in the Chester City Bank, but luckily I built a secret hiding place into the lodging house, so I just keep stashing bags of gold dust in there. And Lydia, I've got a fortune already. One of these days I'm going to come visit you in San Francisco, and I'll take you and Herbert out to every fancy place in town. . . .

He reread the lines about the gold dust once again, then carefully refolded the letter and put it away where it belonged. That certainly explained how those two galoots knew about his gold. But how had they come by the scrapbook?

Turning past the final few empty pages, he discovered an envelope tucked in against the back cover. It wasn't in his handwriting. And it wasn't yellowed with age or addressed to Lydia. It had been sent to a Mrs. Rose Fechner at an address in Las Vegas.

Roy took the letter out of the envelope and unfolded the single typed page. It was dated July 17, 2014, and the return address was in San Francisco.

Dear Sis,
It took me a while after Mom's funeral before I felt up to cleaning out her house, but I've finally finished going through everything. In the attic, I found the enclosed scrapbook in a box of stuff Grandmother Sophia must have stored up there years ago.

The name Sophia made Roy pause. Lydia's second-born had been named Sophia, and that had to be who this letter was referring to. What other Sophia would have stored away Lydia's letters? And that meant that the woman who'd written *this* letter was Lydia's great-granddaughter.

But how could so many generations have come and gone since he'd been alive? And little Sophia...he'd only seen her once, when she'd been a baby in Lydia's arms. She couldn't have been more than five when he was killed. But now she had to be long dead. And her daughter—the mother of this letter writer—was dead as well.

He began reading again, where he'd left off.

...found the enclosed scrapbook in a box of stuff Grandmother Sophia must have stored up there years ago. It contains letters to our great-grandmother from her brother.

Remember the story about her having a brother who got shot in a saloon brawl? Well these were from him—see the final letter from a woman named Mary Beckwith, explaining the circumstances of his death. Sad, huh?

Roy Hardin was his name. I don't recall anyone ever mentioning it—he was always just referred to as the one who died in a saloon brawl. But he'd have been our great-great-uncle, wouldn't he.

At any rate, knowing how interested you are in the family history, I thought I'd send the scrapbook along. There are a few other things you might like to see that I've kept for you to look at the next time you visit.

Your loving sister,
Claire

P.S. Hope both Artie & Chilli are keeping out of trouble these days. Those boys have given you enough heartache to last any mother a lifetime. Tell them their Aunt Claire says hi.

Artie and Chilli? Roy's mind began working, adding facts together.

Artie and Chilli's mother was this Rose Fechner woman who Claire's letter was written to. Rose was Claire's sister. And Rose and Claire were Lydia's great-granddaughters.

So, damnation...that meant those no-account skunks up in the mine were his kin!

IT TOOK A FEW MINUTES for Roy to get over the shock, and he was still feeling a mite shaky when he glanced in the direction of the Cadillac.

Mary was watching him, not even attempting to hide her curiosity. Alanna and John were trying to be less obvious, but they all clearly wanted to know how Artie and Chilli had gotten hold of his letters. And he'd have to tell them—as embarrassing as it was to admit he was related to those two polecats.

He cleared his throat. "Well, I reckon you'd like to know how my letters ended up in that car." Closing the scrapbook, he began to explain. "You're not going to believe this, but those galoots up in Broken Hill are descendants of mine."

"What?" Mary said.

"I'm afraid so. They're great-grandsons...no, their mother's a *great*, so that makes them *great-great-*grandsons of my sister, Lydia. And their mother, who's Lydia's great-granddaughter, ended up with this scrapbook."

"But what's in it that made them come here?" Mary asked.

"Oh..." Hellfire, he still wanted to surprise her when they got back to 1895.

"Well?" she pressed.

"Well...you remember, back at the Magnolia, when I told you I'd stashed a little gold away in it?"

She nodded.

"Well now that I look over what I wrote to Lydia...I guess I was trying to impress her with how well the lodging house was doing. So I...I seem to have exaggerated the amount of that gold."

"Oh, Roy." Mary gave him an exasperated glance. "You mean *that's* why this Artie and Chilli are here causing Alanna so much trouble? Because you exaggerated?''

"'Fraid so." He did his best to look sheepish.

"Well, you're just going to have to tell them the truth, then."

"What?"

"So they'll go away and leave Alanna alone. You'll have to drift back up to the mine and materialize. Then you'll have to tell them you know who they are and why they're here. And you're going to have to explain that there's really only a little bit of gold hidden."

"What?" he repeated.

"Well, you said it wasn't enough to make it worth mentioning to anyone, so—"

"Uh . . . Mary?" John said.

She turned to him.

"Mary, I don't think Roy's going back up to Broken Hill is a real good plan."

"Why not?"

"Well . . . mostly because he's a ghost. I mean, if he materialized, he'd probably scare the blazes out of them."

"Good," Alanna muttered.

John ignored her and kept talking to Mary. "But even if they were scared, I don't think they'd believe him. They'd figure he was just trying to keep them from getting the gold."

Mary eyed John for a minute, then looked at Roy again. "All right. Then you'll have to show them. You'll have to invite them down to the Magnolia and show them your hiding place. Let them have whatever darned gold that's there, love. If there's not much, what difference does it make?"

Roy just stared at her. He wouldn't give those two his gold even if there *wasn't* much of it. And since there was a whole heap... well, his hiding place had stayed a secret all these years, and it was danged well going to stay that way a little longer. At least until he and Mary got back to their world and took the gold out to use themselves.

"Mary," he said at last, "inviting them to take the gold's not a real good plan, either."

"Why not?"

"Because Artie and Chilli might be my kin, but they're a couple of weasely varmints who don't deserve a single speck of my gold dust."

"But—"

"No," Roy said firmly. "I'm not showing those two the hiding place and I'm not giving them the gold. That's my final word on it. Now, let's all go back to the Magnolia and decide what we *are* going to do about them."

He pushed himself down off the bale of straw and managed to lift the scrapbook with no problem at all. His mental energy seemed stronger than it had in ages.

Tucking the book under his arm, he walked, rather than drifted, out of the stable with it, feeling more like a man than he'd felt in decades.

Without a word, Mary hurried after Roy.

"John?" Alanna said as he started after them.

He stopped and looked at her.

"What *are* we going to do about those guys?"

"Don't know exactly. Like Roy says, we'll have to decide. But we're not going to just sit in the Magnolia, waiting for them to make another move."

"But—"

"Alanna, we've got to get rid of them. Fast. Do you think I could leave tomorrow if they were still around?"

"I . . ." She didn't know what to say. If that's what it took to keep John from leaving, she almost wished they would stay.

"Alanna?" he said quietly. "You didn't *really* think I'd leave you here alone unless they were gone, did you?"

She gave him a little shrug. "You've still got to get to Boston. I heard you promise Will's father you'd deliver that letter to him early in the week."

"That'll wait if it has to. Now that he knows Will's all right, it isn't as urgent."

"But what about the big cities . . . the bright lights? I realize how much seeing more of the future means to you."

"What you *don't* seem to realize," he murmured, moving closer, "is how much *you* mean to me."

He took her in his arms, and every ounce of resolve she'd had vanished. His holding her made her feel safe and secure. And when he kissed her, she almost melted on the spot.

It was a hard, hot, searching kiss—so intimate and arousing that she couldn't stop her hands from roaming over his back, then to his hips.

"God, Alanna," he whispered, kissing his way down her throat. "I seem to love you more every minute I'm with you." He slid his hands to her breasts and smoothed his palms across her already-hard nipples.

A tiny voice inside her head whispered that she should stop him. Ignoring it, she let her own hands slip from his hips to the front of his jeans.

"God, Alanna," he said again when she began caressing him through the denim. This time the words weren't a whisper but a groan. "Never mind what we're going to do about Artie and Chilli. What are we going to do about us?"

"I don't know," she murmured. She knew what she wanted to do, though. At least what she wanted to do right this minute. Every nerve ending in her body was alive with desire. And she could feel how much John wanted the same thing. He was hard and heavy against her hands.

She nuzzled his bent head while he fumbled with the buttons on her blouse and undid the clasp of her bra. Then he brushed the fabric aside and let his lips roam tantalizingly across her breasts while his hands slid down to her bare thighs.

Lightly, he started to caress them, his thumbs slipping beneath the cuff of her shorts before retreating. It made her quiver with excitement.

Then, with excruciating slowness, he began circling her nipple with his tongue.

The hot, moist sensation almost undid her. And when he started sucking on her nipple, still teasing it with the tip of his tongue, she moaned with need. The aching between her legs was becoming almost unbearable.

As if he could feel exactly what she felt, he shifted his thigh between hers, backing her against the bale of straw.

For a second, she was aware of loose bits of straw poking sharply into her... then there was only John, practically making her come with just the intimate pressure of his body against hers. She wanted him so badly she could hardly stand it.

"Alanna," he whispered against her skin. "Alanna, I don't want to just pass through your life."

"I don't want that, either," she told him breathlessly.

His thumbs slid a little farther up beneath her shorts and she arched against him. If he didn't touch her higher she was going to die. Her breathing ragged, she tried to undo the buttons of his fly. He was so hard against them that she couldn't. Then she had a sudden flash of sanity and remembered where they were.

"John, we can't do this." She forced the words out in a hoarse whisper, covering his hands with hers and stopping him from doing what she desperately wanted him to. "Not here. Not now. Mary and Roy might come back looking for us. Or Artie and Chilli could show up."

John groaned in obvious frustration, but took a step backward.

Her knees were so weak she wouldn't have been able to stand without the bale to lean against. She fumbled with her bra, closed it and rebuttoned her blouse.

When she looked up, he was gazing at her, still breathing as hard as she was.

"Listen to me, Alanna," he said quietly. "I love you. And I want to make love to you. And I want us to figure out some way of staying together—either in your world or mine."

Wrapping her arms around his waist, she pressed herself to him, whispering, "I love you, too, John."

Wordlessly, he threaded the fingers of one hand through her hair and put his other arm around her, hugging her to him.

She stood listening to the rhythmic thudding of his heart, trying to banish the thought that they might *not* be able to figure out a way of staying together.

But even though she couldn't push the thought aside entirely, she knew she'd no longer be able to resist making love with John. No, it was more than that. She no longer wanted to resist.

Regardless of how things turned out between them, what she felt for him was a once in a lifetime thing. And even if they didn't end up together, she didn't want to spend the rest of her life regretting she hadn't made the most of whatever time they had left.

At the very least, like Mary, she'd have memories of love to treasure.

"WHERE IN TARNATION have you two been?" Roy demanded when Alanna and John walked into the Magnolia. "We thought you were right behind us."

"We were just..." Alanna paused, suddenly realizing the lodging house had been torn apart. Every single one of her books had been taken off the shelves and thrown onto the floor. The air conditioner had been pulled away from the wall—as had both her sleeping bag and John's mattress. The mattress was destroyed, ripped to shreds—its rag stuffing strewn all over the floor.

The doors of the oven stood open and the old wrought-iron kettle had been tossed across the room. Only the things on her worktable appeared untouched.

"Had some trouble here while we were gone," Roy muttered needlessly. "Those varmints must have been watching the place and come in to search for my gold the minute we left."

"They find it?" John demanded.

Roy made a derisive sound and shook his head. "Nobody'd ever find it. But they made a hell of a mess, didn't they. They pulled your stuff out from behind the bar, too, Alanna. And upstairs, all the mattresses look at least as bad as this one down here.''

By the time he'd finished speaking, Alanna was half-way to the bar to see what they'd done back there.

The microwave was sitting precariously on the edge of the counter. The fridge had been pulled out of place, but fortunately was still humming away.

"Did they take anything?" John asked as she shoved the microwave back into place.

She made a quick check of the drawer and nodded. "My guns. I left the Glock back here with the Luger, and they're both gone."

"That gives *them* at least four guns," Roy said. "And we're down to just yours and mine, John."

"Anything else missing?" John demanded, his brow furrowed into a deep frown.

Alanna looked slowly around the room. "Everything's such a mess it's hard to tell. But— Oh, damn, the SCU's gone."

"The what?" Roy asked.

"Satellite communications unit," John told him. "The thing she uses to phone people."

"Oh, that. I didn't know what it was called. But you think those varmints wanted to phone people?"

"Let's just hope," Mary said, "that they didn't take it so they could phone some of their friends to come help them."

The thought made Alanna cringe. It made both John and Roy swear aloud.

"That's all we'd need," John muttered. He gave Alanna a tight smile.

She knew it was meant to be reassuring, but it wasn't.

"I doubt they'd call in any friends," he said. "If they did that, they'd have to share the gold."

"They're not going to get the gold," Roy snapped.

"But what if they did call in friends," Mary persisted. "Maybe they decided they needed help because they saw Roy and me. We've been visible a lot today, so they might think there are four people here now."

"But two of you are women," Roy pointed out. "That wouldn't worry them none."

"Don't be too sure," Alanna told him. "This is 2014. Women are a whole lot more dangerous now than they were in your day."

"Well, look," John said. "Regardless of what they think or don't think, we've got to get moving—in case Mary's right and they do have help on the way. Roy, you got enough energy left to drift up to Broken Hill and see if they've gone back there?"

Roy nodded.

"Good. Then, if they have, I'll go up and deal with them."

"What do you mean, deal with them?" Alanna asked uneasily.

"Tarnation, woman, what do you think I mean? I'll tell them to get the hell away from Chester City."

"And if they say no?"

"Then I'll have to convince them, won't I," he muttered, resting his hand on the butt of his Colt.

"You mean . . . by shooting them?"

CHAPTER THIRTEEN

WHEN JOHN WAS SILENT, Alanna stared at him in disbelief. "You *do* mean by shooting them," she said at last.

He shrugged. "You got a better idea?"

"Not off the top of my head, but just about any idea would be better than that one. You can't—"

"John's right, Alanna," Roy interrupted. "I should have a say in this because they're my kin. And I say they're the kind of polecats that deserve to be shot."

Mary gave Roy an angry look. "If people weren't always so fast to start shooting, you wouldn't have died before your time, and we wouldn't be the way we are now."

"That's not the point. The point is that we've got to get rid of those two fast. And I vote with John."

"Roy, this isn't an election," Alanna said. "And, John, this isn't 1887. You can't just go around killing people."

"I didn't say I'd kill them. Maybe I'll just wound them a mite. Just enough to convince them I'm a better shot than they are."

"John, you—"

"Alanna, I wouldn't shoot at anybody who wasn't armed. But they have at least four guns."

"Yes, they have. But they've also got my SCU. And if they have half a brain between them, they would call the state police if you started shooting. You wouldn't get back down here before someone arrived to arrest you."

"Arrest *me?* Why in blazes would they arrest me when it's Artie and Chilli who are the ones causing trouble? Look at the way they wrecked this place."

"That doesn't matter. If *you* were the one who started shooting, the police would be a lot more concerned about arresting you."

"What? That makes no sense at all!"

Alanna stared at him in frustration. He was right. It didn't make much sense. But she knew how the police would react.

"Things have changed, John," she said at last. "The laws have changed. Artie and Chilli would get a slap on the wrist for coming in here and tearing the Magnolia apart. But if you started shooting at them, you'd be arrested for attempted murder. That means a jail term. A *long* jail term."

"But *they're* the bad guys!"

"That doesn't matter. Not to the law."

"Well what in tarnation's gone wrong with the law, then?"

"A lot of people wonder that very thing," she admitted. "But the bottom line is that the law says you can't go and start shooting at those two without ending up in a whole lot of trouble."

"I don't believe this," John snapped. He whipped his hat off, stomped over to the far wall, then turned back and slapped his hat on his head again.

"So what do *you* think we should do? Sit around waiting to see if Artie and Chilli show up here again? Maybe they'll come bursting in any minute with their guns blazing and that way I wouldn't get arrested, would I? No, I wouldn't, because I'd be dead. And you would be, too. But at least we wouldn't have broken any danged laws, would we?''

He marched back across to the room to where Alanna was standing. "You know," he muttered, toe-to-toe with her, "I'm starting to think there might be a whole lot about the future that I'm not going to like."

She closed her eyes. She could only imagine how much there might be about the future that John wouldn't like. Maybe even as much as there'd be about the past that *she* wouldn't like. And given that, how could they ever hope to end up together in either world?

"I've got an idea," Mary said.

Alanna opened her eyes, gazed at Mary, and waited.

ALANNA CLUNG TIGHTLY to John's hand, doing her best to keep pace with him. It wasn't an easy walk up to Broken Hill, but once the sun had dipped behind the highest peaks darkness sneaked quickly across the mountains, and they wanted to reach the mine while there was still enough light to see.

She tried to lengthen her stride. After the way John had argued that she'd slow them down if she came along, she'd be damned if she was going to.

Of course, he'd used every argument he could think of to keep her from coming with them, but there was no way she was being left behind. Whatever happened, she wanted to be part of it. And if anything happened to John, she wanted to be right there with him, to do what she could.

"You're sure you're not exhausted, love?" Mary asked Roy for about the tenth time.

"I'm fine," he told her again.

Alanna took her eyes off the trail for a moment and anxiously glanced at him. In the fading light, both he and Mary seemed less substantial than usual, but aside from that, he *did* look pretty good.

This was the second time in an hour he'd drifted up to Broken Hill, though—first to check that Artie and Chilli were actually in the mine, and now, to put Mary's plan into action. She just hoped he'd have enough energy left to carry it off.

He caught her watching him and frowned. "Don't look so danged anxious, Alanna. Mary and I can do this—easy."

John squeezed her hand, then draped his arm around her shoulders and pulled her closer. "Everything's going to work out."

"Sure it is," Roy agreed. "Hellfire, it's even going to be fun—getting those no-good skunks. And it's been a long time since Mary and I have had much fun."

Alanna forced a smile, but she was worried sick. It might be fun for Mary and Roy, but they couldn't get killed if the plan didn't work. Whereas John...oh, Lord, she was so afraid that John would get hurt. Or worse.

All he had was his old frontier-model six-shooter, while Artie and Chilli had her two guns plus their own. If this turned into a shooting match...

She pressed even closer to John as they walked on, trying to banish her negative thoughts.

Nothing was going to happen to John, because they were going to figure out a way to spend the rest of their lives together. And they'd be hardly able to do that if he was dead. No, nothing was going to happen to John. She just loved him too much not to have a future with him.

She looked over at Mary, drifting along beside Roy, and a lump formed in her throat.

Mary had found a man she truly loved, then he'd been killed. Life was far from fair. It was just as Roy had warned, people shouldn't live their lives with too much concern about the future—because they couldn't count on having one.

"We're almost there," John said quietly, stopping and turning to face Roy and Mary.

"We'll dematerialize now and go on ahead." Roy pulled out his pocket watch. "I've got 7:48."

John checked his own watch and nodded. "Okay, give us ten minutes to get around to where the secondary tunnel comes out, then start."

"I don't expect you'll be able to hear what's happening from outside."

"Doesn't matter. We'll be ready for them."

Alanna took a deep breath. They'd be ready, all right. She couldn't possibly be wound any tighter than she was.

"Can you manage this okay?" John asked Mary, handing her the length of chain they'd gotten from the blacksmith's shop.

She nodded and Roy drew his revolver, saying, "Here, you take this, Alanna. I won't need it."

His hand was trembling so badly that she realized he wouldn't be able to use the gun if he tried. He wasn't really feeling as strong as he'd been making out, which made her worry even more.

"That wasn't part of the plan," John said as Roy handed her the Colt.

Roy shrugged. "Like I said, I won't need it."

"Good luck," Mary murmured. Then both she and Roy dissolved into mist.

John watched the wisps of vapor fade in the gathering darkness, then glanced at Alanna, hoping Roy's gun had vanished when he had. He didn't want her any more involved in this than she already was. But she was still holding the gun.

Apparently, ghosts' things only came and went if they were holding on to them at the time. Mary's chain was gone, but not Roy's gun.

He held out his hand. "I'll take that as a backup. And Roy said there are a couple of boulders just outside the secondary entrance, so I want you to stay behind them. They'll be good shelter if there's any shooting."

"No." She shook her head firmly. "John, I can handle a gun. And if it weren't for me, you wouldn't be involved in this. So I'm certainly not hiding behind a rock while you risk your life."

"Tarnation, woman, this is no time to be ornery! Don't you know—"

She stepped closer and pressed her fingers to his lips, stopping him midsentence.

"I know I love you," she whispered. "And I know if anything happened to you I'd want to die. So let me help you make sure nothing goes wrong, okay?"

He knew there was no point in arguing. Unless he hog-tied her, she'd do whatever she danged well wanted to. And he didn't have any rope on hand.

If he hadn't given Mary that chain, he'd be tempted to use it to keep Alanna out of harm's way. As things stood, though, there was nothing he could do but hope for the best. So he just wrapped his arms around her, and kissed her . . . a long, loving kiss that used up most of their ten minutes.

"READY?" ROY WHISPERED.

Mary nodded, smiling so broadly he shook his head at her. They wanted to scare these two varmints, not amuse them. When she bit her lip, managing to look at least halfway serious, he turned back to Artie and Chilli.

The two of them were sitting on their bedrolls. Chilli was absently tossing Alanna's SCU from one hand to the other, while Artie was using the dim light from a lantern to look at the most amazing magazine Roy had ever seen. It was chock-full of pictures of naked women.

"So who d'you think I oughtta call?" Chilli asked his brother.

"I told you, it ain't gonna work in the mine, dummy. You wanna call somebody, take it outside."

"Roy?" Mary whispered. "Stop trying to see those dirty pictures and let's get started."

Roy took her hand and drifted backward down the tunnel a bit, so his voice would echo better.

"Okay," Mary murmured, shooting him a conspiratorial look. "Let's do it."

He took a deep breath, then softly wailed "Wooooooooo" in a rising crescendo.

Both Artie and Chilli jumped, giving him a very satisfied feeling.

"What in hell was that?" Chilli asked.

"How do I know?"

Chilli pushed himself up and peered into the darkness. "Don't see nothin'," he muttered, still staring down the tunnel. He started playing catch with the SCU once more.

"Must have been the wind or somethin'," Artie said at last. He looked back down at his magazine.

"Wooooooooo," Roy wailed again, louder this time and putting some agony into it.

The sound caught Chilli midtoss and the SCU clunked to the stone floor of the mine.

"What the hell?" Artie snapped. "You break it?"

Chilli grabbed it and shook it. Something inside clattered around loudly and he tossed it down onto his bedroll. "Never mind if I broke it, what *is* that noise? I never heard no wind like that."

"Look," Mary whispered, almost laughing, "they've gotten nearly as pale as we are."

Roy grinned, and she took the chain, held it out in front of her, and gave it a good rattle.

"Oh, jeez," Chilli whispered. "You hear that? I think there's a damned ghost in here." He bent down and grabbed a gun that had been hidden in his bedroll.

Artie picked up the one beside him and aimed it into the blackness of the mine shaft. "Who's there?" he demanded, sounding decidedly frightened.

"This is the ghost of Roy Hardin," Roy said, dragging each word out slowly.

Chilli swore and became even paler.

"I don't believe that," Artie snapped. "You ain't no ghost. This is some kinda trick and we ain't buying it."

Roy concentrated on gathering his strength. Materializing halfway and holding it was far tougher than full materialization.

Gradually, he began to make himself visible.

"Oh, jeez," Chilli whispered again. "It *is* a ghost."

"Okay, perfect," Mary murmured. "Try to stay just like that."

"It ain't a ghost," Artie told his brother. "It's a trick." He shoved himself to his feet, the naked-ladies magazine still in one hand and his gun in the other.

"Stop playin' games and get the hell outta here before I shoot you."

"*You* shoot somebody?" Chilli muttered. "When's that gonna be. When hell freezes over?" He aimed his own gun directly at Roy and fired.

The bullet passed through Roy's chest and ricocheted off the wall. The roar of the shot reverberated like thunder along the tunnel.

Chilli's gun hand began to shake. "He *is* a ghost," he whispered.

Mary rattled her chain again.

"Hear that?" Chilli practically whimpered. "That guy don't have no chain, so there's got to be more of 'em."

"That's right," Roy moaned. "There are a lot of us in here with you, and we all want you to leave."

"Tell us where you hid the gold," Artie said, even though his voice was shaking as badly as Chilli's. "That's all we want. Tell us where the gold is hid and we'll leave. We won't bother none of you."

"You're not getting my gold. And you're going to leave right now, or we'll kill you. Then we'll keep you with us forever."

Artie glanced nervously at Chilli, saying, "I still think this is some kinda trick. Maybe they's usin' wires and mirrors or somethin'. And even if it's really a ghost, I don't think ghosts can kill people."

"Well you think what you want," Chilli snapped, "but I ain't takin' no chances. I'm gettin' outta here. I'm goin'," he added, looking at Roy. "Right now. Don't do nothin' 'cuz I'm goin' right now like you said, okay?"

"Put down your gun first. You, too, Artie. I want you to leave them behind."

Chilli tossed his onto his bedroll as if the gun were afire.

Artie hesitated.

"Leave it behind," Roy ordered. "And leave that magazine you're holding, too."

Mary turned and glared at him.

"Oh...hellfire, take the magazine with you. But put down your gun."

Artie hesitated another second, then did as he was told.

"Good. Very good."

"What about Alanna's guns?" Mary prompted quietly.

"You have two more guns. Let me see them," Roy called out.

Chilli reached down and pulled Alanna's Glock out of his boot. "Get ridda the Luger," he snapped when his brother didn't move.

Artie muttered something, but pulled Alanna's other gun from his boot.

"Good," Roy said again. "Now turn around and walk out of the mine. Very slowly."

The two men turned and started forward.

Mary scooped up all four guns and tucked them into the pockets of her dress. Then she and Roy drifted along after the Fechner brothers.

"Just keep walking straight ahead," Roy told them when they neared the tunnel entrance.

They were about half a dozen feet out of the mine when John and Alanna stepped into view behind them.

"Don't turn around," John said. "There's a gun trained on each of you. And we're going to walk you on down to your car now."

"IF I EVER SEE EITHER of you again, you're dead men," John said, staring evenly through the driver's window of the Caddy and cocking his Colt for emphasis. "You remember that, huh?"

"Absolutely," Chilli assured him.

"Okay, then. Get out of here."

Artie started the engine and drove the car out of Miller's stable without a backward glance.

Alanna felt weak with relief. Despite all her fears, she and John were both fine. And her troubles with Artie and Chilli were over.

"I still think keeping them prisoners would have been smarter," John muttered.

"Oh, John, that would have been a good idea if we'd been able to call the police to come and get them. But with my SCU smashed, we're cut off from the outside world until Frank Bronkowski gets here. And the last thing I wanted to spend the night doing was looking after prisoners."

John gave her a slow smile. "Yeah, we can find better things to do tonight, can't we. But I'm a mite worried about them taking it into their heads to come back."

"They wouldn't dare. Not after you made them swear about ninety times that they wouldn't."

"Well, I don't entirely trust them to keep their word."

"We've got their guns."

"They could get other ones."

Alanna tried not to let that fact make her anxious, but she didn't entirely trust the Fechner brothers to keep their word, either.

"Come on," John said, taking her hand. "Let's go make sure they remember the way out of town."

Roy and Mary had been waiting in front of the stable, and the four of them stood watching the Caddy drive down Main Street and off into the moonlit desert.

"We did it," Mary murmured when the taillights were nothing but red pinpoints in the night.

"Come on," Roy said. "We'll walk you back to the Magnolia."

They headed down Main Street in silence until they came to the door of the lodging house.

"We made a good team," Alanna finally said. "I think we should all be proud of ourselves."

"Oh, especially Roy." Mary leaned closer and gave him a kiss on the cheek.

"I couldn't have done it without you, darling. It was Mary rattling the chain," he said, glancing at Alanna and John, "that convinced them there were a lot of us."

"You both must have been wonderful in there," Alanna said. "I don't know how I can thank you enough."

"I do," Roy told her. "And if John's leaving tomorrow, there's not much time left."

There was no need for him to elaborate. She knew exactly what he wanted. And even though it was against the rules, she'd been giving the situation a lot of thought. And she'd concluded it could never be reduced to a question of black-and-white.

No matter how hard she tried to find one, there could never be a cut-and-dried right answer. What it actually came down to was deciding what she felt most strongly about. She could blindly insist on going along with what her profession mandated. Or she could do what seemed the only humane thing to do in this particular case.

"So?" John asked her quietly.

"Tell them how they can do it," she murmured.

Roy's relief was visible, but Mary looked strangely upset.

"Well," John began, "that little window of opportunity is going to open up on Wednesday morning right about—"

"Wait," Mary said.

Roy glanced curiously at her. "What's the matter?"

"Roy... I'm not sure I want to try to go back."

"What?" he said incredulously. "What do you mean? You said you did. You said you wanted a second chance at life more than anything."

"I know, but... Roy, please try to understand, but I've been having second thoughts."

"What? What in tarnation kind of second thoughts?"

"I... Oh, I'm sorry. I really am. But I can't help thinking... and the more I think, the more reasons there seem to be against trying."

Roy took a deep breath. "Tell me the reasons."

"Well... I'm afraid that something would go wrong... all those things John told us might happen.... Roy, I couldn't bear to never have existed, to never have loved you. And—"

"Mary," he murmured, putting his arms around her. "Darling, that isn't going to happen. We'll make it back just fine and everything will be—"

She pulled away from him and looked at John. "You aren't sure of that, are you? You said before that you couldn't be certain everything would be fine."

"Well... no, not *certain*, but—"

"Mary, listen to me," Roy said, taking her hands in his. "It's worth the risk."

"Is it, love?"

Alanna felt her throat growing tight as tears began streaming down Mary's face.

"Yes, it is," Roy insisted.

"But what if I lost you forever?"

"Darling, up in the mine . . . I almost felt alive again. Didn't you?"

"Yes, I did."

"And it was wonderful, wasn't it."

"Yes, but it scared me, too. I'd forgotten how marvelous it was to laugh and play tricks but . . ." Mary paused, pulling her hands away from Roy and wiping fiercely at her tears.

"But what?" he asked gently.

"Oh, love, it's so hard for me to explain. But I'm not sure I *want* to be alive again."

"You can't be serious."

"I am! Roy, if we *did* make it back, I'd appreciate life so much more."

"That wouldn't be bad. That would be—"

"No, listen to me. I'd appreciate life so much more, but all the while I'd know we'd have to die again . . . that I'd eventually lose you and everything else again. And I can't stand the thought of going through it a second time. So—"

"Darling, you aren't making sense. Everyone dies eventually. And you can't—"

"No, I don't think I could stand trying to go back. If we failed, things could be even worse. And if we did get to 1895— Oh, Roy, can't you understand?"

He shook his head, clearly bewildered. "What are you saying? That you want us to stay the way we are?"

"No, we can't do that because sooner or later you'd fade away to nothing. Alanna told me that's what would happen. Then I'd be alone, and I couldn't stand that, either. So what I want is for you to give her another chance at talking you over to the other side. That's the only safe thing. Then we'd be together forever and—"

"Damnation, Mary, I don't *want* to be talked over to the other side. I hate being dead."

"But that's because we're trapped in limbo! It wouldn't be so bad if you were at peace."

"No, Mary, don't you understand why I'm still here after all these years? I've been clinging to this side because I haven't been able to give up on the thought of having a life with you. Even though I didn't believe it was possible, I couldn't give up on it. And now that I know it *is* possible..." Roy's voice cracked and he stopped speaking.

Mary turned to Alanna, still in tears. "You understand, don't you? You know all the other options are risky. We might become nonexistent. Or we might end up as ghosts—but in another time, without you to help us. And if that happened and Roy wasted away, I'd be without him forever. Passing over is the only safe solution, isn't it?"

Alanna looked from Mary to Roy and back, caught in the middle and not knowing what on earth she should tell them. Mary was right, of course. All the other options *were* risky. But Roy wanted to try going back so badly.

John finally rescued her, saying, "It's been an emotion-filled day, Mary. I think what we all need is some rest. How about if we get together in the morning before I leave? Talk about this some more then, instead of now?"

"Mary?" Roy murmured. "Let's do that, huh?" He extended his hand to her.

She simply gazed at it.

Eventually, she reached out and took it in both of hers. Then the two of them grew translucent, fading into the night.

CHAPTER FOURTEEN

THE LAST MISTY WISPS were swallowed up by the darkness. Roy and Mary were gone.

"Damnation," John muttered. "This is all my fault. I should never have tried figuring out how to send them back in the first place."

"You did what you thought was right," Alanna reminded him, opening the Magnolia's door.

The heat that had built up inside during the day rushed out to greet her, but she managed to ignore it. Difficult though it was to believe, she was becoming acclimatized to living in this oversize oven.

"John?" she said when he continued staring into the night.

Wordlessly, he followed her inside and closed the door.

When she lit a lamp, she realized she'd completely forgotten the lodging house was a disaster area. In their hurry to get to the mine, there'd been no time for cleaning up the mess Artie and Chilli had made searching the place.

"What's going to happen?" John said, drawing her attention back to him. "Now that Mary's as determined to stay as Roy is to go?"

Alanna slowly shrugged. She really hated to see Roy and Mary at loggerheads. And if John thought he was responsible for it, he had to feel even worse.

"They'll have to decide which option it's going to be," she finally said. "The situation they're in . . . well, it isn't the type of thing they can compromise on, is it."

"And if they just can't agree?"

"I'm sure they will. They love each other too much to ever go their separate ways."

"But what if they *can't* agree?" John pressed.

"Then I guess one of them will just have to give in—do what the other wants so they'll still be together."

John shook his head, saying, "They wouldn't have this problem if I hadn't dangled the idea of time traveling in front of them. Maybe if—"

"John, you were trying to help. And there's no point in second-guessing when you can't take back what you did. No more than you can take back the fact that you came walking out of a different century and into my life. And even though . . ."

"Even though what?" he asked when she paused.

She shook her head, her throat suddenly so tight she couldn't go on.

"Alanna?" He tossed his hat onto a chair, then wrapped his arms around her and pulled her close.

She pressed against his warm strength, trying not to cry. This was their last night together before he'd be leaving for Boston, and she wanted it to be as perfect as possible.

But she was filled with fear that it was going to be their last night together, period. Once John left, she might never see him again.

He'd be so enthralled by the wonders of her century that he'd want to spend all the rest of the time he had in 2014 enjoying them.

"What's wrong?" he whispered.

"Sorry . . . I just started thinking about your leaving in the morning."

"Hey, I'll be back." He brushed her hair away from her face and kissed her cheek.

"But I'll be going home to Elko next weekend. The moving van comes on Saturday and—"

"And if I'm not here again by then, I can find Elko. I'll be back in Nevada before you even start missing me."

That made her smile. She was already missing him—and he hadn't even left yet.

"I love you, remember?" he whispered.

"And I love you," she said softly. "I just . . . oh, I wish there was a better way of saying that. Because people so often say the words without meaning them at all. And I really do mean them. But it's been so sudden between us that I'm scared you'll—"

"Shh." He pressed his fingers to her lips. "I'll go visit Will's parents, like I promised him I would, then I'll come back like I promised you."

Part of her wanted to ask him what would happen if he *did* come back. What he thought would eventually happen to them. Another part was afraid to.

He'd talked about wanting to spend the future with her. But they hadn't talked about how he could possibly do it. And she had an awful fear he simply couldn't.

"What are you thinking?" he murmured.

For a moment she considered telling him, but Roy's advice about not worrying about the future had begun echoing through her mind again. When it came to her and John having a future together, she thought ruefully, Roy's words were even more true. The chance of that had to be infinitesimal.

Then John brushed his fingers gently across her lips and made her stop thinking about how small the chance was.

She caught his fingers and kissed them; he cradled the back of her head in his hand, tilted her face up and gently pressed his lips to hers. Just like last night, his kiss sent her senses reeling.

She wrapped her arms tightly around his neck and kissed him back, forcing her worries away. She and John had tonight, and she wasn't going to let their uncertain future ruin it.

"I guess," she murmured, drawing her lips a fraction of an inch away from his, "since Artie and Chilli tore your mattress to pieces, I'm going to have to share my sleeping bag with you."

John gave her a deliciously evil grin. "Blasted old Artie and Chilli, huh? Even though we got rid of them, they just keep on causing us problems. Wait one second," he added, grabbing a chair and carrying it over to the door.

He slid the chair's back under the door handle and angled the legs to create a makeshift lock.

"Just in case those two varmints *do* get any crazy ideas about coming back," he said, heading over to her again.

That thought made her anxious for a second. Then John scooped her up in his arms and every remaining thought in her head was about him.

Blowing out the lamp, he left nothing but moon shadows to light their path to the sleeping bag.

He lowered her onto it, took a second to remove his gun belt and boots, then sank down beside her—pressing the entire length of his body against hers. His nearness made her pulse leap and her heart begin to race.

"We're going to work something out, Alanna," he murmured. "Work something out so we can be together forever."

"You're sure?" she whispered.

"Positive. And I'm a man of my word."

His breath, warm against her throat, fanned the sparks of desire that had started deep within her. And lying with him this way, feeling him so close to her, she could nearly believe him. Anything seemed possible.

"I love you so much, Alanna. Everything's going to be just fine."

"I love you *more* than so much," she teased, managing to prevent a "but" from slipping out.

She wished with all her heart there were no buts, yet she couldn't manage to ignore them. They were persistently lurking in the dark recesses of her mind, sneaking out to worry her every time they could seize the opportunity.

"More than *so much* isn't possible," John murmured.

That almost made her cry.

He stroked her hair for a minute, his dark gaze locked with hers in the pale light of a stray moonbeam. Then he leaned a fraction of an inch closer and his lips met hers once more.

This time, his kiss was more demanding—that uniquely rough-tender kiss she'd been fantasizing about since the night before. Reality, though, was a hundred times better than her fantasies.

And when he trailed his fingers from her hair to the base of her neck, her entire body quickened beneath his touch.

She pressed even closer, loving the strength of his hardness against her. Resting one hand on his chest, she could feel his heart beating as rapidly as her own.

She traced his chiseled jaw, his five o'clock shadow tickling her fingertips, then she kissed his ear. When that sent a little shudder through him, she began nibbling on his earlobe.

"Oh, Alanna," he groaned, running his hand down her body with excruciating slowness. Tantalizingly, he smoothed his palm across one breast and down over her shorts to her bare thigh.

Aching with need, she started undoing his shirt buttons. But he began caressing tiny circles on her inner thigh, each one venturing a fraction of an inch higher than the one before it, and her fingers fumbled with his buttons.

When she'd finally managed the last of them, she slid her hands across his naked chest. He made a low sound of pleasure at her touch; she followed her hands with her tongue.

His skin tasted salty—the kind of saltiness that was addictive, that made it impossible to stop eating pretzels after only one.

Still kissing him, she let her fingers wander through his chest hair until she found a nipple.

Caressing it lightly, she made him groan again. But all the while, his fingers were working their magic on her, still creeping ever higher beneath the cuffs of her shorts, gradually making every single one of those sparks of desire burst into flame.

She arched against him, silently saying how much she wanted him.

He shifted onto his back and pulled her on top of him, settling her lower body on his. His erection, so obvious beneath her, made her hotter than a fire in July.

Kissing her even more deeply, John slipped her top over her shoulders, trailing his fingers to her naked waist, then drew her up along his body so he could more easily kiss her breasts.

Straddling his stomach, she squirmed against him. She loved what he was doing, but it was almost too much to bear.

She pressed herself hard into him, moving back and forth until she couldn't stand the scorching ache between her legs any longer. It had grown so fierce it had her almost begging for release.

As if he'd been waiting for her to reach just that state, he shifted from beneath her and rapidly tugged off his jeans.

Then, all gorgeous, naked muscle in the moonlight, he made short work of the rest of her clothes.

She reached for him, but he shook his head, murmuring, "Not yet," and captured both her hands with one of his, pinning them above her head.

He teased one hard nipple with his tongue until tiny whimpers rose uncontrollably from her throat. Then, finally, he touched her where she'd been longing to be touched most.

Involuntarily, she arched against his hand, so near a climax she could think of nothing but relief from the torturous pleasure of her arousal.

He caressed her slowly, slowly and gently, keeping her hovering on the brink until her breathing was so ragged she thought she was going to die.

"Oh, John," she managed to whisper. And as she did he released her hands and pressed his entire body down onto hers.

It suddenly felt as if an earthquake were erupting inside her, as if it were only his weight on her that was holding her together. She clung to him while her body quivered with tremor after delicious tremor.

Eventually, their intensity diminished. Gradually, they began to subside.

Finally, a semblance of normality returned—so fragile, though, that she knew it could be shattered by his slightest touch.

She lay breathlessly beneath him, her body covered in a fine sheen of moisture, feeling totally and utterly drained.

"A ten on the Richter scale," she murmured at last.

"What's the Richter scale?" he whispered.

"It measures the strength of earthquakes."

"Oh?" He smiled at her in the moonlight. "Does it measure aftershocks, too?"

Almost afraid to, she nodded.

"Ah." Still smiling, he slowly slid his hand down her body once more.

JOHN WOKE to the early-morning light with Alanna naked in his arms and the nether parts of his body aching from overuse.

They'd made love off and on all night long. It couldn't have been more than an hour or two ago that they'd finally drifted off to sleep, and he felt like— Hellfire, there was nothing to compare the feeling with.

He'd never in his life been so exhausted yet so exhilarated...or so in love. For the moment, he was content to do nothing more than lie beside Alanna and watch her sleep.

Her lips were swollen from the passion of their kisses. Her hair was damp and lank from a combination of the heat in the Magnolia and the heat they'd generated. She looked more beautiful than he'd ever imagined any woman could.

And she was *his* woman. Unbelievable as it seemed, this incredible woman loved him.

Half tempted to kiss her awake, half wanting to let her go on sleeping, he hesitated, thinking it wouldn't be long before her delivery fellow arrived. And he had no choice but to leave with the guy.

He'd given Will his word he'd get that letter to Boston just as soon as he could, and his little detour through 1850 meant it was already long overdue.

And he'd promised to deliver it in person, so he could answer any questions Will's parents had. But he sure didn't cotton to the thought of leaving Alanna here on her own. Not even for a few days.

If Roy and Mary decided to take their chances tomorrow, Alanna wouldn't even have them around. And the idea of her being totally alone made his blood run cold.

A knock on the door interrupted his thoughts. Beside him, Alanna's eyes flew open.

"Oh, Lord, Frank Bronkowski's here already," she whispered, grabbing John's shirt off the floor and doing her best to cover herself with it.

"John?" Roy called from outside. "John, gotta talk to you."

"Oh, thank heavens they promised never to come drifting in on us again," Alanna murmured.

"John?" Roy called once more.

"Hold on a minute. Just getting dressed." John scrambled into his jeans and boots, strapped on his Colt, then reached for his shirt.

Alanna gave him a horrified look and pulled the garment more tightly around herself, so he simply pushed himself up and headed across the room, grabbing his hat on his way past.

Moving the chair he'd propped against the door, he opened it and stepped outside. "Alanna's not up yet, Roy. So we'll talk out here, huh?"

"Sure. Sorry to come by so early, but I didn't know what time you were leaving. And I didn't want you forgetting to give me the instructions."

"Mary's agreed to try the trip back, then?"

Roy shook his head wearily. "We talked on it all night, but the more we talked, the more upset she got. She's so danged scared that something will go wrong.... John, I just don't know what else I can say to convince her."

"What will you do if you can't?" he asked quietly.

"I don't know. I really don't. She wouldn't even come along with me now—seemed like she didn't want to see you because she was scared you'd try to talk her into going—and she's determined she doesn't want to be persuaded."

"Alanna and I wouldn't try convincing either of you, Roy. You've got to make up your own minds."

"That's exactly what Mary says. She has to make up her own mind. But if she doesn't make it up soon...well, you can't hog-tie a ghost, so if she won't agree... Tarnation, John, what *will* I do?"

"I don't know, Roy."

Roy kicked at a stone in the street, then swore when his boot went right through it.

"Well, I'm sure not passing over to the other side,"
he snapped. "That's the way Mary still wants things
decided, but I'm not doing it."

"No matter what?"

"No, no matter what. I haven't done it in a hundred
and twenty years and I won't do it now. Not now that I
know I can have my life back. Only what good would it
do me to be alive again if Mary wasn't there with me?
Anyway, I came to find out how to go so if we *do* decide... but what if Mary plain refuses to go when the
time comes?"

"I wish I had an answer for you," John said slowly.
"I really wish I did. But all I can do is tell you exactly
how to go about making the trip. You've got to swear,
though, that if you do, neither you nor Mary will ever
say a word about having traveled through time."

"But people will know *something* strange has happened. I mean, they'll know I got killed, and that Mary
died. But suddenly we'll be around again and—"

"No. If you go back, you'll be arriving on July third,
remember? So you won't have been killed. But I know
you'll be mighty tempted to say something to someone
and—"

"I swear we'll never tell anyone, John. On my mother's grave, I swear."

"All right, then listen careful because I can't write
anything down. If there was a record of how you did
this, and the wrong people got hold of it..."

"I understand. Just give me a minute to muster all my
concentration."

John waited until Roy nodded that he was ready, then
knelt down and drew a map in the sandy dirt of Main
Street.

He carefully indicated Broken Hill's main tunnel, the secondary shaft Roy and Mary would have to be in, and the three side shafts where the shimmering blue lights occassionally appeared.

"This is the one you'll see the light in." He tapped the center one with his finger. "But even if there's another light, in one of the other shafts—"

"You're saying there might be more than one light?" Roy interrupted.

"Well, it happens sometimes, but even if it does, it's the middle shaft you want to take," he said, hoping he sounded certain enough that Roy wouldn't start worrying.

After all, he'd tried both of the other two himself, which had made his figuring a lot easier this time around. And he was *almost* positive it was the center one Roy should take.

"You should see the blue light at exactly 10:04 tomorrow morning. And as soon as you do, start down this shaft." He stabbed the line again with his finger. "When you reach the end, you'll come out in 1895."

"On July third," Roy said. "Then we just get out of Chester City until after July fourth."

"Right. Now, you've got the map memorized?"

"I'm getting it. Let's just run through things one more time."

One more time turned into five more times before Roy decided he had everything straight.

"Well, I reckon I've got it now," he finally said. "And I reckon this is goodbye," he added, starting to extend his hand to John.

Then he remembered it had no substance and withdrew it. "Come tomorrow," he said, "I'll actually be able to shake hands again, won't I?"

John nodded.

"Well...I'm danged grateful, John. More grateful than I can rightly say. I just hope Mary... I just hope..."

"Why don't you head on back and see how she's doing," John suggested, seeing tears at the corners of Roy's eyes.

"I reckon I should do that. I just wish I could thank you better." Roy tipped his hat, then turned and started along Main Street in the direction of the Miner's Saloon.

John watched for a minute, absently rubbing his boot back and forth over the map, erasing it.

He wished he'd been able to give Mary the instructions, too. But if she didn't want to see him, there wasn't much he could do about it.

And Roy *did* have all the details straight—for the moment, at least. It was just that his memory was more than a mite poor. But after they'd gone over everything all those times, surely he'd be fine.

Or would he? Even if he remembered the instructions perfectly, what would happen if, come tomorrow, Mary was still refusing to go?

It hadn't sounded as if there was any way Roy would ever go along with what she wanted and pass over to the other side. But they were going to have to agree on one option or the other. At least, Alanna seemed sure that's what they'd do.

"They love each other too much ever to go their separate ways," she'd said. "And the situation they're in...well, it just isn't the type of thing they can compromise on."

He turned back toward the Magnolia and stood gazing at the door. Maybe, rather than worrying so much about Mary and Roy, he should be doing some of his worrying about himself and Alanna.

There couldn't be any more compromising in their situation than there could be in Roy and Mary's. If they wanted to be together, he'd have to live the rest of his life in a century he didn't really belong in. Either that or Alanna would have to go back with him.

He loved her so much he couldn't conceive of a future without her. But he hadn't forgotten about the enormous stumbling block to his staying in her world—all those credentials Will had said people needed before they could get jobs in 2014.

And John McCully, of 1887 Nevada, didn't have a single danged 2014 credential to his name.

He'd been mulling that problem over a whole lot, but he just couldn't see any way around it. Which meant, as far he could figure things, the only possible solution would be for Alanna to come back to 1887 with him and live there.

She'd said she really loved him. But that didn't mean he had any illusions that she was eager to give up her life here. Far from it.

He was certain she'd absolutely hate the idea of living in the past. So maybe, whether they could be together forever or not was going to come down to how much she honestly did love him. And would it be enough?

He rubbed his jaw uneasily. She'd said that if Roy and Mary couldn't agree, one of them would eventually give in—do what the other wanted so they'd still be together. But what about Alanna and him? If he *couldn't* give in, because of all those danged credentials . . .

He stood staring at nothing, trying to recall if Alanna had given in on anything since the moment he'd met her.

Then he took off his hat and wiped his brow, realizing he couldn't recall a single instance.

CHAPTER FIFTEEN

ALANNA GOT DRESSED, stuck some water in the microwave for coffee, then wandered over to the front window to see if John was still talking to Roy.

He wasn't. He was standing alone, looking totally lost in thought.

Just watching him made her so happy she felt like laughing out loud. He was quite a sight—shirtless, but wearing a gun and Stetson.

She didn't care how silly he looked, though. He was the most wonderful man she'd ever met, and it was an absolute miracle that they'd fallen so deeply in love. And they *were* going to figure out a solution to their little problem.

She smiled to herself. It wasn't really little, of course, but their love would let them find a solution to it, anyway.

The microwave pinged and she started to wave at him, but he turned and looked down Main Street as if he'd heard something. A few seconds later, she heard it, too.

Frank Bronkowski's van.

Her smile vanished and her heart sank. Frank was here already. And when he left again, he'd be taking John back to Branchwater with him. Suddenly, she didn't feel nearly as certain about that future.

She stood rooted to the spot while the faded blue van rolled into sight. Frank was going to wonder who on earth the half-naked man wearing a gun was, so she should go outside and explain things.

But before she could move, she was immobilized by a bizarre thought. Maybe, if she stayed perfectly still, she could freeze time and prevent this scene from unfolding.

Not surprisingly, that proved as effective as her childhood trick of making herself invisible by hiding her head under the blankets. The scene continued to unfold before her eyes.

Frank pulled the van to a stop in front of the Magnolia, cut the engine and got out, eyeing John curiously the whole time.

John walked over to the van, his hand extended to the older man, and she could see his lips moving as he introduced himself. Given the length of time he talked, she figured he was explaining that he was stranded here and asking Frank about a ride.

Her throat caught when Frank nodded—silly, when she'd known he'd agree. Besides, she was being totally selfish about not wanting John to leave. He'd given his word about going to Boston, and John McCully was a man of his word.

At this precise moment, she almost hated him for that.

A minute later the two men began unloading her supplies, and she went to open the door for them.

"So," Frank greeted her. "John, here, tells me you've had yourself some unwanted company. Whooeeh," he added, stepping inside. "It's hotter than Hades in here, isn't it."

Alanna managed a smile. "Does that mean you don't want any of the coffee I'm making?"

"I think I'd rather have somethin' cold if you got it. I brought you enough soda to last till you leave. Boy, those fellows sure did a number on this place, didn't they."

He glanced slowly around, making Alanna feel like a nominee for the world's worst housekeeper award. Frank undoubtedly figured she should have cleaned things up by now, and she couldn't help wondering what he'd think if he knew what she'd been doing instead.

She glanced at John and he shot her a lecherous grin—obviously reading her thoughts.

Gingerly, Frank picked his way through books and mattress remains, and set the box of groceries he was carrying onto the bar.

John deposited his carton next to it, saying, "I'll bring in the rest, Frank. You go ahead and have that cold drink."

Alanna dug into the fridge for the last bottle of Friztee. When she looked back over at John, he'd put on a shirt and was rummaging around in his things.

She looked away. He was getting organized to leave. Her throat started aching.

"Too bad I didn't know about your problems earlier," Frank said as John headed out for the rest of the supplies. "I coulda brought you a replacement battery for the air conditioner. And I've usually got an SCU in the van I coulda left for you to use, but I was running late this morning and forgot to grab it."

"That's all right. I'll only be here until Saturday. But maybe you could call the university for me? Just let someone in my department know why I can't be reached? Chris Schuller, if you can get hold of him."

"Sure. I'll do that as soon as I get back to town. But you won't be nervous out here, cut off from the world at large, will you?"

"No, I won't be nervous," she lied. After everything that had happened during the past few days, she'd be an entire bundle of nerves.

John carried in the final carton and put it with the others, then dug a slip of paper from his pocket and handed it to Frank, saying, "There's the number. And you're sure I can't pay you?"

"Nah, I don't know how much it'll be, so it's easier if I just put it on the university's bill. Alanna can settle up with them later."

"Settle up for what?" she said.

John gave her a nonchalant shrug. "I asked Frank if he'd mind calling Boston for me and explaining to Will's father that I'm going to be delayed in Chester City a mite longer."

"Oh," she murmured, a warm sensation starting around her heart. She was honestly beginning to believe that someone, somewhere, had assigned her a fairy godmother, because she'd never in her life done anything to deserve a man as wonderful as John.

She gazed across the bar at him and silently mouthed a "thank you."

Thanking him properly would have to wait until they were alone.

ROY STOOD GAZING across the bar at the mirror behind it, trying to imagine what it would be like to see his reflection for the first time in almost a hundred and twenty years.

But that wasn't going to happen if he didn't end up alive again. And if Mary didn't agree to go back with him... Damnation, she just *had* to.

He turned and looked across the saloon at her, still racking his brain for the elusive words that would convince her.

She was sitting at the piano, but she hadn't touched the keys. The keyboard cover was down and her elbows were resting on it. Her head was in her hands and she looked every bit as miserable as he felt.

Outside, the bright light of day had given way to a purple glow of twilight. John McCully would have left town hours ago, and Chester City would soon be completely shrouded in darkness. Then morning would come once more.

Wednesday morning. And at 10:04 on Wednesday morning that little window of opportunity would open up. But if he and Mary weren't in Broken Hill, ready to go, they'd miss it.

Taking off his hat, he raked his fingers through his hair. Normally, he couldn't feel any sensations even close to those he'd felt when he was alive. But right now he was feeling more danged frustrated than he'd have thought a body possibly could—dead *or* alive.

He just *had* to convince Mary that trying the trip was the only thing to do. But he'd used every argument he could think of and she was still refusing to go.

From the way she'd been talking—although her logic hadn't been any too clear much of the time—she had two entirely different fears.

The first was that they'd have a mishap and end up someplace either too far back or not far enough. In either case, they'd both still be dead.

He could understand her fear about that happening, even though he had complete confidence in John's calculations. It was her second worry that he was having a heap of trouble puzzling through, because it was the precise opposite of the first. She was afraid they *would* reach 1895.

She didn't think she wanted to be alive again—because it would mean they'd both eventually have to die again. And she said she could never bear that.

It apparently made sense to her, but it struck him as completely ridiculous—a woman's harebrained logic. As he'd told her last night, *everyone* eventually died. And everyone lived their lives knowing they would.

But she was fretting so about the pain of it all that he couldn't see how in tarnation he was ever going to talk her around in time.

He glanced along the bar and his gaze fell on Lydia's scrapbook. He'd read through his letters to her a second time, remembering so many more wonderful things about being alive. Maybe, if he asked Mary to read some of them...but he wasn't sure that was a wise idea.

Oh, he could show her the letters he'd written after they'd met—the ones that told Lydia how in love he was. But Mary already knew how much he loved her. And it wasn't *his* thoughts and feelings that were the problem. It was hers.

The longer they argued, the more convinced he became that she didn't *really* remember how incredible it had been to be alive and in love. Because, if she did, surely *nothing* would keep her in this world that was a never-ending void.

Uncertainly, he wandered along the bar and opened the scrapbook to the final letters Lydia had put in it. Then, deciding, he took the very last one from its envelope—the one Mary had written, informing Lydia of his death—and headed across to the piano.

"Mary?"

She looked up, her eyes red from crying.

"I want you to do something for me. Will you?"

"Roy, I—"

"I only want you to read this letter. That's all I'm asking. Will you just do that?"

"Of course." Dabbing at her eyes with her lace handkerchief, she took the letter from Roy and unfolded it, then simply sat gazing at it, surprised to see her own handwriting.

"I wrote this," she finally murmured. "To your sister," she added, focusing on Lydia's name. "I don't remember doing that.... I never even met her."

"You wrote it right after I was killed," Roy reminded her gently. "To let Lydia know."

Tears threatening again, she shook her head. "Then I don't want to read it. I—"

"You just told me you would...please?"

She looked down at the page again. The words swam before her eyes and it took several blinks before she could see them well enough to read.

The letter was dated July seventh, 1895.

"Oh, no," she whispered. "Roy, I wrote this the day we were supposed to get married. I just can't read it. I really can't."

When she held it out to him he took it, but instead of refolding it he straightened the page and cleared his throat.

"Dear Lydia," he began.

Mary stared at the floor and tried to block out the sound of his voice, but it was impossible.

"It makes me sadder than I can say to write this letter. And sadder still when I think about how unhappy you will be to read it. But I must let you know what has happened. Three days ago, on Independence Day, your dear brother was killed."

"Roy?" Mary whispered, her throat thick with tears. "Roy, why are you doing this?"

"It happened in my own brother's saloon. Just before midnight, some of the men took to shooting off their guns in celebration. Then one of them was shot in the arm and a brawl broke out. Roy and Charles were trying to stop the fighting when a stray bullet hit Roy in the chest.

"He died in my arms, Lydia, and a large part of me died with him."

"Roy, stop! I can't bear this!"

"Shh," he whispered, resting his hand on her shoulder. "I know it hurts, but please listen to just a little more.

"I am still numb with the pain of what happened, Lydia, but I have been trying not to think about the tragedy of Roy's death. Instead, I have been doing my best to remember how much he enjoyed his life. I want you to know that you were an important part of what he loved. I'm sure you realize that, but perhaps you have no idea how often he spoke to me of you and your family.

"And Roy treasured so many things most people don't even notice. The day he was killed . . ."

Roy's voice cracked on those words.

Hearing his sadness would have broken Mary's heart—if it hadn't already broken, all those years ago.

In the ensuing silence, she tried to recall that blessedly numb feeling she'd mentioned to Lydia, tried to feel nothing at all. It was the numbness that had gotten her through the months after Roy's death. The months until she'd followed him to her own premature grave.

Then Roy began reading again.

"The day he was killed, we'd gone out into the desert just before dawn, to watch the sunrise. You couldn't begin to picture what a beautiful sight it is here, Lydia. In the distance, a pink glow appears behind the buttes. Gradually, you start to see a reddish color, as if the desert was afire. Then, suddenly, the sun has risen above the horizon, stretching its rays out across the land, bathing the plains that surround Chester City in gold.

"In fact, for a few minutes, the entire world turns golden. The air begins to grow warmer, and it comes alive with the chatter of cactus wrens and little roadrunners.

"Roy and I often watched the sunrise together. It always gave us such a warm feeling, a feeling of utter happiness and contentment. Later that day, we took his carriage and rode out for a picnic—at a small stream that splashes down from the mountains a couple of miles from town. It has the coldest, purest water I've ever tasted, and we spent the afternoon beside it, talking about all our hopes and dreams.

"Sitting beside a stream sounds like nothing special, I know, but what I am trying to do is help you imagine how happy we were, how happy Roy was.

"Lydia, I loved your brother with all my heart and soul. And I would give anything in the world to have him with me again, to live out those hopes and dreams with him. If I could go back in time and be with him again, I would do it in a minute.

"Of course, that isn't possible. The only way I can ever be with him again is by dying. And I feel so lost without him I truly wonder if that might not soon come to pass.

"But I apologize, Lydia. I did not mean to write about my own sorrow, when I know how distraught you will be by this news. I only wanted to assure you that Roy was happy. And tell you that neither of us would ever have given up our time together, even if we'd known it would be so short, and ultimately end in such pain.

"If I ever visit San Francisco, I would very much like to meet you. In the meantime, please keep Roy alive in your heart, as I always will in mine.

Your late brother's fiancée,
Mary Beckwith"

Mary swallowed past the lump in her throat and gazed up at Roy, seeing little through her tears.

He slowly put the letter down on top of the piano.

"Do you recall how wonderful it was?" he murmured. "Can you *really* remember how incredible it felt when we were alive together? The sunrises? The picnics? Just talking? Mary, we can have it all back."

She wiped at the tears, whispering, "But if we did, we'd have to lose it all again. And that would hurt so much."

"Eventually. But maybe not until we were old and gray. And however much time we had together would be worth it, darling. You've forgotten so much about what being alive is like. Your own words, though...don't they remind you?

"Mary...darling, even when the pain was at its worst, you said you wouldn't have given up our time together. And if you'd had the chance... Mary, now we *do* have the chance. We *can* live out our hopes and dreams. All you have to do is say yes."

She took a deep breath, still terribly afraid.

Roy gently brushed a stray wisp of hair back from her cheek and she could almost feel warmth in his fingers. Then he leaned down and brushed her lips with his, and she could almost feel passion in his kiss.

It made her want more than "almost," more than anything.

ALANNA WALKED hand in hand with John, the moon playing hide-and-seek behind lazily floating clouds, the town completely quiet. Everything was at utter peace—except her.

She and John had finally taken time to sit down and discuss the problem of belonging in two different centuries. And if there was an easy solution to it, it had managed to elude them entirely. Even trying her hardest, she could no longer pretend to be certain that she and John would work things out.

"Time to head back?" he asked when they reached Main Street again.

She nodded. They'd walked up and down every side street in town, trying to clear their heads. But hers, at least, was still muddled.

She'd promised John she'd consider the possibility of going to live in 1887 with him. That was only fair when he was more than willing to consider staying in 2014. But none of her worries about facing a life in the past would stop nagging at her.

Going with him would mean giving up every single thing she loved—every single thing except him, that was. Her family, her research, her teaching.

She wouldn't even have a chance at a job teaching *grade* school in 1887. Not when the only degrees she could trot out were dated in the twenty-first century.

Showing them to anyone would only get her thrown out of a job interview—fast. It might even get her thrown into a loony bin.

"Look," John said, gesturing toward the Miner's Saloon as they neared it. "It's in darkness. What do you think that means?"

"I don't know. Ghosts don't actually need lights to see by, but Roy usually likes to have a lamp on—part of his not giving up on life, I guess. Maybe he just turned it off because he and Mary are done talking for the night."

"Then they've decided what they're going to do."

"Could be."

John said nothing more, but she knew he was wondering the same thing she was. Had Mary finally agreed to try the trip to 1895? And what would happen if she hadn't?

Alanna took a deep breath and did her best not to remember that she and John were in an almost parallel situation. But what if things came down to her having to choose whether to go with John or lose him forever?

She'd fallen so in love with him, it was almost impossible to imagine a life without him. But the scientist in her was insisting she think with her brain, not just her heart.

And everything she knew about the way women were treated in the nineteenth century told her that she'd find living there incredibly difficult. And the prospect of leaving everything and everyone in her life behind forever...

She tried telling herself it wouldn't come down to her having to choose. John didn't seem to have any of the negative feelings she had about being the one to jump ship—or jump century, to be more accurate.

In fact, the longer they'd talked about it, the more she'd realized how much he liked the idea of staying in the modern world.

So, if he could just see his way past the archaic attitudes men of his time had about relationships, their problem wouldn't seem so insurmountable.

But thus far, he hadn't been prepared to see his way beyond his nose.

Her mind drifted back to that discussion. *Those* discussions, actually. They'd kept coming back to the same issue all afternoon.

"But things have changed," she'd tried to explain. "Men's and women's roles are entirely different now. They're not strictly defined, the way they used to be."

"I could never be a *househusband*," John had snapped. "I'd never even heard of such a thing until today."

"You don't have to be a househusband. All I'm saying is you don't have to earn an executive salary. I know several women who earn more money than their partners."

"Their *husbands*, you mean? Damnation, Alanna, what kind of word is partner? I don't want to go into business with you. I want to marry you."

"Yes . . . well, I want to marry you, too. That's not what we're arguing about. All I'm trying to tell you is that supporting a household is not solely the man's job anymore. It's not important."

"Well it's important to *me*. Alanna, I know I couldn't change all my attitudes overnight. No more than you could. And that's one thing I just wouldn't be able to tolerate. Damnation, I've got my pride. The husband of a university professor has to have a danged good job."

"I'm not a professor, only a lecturer."

"You *will* be a professor, though. And you don't want to be embarrassed by what your husband does. You sure couldn't be married to a man who drove cattle for a living, or anything like that."

She bit her lip, not pointing out that there wasn't much call for that, anyway. Instead, she said, "John, I'd never be embarrassed by what you did. No matter what it was."

"Well *I* would be. No, Alanna, if I can't get the right work, I won't be able to stay here. It's as simple as that. I'd never be able to live with myself."

And that was the way things had been left.

The man was as obstinate as they came. She snuck a sidelong glance at him, trying to decide if he rated higher on the stubborn scale or the gorgeous scale. A ten on both, she concluded.

Then he caught her looking and stopped midstride, turning and gazing at her in the moonlight. "You *are* considering the possibility of living in 1887, aren't you?"

"Of course. I said I would."

That made him smile and he wrapped his arms around her, drawing her close. Instead of making her feel better, though, his hug made her feel hollow inside.

They both knew how tough it would be for him to find a job. He had no record of an education, no record of previous employment, no references.

And on top of that, if he *was* going to find a job, he'd have to do it fast. He hadn't realized that yet, but she certainly had.

He didn't have the slightest idea how much things cost in 2014, and the money Will had given him had been little more than pocket change.

But another of John's engraved-in-stone messages had been that he wouldn't let her support him, even temporarily. So when Will's money ran out...well, the bottom line was that John would have to find a job fast. And he didn't even have a social security number.

"So," he said, releasing her from his arms with a quick kiss on the forehead, "do you think Roy and Mary will come by and tell us what they've decided?"

"I hope so. If they don't...well, I think if they don't it will mean they just can't agree."

"You said you were sure that wouldn't happen," he reminded her.

She shrugged unhappily and they walked on in silence until they reached the Magnolia.

"You know what I was just thinking?" John asked as they stepped inside.

"No, what were you just thinking?" She smiled. His words had her hoping he'd miraculously come up with a solution.

If he had, though, he didn't get the chance to tell her what it was.

"Shut the door," a man said from across the room.

CHAPTER SIXTEEN

FOR A SECOND, only the sound of Alanna's sharp intake of breath penetrated John's shock. Then the man spoke again and he recognized the voice.

"I told you, shut the door," Chilli repeated. "Then don't move a muscle or you's both dead meat."

John kicked the door closed behind him, shutting out all light except for a stray moonbeam drifting in through the window.

He found Alanna's hand and squeezed it, trying to reassure her—all the while silently swearing at himself. He'd *known* he shouldn't have trusted those polecats to keep their word.

"You always get the drop on folks by sneaking around in the night, Chilli?" he asked.

"Yeah. Works pretty good. And if they turn out to be guys with big mouths, I shoot 'em, too."

John stared hard into the darkness, in the direction Chilli's voice was coming from. But he couldn't make out any shapes.

And even if he had, he wouldn't dare make a move. Not with Alanna right in the middle of things.

Chilli would have been here long enough for his eyes to adjust to the dark. And he wouldn't be alone. Big brother had to be here, too. Chilli would never have come back on his own. Artie, maybe, but not a yellow-livered whelp like Chilli.

John cleared his throat, not wanting to sound near as alarmed as he felt. "I reckon you're still after Roy's gold, huh?" he ventured, playing for time until his own eyes adjusted.

"Yeah, you *reckon* right, cowboy. So why don't you save time and tell us where it is. Maybe help us carry it to the car, too. We're just parked down in Miller's stable again."

Alanna muttered something about them not being very original thinkers. Her words, themselves, sounded ten times braver than her tone of voice.

"'Fraid we can't help you with anything," John told Chilli. "If there really *is* any gold, we haven't got a clue where it's hidden."

"No? Well, maybe you'd get a clue if I was to shoot up your girlfriend, huh?"

John's heart began to pound; Alanna was suddenly clenching his hand so tightly he was sure her nails were drawing blood. What in tarnation was he going to do?

"*I* know where it is," she said at last, her voice a mere whisper.

His heart stopped pounding. In fact, it almost stopped entirely. He knew Alanna didn't have any more of an idea where that gold was than he did. And playing games with a guy like Chilli was dangerous as all get-out.

If whatever she was up to didn't work, she'd be dead. So they had to make sure her plan worked—which would be a danged sight easier to do if he knew what in blazes it was.

"Well, atta girl," Chilli was saying. "That's all we wanted, just a little c'operation. So where is it?"

"I'll show you. But I need some light."

"Whatcha think, Artie?"

Big brother didn't say a word, but a moment later one of the lamps flickered to life—eerily throwing light up onto Artie's face. It made him look more like a ghost than Roy.

Artie was standing on the side of the worktable closest to the fireplace, while Chilli was on the other side, between the table and the bar. Both of them had pistols trained in Alanna and John's direction.

Obviously, they hadn't had much difficulty getting replacements for the ones Mary had collected from them up in the mine last night. And since there were two of them he wouldn't have a prayer if he tried to draw his Colt.

"Take your gun outta its holster, cowboy," Chilli ordered. "Real slow or I'll shoot your girlfriend. And slide it across the floor to Artie."

With no other choice available, John followed Chilli's instructions—watching the only chance he might have had sliding away with his Colt.

It stopped partway between them, but much farther from him than from Artie.

"So where's the gold hid?" Chilli demanded.

"Behind the bar," Alanna told him. "I'll show you."

This time, John's heart did stop entirely. Now he knew what her plan was.

Her guns, along with the two they'd taken from the Fechner brothers, were in the drawer behind the bar. And she wanted a shot at getting her hands on them. But she was going to get herself killed trying it.

When they'd first met, he'd grabbed her gun away as easy as a coyote grabs a prairie chicken. She wasn't fast enough to be any match for Artie and Chilli.

"Alanna," he tried, "I don't think you should show them the danged gold. It's not yours to—"

"Mind your own business, cowboy," Artie snapped.

"And stay right where you are," Chilli added. "Keep him covered, Artie. And you…" He looked at Alanna. "You come show me."

She started across the room.

John frantically tried to think what to do. Maybe, if she actually got to the guns, and he caused a distraction…

If he did, Artie would drill him for sure. But, just maybe, he could buy Alanna the time she needed.

And then, from nowhere, another voice spoke up. "You stop right where you are, Alanna," an invisible Roy ordered. "These skunks don't listen right well. I told them *last* night I wasn't letting them have my gold."

"Who said that?" Chilli asked, his face suddenly white.

John felt a small surge of hope. With Roy's help and a little luck, things might turn out all right.

"Who the hell said that?" Artie demanded this time.

He sounded nervous, which John would have appreciated more if he hadn't still been holding a gun.

"I did," Roy said, beginning to materialize not far from Chilli.

His revolver was drawn and John almost smiled. Suddenly, the Fechner boys *weren't* the only ones with guns.

Then he recalled Roy saying that actually using his gun was more than middling hard, and the thought that there was anything to smile about vanished.

"Oh, jeez," Chilli whispered. "Artie? What the hell do we do now?"

"Shut up," Artie snapped. "This is just more of their damned tricks. You," he said to Roy. "Don't you move."

"But Artie," Chilli wailed. "It's that same ghost from last night."

"I said, shut up. It weren't no ghost last night and it still ain't. It's still just a trick. But this time it ain't gonna work. What we's gonna do tonight is—"

While Artie was midsentence, Chilli's gun suddenly roared to life. He pumped several shots through Roy.

Roy calmly leveled his Colt at Chilli's chest. "You want to drop that gun now? And tell your brother to drop his? Or you want me to shoot you?"

Chilli looked utterly terrified, but he shot the rest of his rounds through Roy.

Roy shook his head, then *his* gun blasted.

Chilli screamed.

The next second he was clutching his arm, his pistol lying on the floor.

"Shoot," Roy muttered. "I was trying for his hand. My aim's off after all these years. What about you?" he asked, waving his gun in Artie's direction.

John froze in fear. Alanna was standing directly in the line of fire, and he doubted Roy had near as much control over that gun as he seemed to.

"I'm droppin' it," Artie muttered.

Before it even hit the floor, John dived for it, grabbing it and covering Artie. He didn't think the polecat would try anything more, but he stepped away a few feet, just in case, and retrieved his Colt. He stuck Artie's gun into his boot, then glanced back across the table to make sure little brother wasn't up to anything.

He was still just standing, holding his arm. His face was contorted in pain and a little blood was visible, but it didn't look as if he was seriously wounded.

Beside him, Mary had materialized and was in the midst of picking up his gun and sticking it into the pocket of her dress.

Alanna simply stood where she'd been, looking as if the proverbial feather could knock her over.

"Hey," John murmured, gesturing her to him.

When she managed the few steps to his side, he wrapped his free arm around her.

She was still trembling with fright. Roy and Mary, on the other hand, looked as if they'd enjoyed the excitement immensely.

"Didn't think you'd still be in town, John," Roy was saying. "We were just coming to talk to Alanna . . . reckon it's a good thing we were, huh?"

John grinned. "I reckon it was, Roy."

"You did right fine with that gun, love," Mary said, fixing an adoring gaze on Roy.

"Yes," Alanna agreed in a strangled little voice. "You did, Roy. Right fine. You must be feeling very strong tonight."

"I'm feeling plumb perfect tonight, Alanna. We were coming to tell you that Mary's decided she's going to make our little trip tomorrow. And since you're still here," he added to John, "maybe you wouldn't mind seeing us off in the morning? Just to make sure I remember all the instructions right?"

"I'll see you halfway down the mine shaft if you like, Roy. It'll be my pleasure."

"I need a doctor," Chilli whined. "You guys gonna stop talkin' and take me to a doctor or what?"

"Let me look at that arm," Mary said.

"It's nothing," she announced after a quick inspection. "We could bandage it up, but it's practically stopped bleeding already. Roy barely nicked him."

"Barely nicked me? He almost killed me! One of you's gotta get me to a doctor."

"Pish," Mary snapped. "The bullet went right on by. Why I've seen cat scratches worse than what you've got there."

"What do you want to do with them?" Roy asked John.

"Well, we sure in tarnation aren't letting them go again."

"Could tie them up for the night," Roy suggested. "The blacksmith's shop would be a right good place. There's lots of rope there. Then, after Mary and I are gone in the morning, you could drive them into Branchwater and call the police."

"Or just leave them in the blacksmith's while the two of you drive in and call," Mary suggested.

John nodded. He liked Mary's idea better. "You can drive?" he asked Alanna, realizing he'd never thought to ask her that.

"Yes, just be sure to get the car keys from them. But, John, I—"

"No buts. We did it your way last night. Tonight, we do it mine. You feel up to helping me with these two, Roy?"

"I feel up to just about anything you could name, John. Just about anything you could name."

"Let's go then." John gave Artie's gun to Alanna and used his own to gesture the Fechner brothers out into the night.

"Here," Mary said, pulling Chilli's gun from her pocket. "Take this one, too. Guns make me very nervous."

Alanna headed behind the bar, opened the drawer and tried to put the two latest acquisitions in on top of the others. There wasn't room.

Over the past twenty-four hours they'd collected a miniarsenal. In addition to her Glock, and the Luger she'd kept behind the bar all along, were the two guns they'd taken from Artie and Chilli the first time around.

Adding these two took them up to half a dozen. "This is ridiculous," she muttered. "We've got so many guns now we could practically open a gun store. I can't even get these new ones into the drawer."

"Put them someplace else," Mary said.

"Right." Alanna started to close the drawer.

"No, I mean all of them. I ... I've got a funny feeling that you shouldn't leave them there. Before Roy materialized, we heard you telling those fellows the gold was hidden behind the bar. So if they ever got in here again they'd head straight back there and—"

"But they're not going to get in here again."

"No ... no, of course they're not. So my feeling probably has nothing to do with them. In fact, I don't know *what* it has to do with. But sometimes I get vague impressions that make no sense at first, then later ... "

Alanna shrugged. No paranormalist worth her salt would ever ignore funny feelings—no matter how vague they were or how little sense they seemed to make. She took out the four guns that were in the drawer, then looked around for someplace else to put the entire collection.

ALANNA STOPPED at the entrance to Broken Hill, unable to force herself to take another step forward.

An image of her parents floated before her, bringing tears to her eyes. She just couldn't give up her entire life.

No matter how much she loved John, she just couldn't do it.

"Come on," he said, pulling her by the hand. "Come on, Alanna, it's the only way we can be together."

"I can't," she whispered, the tears starting to stream down her face. "I can't go with you. I'd never be able to live in the past."

"But I can't stay!"

"I know... but I just can't—"

"Alanna? Alanna, you're dreaming."

She woke with a start. She wasn't crying and she wasn't at the entrance to Broken Hill. She was lying on her sleeping bag, in the warmth of John's arms.

"You can't what?" he murmured, nuzzling her ear. "You were mumbling about something you couldn't do."

"Nothing. I mean, I don't know. It was one of those dreams that vanish the second you wake up."

He gave her a long, lingering kiss that started her pulse racing, then he slowly trailed his hand down her naked body.

"Mmm," she murmured, trying to banish thoughts of anything but the moment.

"I'm afraid you're going to have to save that 'mmm' for later," John said. He gave her a final quick kiss, then pushed himself up and grabbed his clothes. "It's almost nine. We overslept."

She rubbed her eyes, thinking it was no wonder. Roy and Mary had kept them up half the night—too excited by the prospect of their trip back in time to stop talking about it.

"They're going to be here any minute," John warned her.

Needing a wake-up jolt, she grabbed the radio remote and clicked the Power button. The radio blared to life and John shot her a disapproving glance.

"Just for a couple of minutes," she assured him above the music. "It helps me get moving."

While she dressed, she decided she was really going to have to do something about loosening John up when it came to music. The only music he'd liked since they'd met was the sad old tune Mary played on the piano.

"Alanna, did you hear something?" he asked as she began to brush the tangles out of her hair.

She shook her head, then listened intently, and sure enough, a moment later she heard a knock.

"I thought so," John muttered. He picked up the remote and turned off the radio.

"It's us," Roy called from outside.

"You know, I don't think you should be trusted with this thing," John said, waving the remote. "Just for temporary safekeeping," he added, sticking it into his shirt pocket.

He flashed her a quick grin, assuring her he was joking, then headed for the door. When he opened it, both Mary and Roy were standing outside. Roy was holding a lantern in each hand and Mary was clutching the scrapbook.

"You two ready to go?" Roy asked. "We've already been along to the blacksmith's and checked on those skunks—wanted to make sure they were still tied up tight, but it didn't look like either of them had even twitched all night."

"We gave them some water and such, too," Mary added. "So they'll be all right until you get back down from the mine."

"And we loaded these lanterns up with oil," Roy said. "We won't need them to see by, but we thought it would make things easier for you...if you really are going to walk with us into the mine, I mean."

"'Course I am," John assured him.

"Me, too." Alanna smiled across the room. "You're taking Lydia's scrapbook with you, Mary?"

Mary nodded. "Roy let me read the letters he wrote, and some of the things he said to Lydia about...about his feelings for me...well, I can't tell you exactly, because they were personal. But it made me feel wonderful to read them. So I thought that someday, when I'm an old, old woman, I'd be glad to have them to look at. They'll help me remember how beautiful he once thought I was."

"I'll always think you're beautiful," Roy murmured.

The words were clearly meant for Mary alone, but they were loud enough for Alanna to catch.

Hearing them made her smile again. Roy and Mary looked as if they were ready to burst with happiness.

But why shouldn't they? In another hour or so, they'd be alive again. Alive and together and back in their own time.

Unless something went wrong.

That thought was still enough to send a shiver of anxiety through her—no matter how often John had reassured her that Mary and Roy would be fine.

"Here, why don't I take those, now," John said, reaching for the lanterns and scrapbook.

Roy handed over the lanterns, but Mary shook her head and said she could manage.

"We're on our way, then?" Roy asked eagerly. He glanced at the hairbrush Alanna was still holding.

"Yes, on our way," she said, tossing it down and telling herself nothing would go wrong. John couldn't have made an error in his calculations, so Mary and Roy were going to end up exactly where they expected to. Or, rather, *when* they expected to. They'd be back in 1895, on the third of July.

She repeated that to herself at least a thousand times during the trip up to the mine, and by the time they reached the entrance, she'd *almost* convinced herself.

Roy pulled out his pocket watch and checked it. "Nine-forty. It's not too early to get ourselves in position, is it?"

John shook his head. "No. That little window of opportunity isn't going to be open for very long, so we want to be right in place when everything comes into alignment." He lit the lanterns, handed one to Alanna, and the four of them started off in single file, down the main tunnel.

Once a bend had taken them out of sight of the entrance, there was absolutely nothing but the dim lantern light to see by.

John pressed on in front of the others, holding his lantern chest high and anxiously watching for the side tunnel. The light barely reached the walls in many places, and even where it did, nothing looked familiar.

On both his own trips, he'd been coming at the secondary shaft from the opposite direction. It had been on his left, then, so this time it would be on his right. But they seemed to be walking forever and there was no sign of it.

He swore silently. If he missed the danged thing, he'd ruin this entire venture.

"There aren't bats in here, are there?" Alanna asked, her voice nervous. "I have a thing about bats."

"They generally sleep during the day," Roy told her.

"Oh," she said, sounding more nervous yet. She'd obviously been hoping there were none—either awake or asleep.

Finally, to his great relief, John saw what he'd been watching for. He held his lantern over to the right and stopped outside the entrance.

"This is it?" Mary said.

He nodded.

"You're sure?"

"Positive. I recognize it by that jagged little vein of gold running along the ceiling of the shaft. See?" He held the light higher yet, then remembered Mary didn't need it to see by.

"It looks like a snake," Alanna murmured.

"Is that better or worse than bats?" John teased. Now that they'd found the shaft, his mood had improved a whole lot.

Alanna, though, gave him a look that said she didn't appreciate his humor.

"Well, let's get going," Roy said.

John led the way forward once more, down the narrower shaft until they reached the fork. Then he stopped again, slowly moving his lantern along the walls to light each of the side passages in turn.

The first time he'd tried to travel, he probably wouldn't have even realized this fork existed if a shimmering light hadn't appeared down each of the three shafts.

That had sure taken him aback. Will had only talked about seeing *one* light, down *one* shaft. Until John had been faced with three of them, it had never occurred to him there'd be more than one possible way to go—each with an equally bright beckoning light.

Hopefully, this time, there'd only be one light. If that turned out to be the case, he'd feel certain he was sending Roy and Mary down the right shaft. Otherwise, he knew he'd be left with a nagging doubt.

"Ten o'clock," Roy said, checking his watch again, then looking at John. "I thanked you the best I could yesterday, and I still wish I could do it better but...well, take this note. There was something I wanted to put down in writing."

He fumbled in his vest and produced a folded piece of paper. "It's just something I wanted to tell you and...well, don't read it until you get back to the Magnolia, huh?"

John nodded and stuck the note in his shirt pocket, realizing when he did that he was still carrying the radio remote.

"And thank you, too, Alanna," Roy said. "If you hadn't agreed to this... Well, thank you for seeing your way clear."

"You're welcome, Roy. Even though I had my qualms at first, I'm really happy it's working out."

"So are we. And if anyone can understand how very much this means to us, it's you. This is it, darling," he went on, turning to Mary. "In just a few more minutes, we'll be alive again."

Mary gave him an anxious nod, then looked at John. "I want to thank you, too, John. From the bottom of my heart. And I want you to know that even if...even if something goes wrong, it's all right. We'll know you tried your best to give us back our lives."

"Nothing will go wrong," he said, hoping even harder that there'd be only one light.

Mary smiled tentatively, then looked at Alanna, not saying a word.

Even in the dimness, John could see they both had tears in their eyes.

"I wish I could hug you goodbye," Mary whispered at last. "I wish so much that I could. You're the best friend I ever had."

"I wish I could hug you, too," Alanna murmured. "And I hope you have a long and happy life."

"And a lot of healthy babies."

"And a lot of healthy babies," Alanna agreed. "You, too... you and John."

"I want to give you this," Alanna said, twisting the silver ring she always wore from her finger. "It's a friendship ring I've had since high school. But I know the friend who gave it to me would understand why I want you to have it now."

Mary dabbed at her eyes with her hankie, then held out her hand so Alanna could drop the ring into it.

"I'd like to give you something, too, Alanna. But I don't know what I could possibly— Wait, I do know. I'll leave my wedding dress for you. After the boom is over in Chester City, and Roy and I move on, I'll leave my dress behind for you."

"No, you'll have daughters, Mary. You—"

"I wouldn't be getting the chance to have daughters if it weren't for you and John. So I'll leave the dress right where you saw it, where my brother stored it after I died. It'll be there in that trunk, in the attic of his house. And maybe you'll decide... well, you might want to consider wearing it for *your* wedding. I'd like that. In a way, it would be like a part of me being with you on your wedding day."

"I'd be honored to wear it, Mary. It's the most beautiful dress in the world."

"All the way from New York City." Mary smiled through her tears.

As she murmured the words, John saw a faint glimmer of light appear down the middle shaft of the fork.

Not wanting to, he made himself check to either side.

Blue lights were beginning to shimmer in all three shafts. Despite how hard he'd been hoping, he was never going to be certain he'd sent Roy and Mary to the right destination.

"There it is," Roy said. "Just like you told me, John."

"What about those other tunnels?" Mary whispered. "Why do they have lights, too?"

"It doesn't matter," Roy said firmly. "John told me yesterday that might happen. But it was definitely the middle one we should take. It leads to the past. Right, John?"

"Right." But he'd give anything to be positive he'd calculated the precise timing for 1895. If he'd ended up even a tiny fraction out, Mary and Roy could end up as far back as prehistoric times.

His imagination began conjuring up dinosaurs...a Tyrannosaurus rex devouring Roy and Mary. But that wasn't going to happen. It just couldn't happen.

"We'll walk with you a ways," he said. "Alanna?" He offered her his hand and she silently took it.

"You two walk in front, now," he told Roy and Mary. "But we'll stick with you for a bit."

Mary tucked her arm through Roy's. Roy squared his shoulders. Then the two of them started toward the shimmering blue light.

"John?" Alanna murmured anxiously after they'd followed along for a few yards. "John, how far is it safe for us to go? I don't want to end up in 1895."

"No...no, I guess this is far enough."

"Mary? Roy?" Alanna called. "We're stopping here. You go on ahead. And good luck. Remember us sometimes." Her voice broke on the words.

When John looked at her, fresh tears were streaming down her cheeks.

"It's okay," he whispered, wrapping his arm around her shoulders.

Mary had glanced back to wave, and she was crying again as well. "We'll *always* remember you," she called. "Both of you. We'll never forget."

Roy touched the brim of his hat in a little gesture of farewell, then they both turned back toward the light and began walking again.

With each step they took, the blue light grew brighter, as if it was moving forward to meet them.

Eventually it surrounded them in a blinding blue glare. And, when it gradually receded, the tunnel ahead was empty.

CHAPTER SEVENTEEN

SOMETHING HAD LULLED John and Alanna into what her favorite poet called a lucid stillness.

She suspected it had been their exposure to the magical power of the shimmering blue light. But whatever the cause, they hadn't talked since leaving the mine.

She finally broke the silence when they reached the street Mary's brother had lived on. "Can we go and see if the wedding dress is really there? It won't take a minute."

"Sure. After all the trouble those Fechner brothers have given us, I wouldn't care if we left them tied up for days."

"Mmm...I think I'd rather get rid of them fast. We could drive into Branchwater just as soon as we've checked for the dress."

"And after someone comes and arrests them?"

"After that, I don't want to do anything except spend time with you."

John squeezed her hand and gave her a smile that told her she'd said exactly the right thing.

"No more work?" he asked. "No more interviewing ghosts?"

"I don't think there'd be much point even trying. There's only tomorrow and Friday left before the movers come to collect my things. And with all the excitement we've had, most of the ghosts will be laying low.

So I'd probably spend a lot of time for nothing. Whereas, spending my time with you,'' she teased, "produces some awfully nice rewards."

He smiled again, making her two for two.

She was thinking about going for three when they reached the weather-beaten old house. Once inside, they started directly up the ladder to the attic. The air grew hotter with each rung they climbed.

The humpbacked leather trunk was sitting exactly where it had been when Mary had shown Alanna the dress. She sank to her knees on the dust-covered floor, and when she undid the hasp and lifted the lid, there the gown lay—just as it had the first time she'd seen it. Neatly folded and carefully wrapped inside a protective muslin sheet.

She glanced at John, saying, "It *is* here. I thought she might have changed her mind and decided to save it for her daughters, after all. But she left it for me, just like she promised."

"Yeah."

The way he mumbled the word told her something was wrong. When she asked what, though, he merely said, "Nothing. Are you really going to wear it when we get married?"

"Of course." She did her best to ignore the imaginary voice in her head that was changing his "when we get married" to "if we get married."

They might not be any closer to solving their problem than they'd been yesterday, but if they spent the next couple of days alone together, they'd have endless time to figure out a solution.

"Just look at it," she added when John said nothing more. "It really *is* the most beautiful dress in the world. Don't you like it?"

"Sure. Sure, it's right fine. But I thought women liked new things. That's from the nineteenth century."

"Well, *this* woman is extremely fond of things from the nineteenth century. I can't believe you haven't noticed that."

He grinned at her. She'd made three for three without even trying. How could she have ever thought John was a difficult man?

"I think I'll take it with me now, all right? Then we won't have to bother coming up here again."

"Sure."

She hesitated, still getting the sense that he felt uneasy about something, but she couldn't put her finger on what it might be. And then it came to her.

The first time she'd seen Mary's wedding dress, it had been in this trunk because her brother had packed it away after she'd died.

So what was to say it had ever been touched after that? What was to say Mary had actually worn it, then left it here as she'd promised. What proof did she have that Mary and Roy really *had* gotten their lives back and had their wedding?

Alanna looked at John again, doubting he knew the answers but knowing she had to ask the questions. "John? Is there any way we can be *positive* Roy and Mary made it back to 1895?"

He shrugged. "That's where my calculations said the shaft would take them."

"I know. But is there any way we can tell for certain that it did?"

He didn't say a word, simply shook his head.

"Oh," she murmured. Seeing that awesome blue light had finally convinced her Roy and Mary would be just fine. But if John wasn't completely sure... Oh,

Lord, what if they'd become lost souls, wandering on their own in time and space? Thinking about that possibility made her so sad she felt like crying.

"Alanna?" John said quietly. "We're just going to have to believe they made it back safely. If we don't, we're always going to worry that we did the wrong thing. You think you can do that? Just believe everything turned out all right, I mean?"

"I don't know. I can try to, but I really wish there was some way— The scrapbook!" she exclaimed, her spirits soaring.

John gazed at her blankly.

"The letters to Roy's sister. If the wedding took place as planned, there'd be a letter telling Lydia all about it. And maybe more letters over the following years, talking about all kinds of things that—"

"Alanna, Mary took the scrapbook with her, remember? It's not here for us to look at."

Her spirits plummeted as quickly as they'd soared, and she sat gazing at the trunk, trying to think if there was any other way.

She supposed she could go through whatever old records were available in archives, looking for a post-1895 mention of Roy and Mary Hardin.

But people in the Old West hadn't worried much about keeping records. And most of the ones that had existed had disappeared or been destroyed over the years. So her odds on learning anything would be awfully low.

"You still want to take the dress with us now?" John asked.

She nodded. Mary had wanted her to wear it when she got married, and she was going to.

"*If* you get married" that horrid imaginary voice piped up again. "*If* you can figure out how on earth to make a life with John feasible."

She took the dress from the trunk and closed its lid, then they made their way down from the attic and headed for the Magnolia, John carrying the wrapped up wedding gown.

"Here," he said, handing it over as they neared the lodging house. "I'll walk along as far as the blacksmith's while you put this away. I want to make sure those two polecats are still tied up tight."

"Roy said they didn't look as if they'd even twitched all night."

"Yeah, well, that was a couple of hours ago, and most critters get more active during the day. Besides, I'll feel better checking on them. Then we'll head for Branchwater and call the state police."

When Alanna nodded, he started off down the street again, smiling to himself. He was plumb looking forward to the trip into Branchwater. At long last, he'd be getting to ride in a danged car. And a big pink one at that.

Maybe Alanna wouldn't even mind if he did some driving. Will had said there was nothing to it, and that was probably true. None of the newfangled things he'd encountered so far had been very difficult to use.

Not that he liked all of them. For one thing, he could sure do without that noise Alanna called music. In fact, he thought, remembering he still had the radio remote in his shirt pocket, he had half a mind to not-quite-accidently lose the danged thing before he got back to the Magnolia. Then she wouldn't keep scaring the blazes out of him by switching the radio on when she was nowhere near it.

But he liked *most* of the new things he'd seen or heard about. And he really wasn't having much trouble getting used to the differences between 2014 and 1887.

State police instead of a marshal. Weekends and even *long* weekends, instead of working every day. Drinks like Almondpear and Friztee instead of good old sarsaparilla. Cars instead of horses. Airplanes instead of... well, airplanes and other things that didn't even have counterparts back in 1887. And respectable women who enjoyed making love.

Thinking about that made him smile even more broadly. If he hadn't already wanted to marry Alanna *before* they'd made love, he sure would have afterward.

Making love with her was the most incredible thing he'd ever experienced, and the thought of spending the rest of his life with her...

All he had to do, to make that possible, was puzzle out how he was going to earn a good living here. If only that was as easy as everything else, he'd be right fine.

There had to be a way. It was just a matter of thinking on it some more.

He turned into the blacksmith's, then stopped in his tracks, his heart suddenly hammering against his ribs. Artie and Chilli weren't there.

ALANNA TRIED to wiggle her hands again, but they were tied as tightly to the chair as her ankles were. And with her mouth taped shut, she could scarcely make a sound. So how on earth was she going to warn John?

She sat staring across the room at Chilli, having trouble thinking past her terror.

The moment John discovered Artie and Chilli weren't where he'd left them, he'd come roaring back to the Magnolia to see if she was all right. And there was Chilli, watching out of the corner of the window for him, ready to welcome him at the door with a crowbar.

The blacksmith's hadn't proved a good place to leave the Fechner brothers after all. In fact, it might have been the worst place possible. Not only had they found knives to cut themselves loose, but they'd also found those damned crowbars.

Her gaze flickered to the knife handle sticking out of Chilli's boot. It made her more frightened yet.

She reminded herself that at least they didn't have guns. Thank heavens she'd paid attention to Mary's funny feeling last night and moved their little arsenal from behind the bar. If she hadn't, Artie would have discovered it right off.

Her gaze strayed to the fireplace. She'd stashed the guns inside the bake oven that was built into one side of it, and they'd be perfectly safe there—unless the Fechner brothers got around to searching it.

For the moment, though, Artie and Chilli had no guns. She just wished she didn't have the horrible sense that a crowbar could be every bit as deadly as a gun.

John would take one step inside and Chilli would knock him over the head with that thing. And a hard-enough blow could probably be fatal, so she just had to come up with a plan—fast.

She looked over at Artie, still trying desperately to think. He had his own crowbar and was in the midst of demolishing the wall behind the bar with it, trying to find the gold.

"Don't think you's so damned smart anymore, do you, lady?" Chilli said, glancing away from the win-

dow and over at her. "Not now that your ghost bud-
dies are gone, huh?"

His sneer gave her a creepy-crawly feeling—above
and beyond her fear.

"Where the hell'd they go, anyways? They couldn'
shut up this mornin'. Kept talkin' about leavin' through
the mine. What'd they mean by that?"

He paused, shooting her an evil grin, but she knew he
wouldn't be feeling so damned sure of himself if he
thought Roy and Mary might still be around.

"Guess you can't answer me, huh? Well, maybe later.
We'll take off that tape after we's done takin' care o'
your boyfriend."

His words sent a fresh shiver of fear through her.

"Why don't you leave her alone?" Artie said.

Chilli glared across the bar. "Why don't *you* stop
wastin' time? She'd tell us 'zactly where the damn gold
was if we smacked her 'round some."

Artie stopped in the middle of prying out a brick and
glared back at his brother. "Chilli, how many times do
I gotta tell you to shut the hell up about that kinda
stuff? You gotta record, remember? You's a two-time
loser. That means you beat up some broad and get
caught, and you'll be an old man before you get outta
the slammer."

"How we gonna get caught, Artie? You's been goin'
on 'bout how we's gonna get caught since we got here.
First you keep sayin' we don't wanna kill nobody 'cuz
we's gonna get caught. Now you's sayin' we can't even
rough her up 'cuz we's gonna get caught. Know what I
think, big brother? I think you's...whadda they call it?
Paranoid, that's the word. I think you's paranoid."

Alanna closed her eyes, wishing she could close her
ears as well. Artie seemed reasonably sane. He wanted

the gold, but he clearly didn't want to murder anybody to get it. Chilli, though, was a psychopath. And it was Chilli who was waiting over there to "take care of" the man she loved.

Knots began forming on top of the knots already in her stomach. She was surprised John hadn't come bursting in by now. He had more than enough time to discover the Fechners had escaped and make it back here.

She couldn't help imagining him racing toward the Magnolia this very second. And she was powerless to keep him away.

Hot tears began to sting her eyes. The entire situation was insane. All this trouble over a little bit of gold.

But, because of that gold, John was going to die. Regardless of what Artie wanted, Chilli would as soon kill John as look at him.

And if John died, she wouldn't want to live.

JOHN YANKED OFF HIS BOOTS, then eased one leg through the window frame at the top of the Magnolia's fire escape and straddled it. Swinging his other leg inside, he put his feet on the floor, careful not to rest enough weight on them to make a board creak.

He hadn't dared risk going near the front of the building, let alone looking through the window, but he was almost certain the Fechner brothers were right downstairs.

He had Artie's car keys, so he knew they hadn't left town. And he'd lay odds they'd decided to have another crack at finding the gold—which meant they were in here with Alanna.

His gut clenched again. He tried to ignore it, sitting quietly on the window ledge, just listening. With all those cracks between the boards, he'd hear them for sure if they were down there.

The problem was, if he tried to make it over to the stairs, they'd hear *him,* too. Unless his plan worked, that was. And it had better, because he had no idea what he'd do if it didn't.

It wasn't two seconds before he heard a noise from the main floor. A whole series of noises, actually—it sounded like someone banging away at something.

That had to be Chilli or Artie. So they *were* here. And from the sound of things, they *were* having another shot at finding Roy's gold. But what about Alanna? What had they done with her?

They wouldn't have harmed her, he told himself firmly. There was no reason for them to. But he knew yellow-livered skunks like Chilli never needed a reason.

Wishing he could be sure she was all right, he took the radio remote from his pocket. Alanna had told him it would work from a different room, and he didn't see that there was much difference between a wall and a ceiling. So, just as long as she hadn't been exaggerating...

He aimed the remote at the far end of the hall and angled it down, so it was pointing roughly in the direction of the radio. Then, his finger almost trembling, he pushed the Power button.

Downstairs, loud music suddenly filled the Magnolia.

Leaping to his feet, he sprinted down the hall in his socks, praying nobody would turn the danged radio off before he made it to the end.

Halfway there, he could hear a man yelling above the music. He neared the staircase and dropped to his haunches, taking a quick glance down the stairs to make sure the door at the bottom was closed.

"How'd that happen?" Artie snapped as the music abruptly stopped.

"How the hell do I know?" Chilli snapped back. "But I got it shut off, didn't I?"

John waited, praying he'd hear Alanna say something. When there was only silence, his heart began pounding again—so hard he was afraid Artie and Chilli would hear it through the ceiling.

Wouldn't they have asked *Alanna* why the radio had suddenly come on? If she was alive and conscious, wouldn't they have asked her about it? His gut clenching worse than ever, he bent over and peered through one of the cracks.

Relief flooded him. Alanna was both alive and conscious. She was sitting just within his line of vision, about halfway between the bar and the worktable—tied to a chair and with some kind of gag over her mouth. He couldn't see any blood, so maybe they hadn't hurt her.

"Hey, little brother," Artie said, "you come have a go at this wall for a while, huh? I'm beat."

"Nah," Chilli muttered. "My arm's shot up, 'member? Besides, I wanna take care of John."

"Chilli, your arm's hardly nicked, so get your butt over here."

A moment later, Chilli crossed the floor beneath John, heading for the bar, and Artie walked past him toward the front of the lodging house. Both men were carrying crowbars.

They disappeared from John's line of vision again and the banging noises started once more. They'd obviously believed Alanna last night, when she'd told them the gold was hidden behind the bar.

So now Artie was near the front door, waiting for John to show up, and Chilli was behind the bar... and far too close to Alanna for comfort.

"Where the hell is he?" Artie muttered.

His question jolted John into realizing there was no time to waste. The Fechner brothers were none too bright, but another minute and even they were going to decide he was up to something. If that happened, things would only get tougher.

Aiming the remote once more, he turned the radio on a second time. As the sound blared again, he pushed himself up and hurried down the stairs, stopping when he reached the door.

Suddenly there was a loud smashing-crashing noise, followed quickly by a second and third. The music died, and Artie said, "Crowbar one, radio nuttin'. Damned thing ain't gonna be turnin' itself on no more."

"Get back to the door," Chilli snapped. "Our friend's gonna be here any second."

John silently drew his Colt, then rested his hand on the doorknob. He hadn't gotten a good-enough look at Artie and Chilli to know if they were armed or not, but they could be. They might have discovered where Alanna had hidden the guns, or forced her to tell them where they were.

But even if all they had were those crowbars, he could be in for a rough ride. It was two against one. This time, there was no chance of Roy materializing to lend a helping hand.

And even though John had his gun, he wouldn't be able to cover both those polecats in the first couple of seconds. He stood on the bottom step, desperately trying to figure out how he could manage to.

Finally, he decided it just wasn't possible. The way the angles were, he wouldn't even be able to see Chilli at first. He'd just have to pray for luck.

Taking a deep breath he threw open the door and yelled, "Neither of you move!"

Artie didn't.

Chilli did.

Even as John went for Artie, he could hear Chilli scrambling across the floor.

With the element of surprise, it was only a second before John had his gun pressed to Artie's temple. "Drop the crowbar," he ordered.

The tool clattered to the floor.

John shoved Artie toward the main part of the room. But by then, Chilli was standing behind Alanna's chair, holding a large knife to her throat.

CHAPTER EIGHTEEN

ALANNA WAS paralyzed with terror.

She could feel the sharp blade of Chilli's knife against her neck, the rope was cutting into her wrists, and the tape over her mouth suddenly seemed suffocating. Or maybe it was the panic filling her throat that was making breathing impossible.

Across the room she could see her own fear reflected on Artie's face. But she knew John was far less likely to blow Artie's head off than Chilli was to slit her throat.

"Drop the knife, Chilli," John said, his voice unbelievably calm.

"Go to hell," Chilli snarled. "You drop the gun or I'll start slicin' up your girlfriend."

She wouldn't have believed it was possible to be *more* terrified, but she almost began to shake at his words. Even if John *did* drop his gun, she didn't trust Chilli not to start slicing her up—just for the fun of it.

"You want me to kill your brother?" John asked. He cocked his gun, the click punctuating his question.

"Who the hell cares?" Chilli muttered. "He's a pain in the ass. But while you's shootin', I'll be carvin'."

The term *Mexican standoff* popped into Alanna's head. There couldn't be a winner here. There was really nothing more John could do.

And that meant *she* had to do something. Otherwise, this was going to end in a bloodbath, and a whole lot of the blood would be hers.

Gathering all her courage, she threw every ounce of her weight to the left, away from Chilli's knife hand.

The second he saw Alanna's chair begin to topple, John shoved Artie to one side and started shooting— aiming for Chilli's extremities but not really caring if he killed him.

The smell of gunpowder filled the air; the Magnolia was transformed into a thundering echo chamber of gunshots and Chilli's screams.

John emptied his gun before he realized his mistake, then whirled toward Artie—expecting to find himself out of bullets and facing a crowbar.

But Artie hadn't even made a move to pick it up. "Hey, everythin's aces, man," he said, raising his hands chest high, palms out. "I've had it with all this."

In a single motion, John scooped up the crowbar and started across the room to Alanna.

"It's over," he murmured, grabbing Chilli's knife off the floor and going to work on the ropes. "It's over and you're alive. You're just fine," he added, praying she really was.

Chilli was lying a few feet away, bleeding but not dead.

"Artie?" he called, his voice a rasping ache. "Artie, take him. His gun's empty."

"Who the hell cares," Artie muttered. "You's a pain in the ass."

JOHN STOOD OUTSIDE the Magnolia with his arm around Alanna, watching the pink Cadillac shrinking to toy size as it headed off across the desert for Branchwater—Artie driving, Chilli bandaged well enough to stop him from bleeding to death.

Five of John's six bullets had hit him, but the wounds weren't so bad he'd die from them. Not as long as Artie got him to a hospital pretty soon.

"What are you thinking?" Alanna asked, once the car had vanished into the glare of the midday sun.

"The truth?"

"Of course."

"Well, the truth is, I was thinking that the way things are going I'll *never* get a ride in a danged car."

That made her laugh. And her laughing made him want to kiss her, so he did—a long, deep, searching kiss that assured him she really was just fine.

"You figure we did the right thing?" he asked after he'd released her. "Letting them go a second time, I mean?"

"Don't you?"

He shrugged. They didn't deserve to get away free and clear, and even though Alanna had assured him they wouldn't, he was a mite worried about it. But he hadn't argued about letting them leave because he'd wanted to be alone with Alanna. And because he hadn't wanted to spend an hour cooped up in that car with Artie and Chilli. And because, this time, there was no risk they'd try coming back to Chester City. Not before he and Alanna were long gone, at least.

Chilli was in no condition to be anywhere except in a hospital. And Artie was completely fed up with the whole idea of trying to find Roy's gold—to say nothing of how he was feeling about his brother.

"We didn't *exactly* let them go," Alanna was saying. "I told you, as soon as a doctor sees those bullet wounds, the police will be called in. It's the law. So Artie and Chilli will have to explain what happened, and after they do that they'll be arrested.''

''You don't think they'll lie?''

''Well…yes. I think at the very least they'll twist the truth. But the police will get the whole story from us. The first time we get to a phone, we'll call and give them the real facts.''

''And Artie and Chilli will eventually end up in jail.''

''Chilli will, for sure, because of his priors. Artie might get off with a suspended sentence. After all, they didn't *really* hurt anyone.''

John nodded, thinking it sure wasn't Chilli's fault they hadn't hurt anyone. That polecat deserved a stretch in jail. And once he and Alanna told the whole story…

''You know,'' he said, thinking, ''maybe we shouldn't give the police all the facts. Saying I come from 1887 would mean a heap more questions, right?''

''I guess it would. So we should probably leave out that bit. And we should think up something reasonable sounding to say about Roy and Mary—in case Artie and Chilli mention them.''

''I'll bet they don't mention a danged thing the police don't drag out of them.''

''You think we should have gone with them, then? Straightened everything out right now?''

''Uh-uh. I didn't want to spend the rest of the day answering police questions.''

''Oh? How did you want to spend it?''

He grinned at her. ''Well, for starters, I thought we could just go back into the Magnolia for a spell.''

''And talk?'' She managed to look so knowing and so innocent at the same time that he couldn't help but laugh.

"Talk. Yeah, I guess we could do some of that, too." He draped his arm over her shoulders and they headed inside.

"You were pretty clever," she said as he closed the door. "Causing that diversion, I mean. It really got those two upset."

She gestured toward the radio—or what was left of it. Artie had crunched it almost flat with his crowbar. "Lucky you confiscated my remote, wasn't it?"

"It wasn't luck," John teased. "I was planning ahead. I'm good at things like that." He reached into his pocket. Now that the radio was broken, it was safe to give Alanna back the remote.

When he pulled it out, a piece of paper fluttered to the floor. He bent down and picked it up, not realizing what it was until he unfolded it and looked at the signature.

He glanced at Alanna again. "It's Roy's note. He gave it to me in the mine, remember?"

"Uh-huh. A thank-you note. He said he wanted to put his thanks down in writing."

"That's what he said, but it's not what he wrote. Listen:

"John,
One of the stones on the left side of the bake oven's base is loose. Take the plug and shelf out to get at it, then move the stone aside."

"What's the plug?" Alanna asked.

"The metal door," John told her, heading over to the fireplace.

She followed him and stood watching while he worked the stiff old door loose and took it off. Then he took the guns from their hiding place, slid the shelf out and felt around on the bottom of the oven—trying every one of the flat stones that formed the base.

"Find it?" Alanna asked.

"No." He pushed himself to his feet. His hands and arms were covered in soot.

"Let me try."

"You'll get dirty."

"I wash up just fine, John."

He moved out of the way and let her have a go at it.

"Here," she said after a minute. "Roy didn't really mean it was part of the base. It's one of the stones along the bottom of the wall. I can wiggle it, but my hands aren't strong enough to pull it out.

"Right near the front," she told him as he knelt down to try again. "I think it's the second one back."

This time he found it. He worked it out and shoved it aside, then reached into the space and pulled out an envelope.

"Well, I'll be," he muttered.

"What?" Alanna demanded.

He held it so she could see the front.

"'Alanna and John,' it says," she murmured. "In Roy's handwriting. Open it."

He wiped his hands as clean as he could on his jeans, then took the single sheet of paper from the envelope and unfolded it.

His throat grew dry as he read what Roy had written.

"What?" Alanna said again. "John? You're pale as a ghost. What's wrong?"

He shook his head. There was nothing wrong, but he was too amazed to speak.

"John, what does it say?"

"It's dated July third," he managed to say. "July third, 1895."

"They made it back, then," Alanna whispered. "Oh, John, they *did* end up in exactly the right time. You gave them back their lives."

Tears began making good their escape down Alanna's cheeks and John felt more than a little choked up himself. "Listen to this," he said over the lump in his throat. "Alanna, listen to this.

"Dear Alanna and John,
As you can see from this letter, Mary and I had a safe trip. We will be eternally grateful to both of you for your help, and I thought perhaps I could help you some in return.

"I didn't want to say much about my gold in front of Mary, because I wanted to surprise her when we got back. But I saved a fair amount during the time I had the Magnolia, and I hid most of it away there."

"But he told us there was only a *little* hidden in here, remember?" Alanna said. "Not even enough to make it worth mentioning to anyone."

"Well, that's not what he's saying now. Listen to the rest of this.

"...I wasn't sure exactly how much I had stashed away, but it turned out to be a heap. Far more than Mary and I are going to need over our lifetime, even if we live to be ninety. So I've left some of it here for you two. There's a strongbox back in that

hollow space you uncovered. Just reach farther in
and pull it out. The contents are for you, with love
from Mary and all the best from me.

                                        Your friend,
                                  Roy Hardin, Esquire''

John handed the letter to Alanna, then turned to the
oven again. He reached farther into the opening this
time and his hand hit metal.

"Tarnation, this is heavy," he muttered, working the
box out of its hiding place. "I can hardly move it."

He dragged it up through the opening in the oven, set
it on the floor and undid the latch. When he lifted the
lid, the strongbox was almost half-full of small cotton
bags.

"There's gold in those?" Alanna whispered, sinking
to her knees on the other side of the box.

"Gold dust." He untied one of them and showed her.

"Oh, my...oh, John, they'll *all* be full of gold dust?"

He nodded. "That's what the letter says." He gazed
down at the box, his excitement growing, then looked
across it at Alanna.

"Back in 1887, this much gold would be worth a
danged fortune. But in 2014 . . . ?"

"I...oh, John, it's worth a fortune now, too. I'm not
really up on the price of gold, but I know an ounce is
worth more than a thousand dollars. And there are
pounds of it in here. Pounds and pounds."

He started to smile. Alanna started to smile. And then
he reached for her and wrapped his arms tightly around
her—not worrying a whit about the soot.

"Roy was one hell of a good friend, huh?" he whispered against her hair.

"And Mary, too. Oh, John."

Alanna drew back a little and traced his jawline with sooty fingers. "John, having the gold means you can afford to stay in this century for as long as you want...*if* you want, that is."

He tried to stop smiling, but it was impossible. "Give me a good reason to stay," he teased.

She wrapped her arms tightly around his neck and proceeded to give him an incredibly *great* reason.

EPILOGUE

New York City
June 21, 1919

"WHO GIVETH this woman into holy matrimony?"

"I do," Roy said, then stepped back and slipped into the front pew beside Mary.

She blinked back happy tears. It seemed like no time at all since Alanna had been born, but now she was a bride. And it wouldn't be long before her sisters married as well.

Mary let her gaze wander to her other three girls, today their eldest sister's bridesmaids. They were all so beautiful. And her sons were all such fine-looking young men.

She glanced at them, seated in a row beside her now that their ushers' duties were done. Roy Junior, John and Charles—named after her brother.

Roy covered her hand with his and she smiled at him.

"Any regrets that you didn't keep your wedding dress for today?" he whispered.

She shook her head. She'd never had the slightest twinge of regret about leaving it behind in Chester City. If it hadn't been for Alanna and John, she and Roy wouldn't be here now, living a wonderful life back East, where they'd both started out.

The West had been an adventure, but the East was where they'd decided they wanted to raise their family.

"I now pronounce you man and wife," the minister said. "You may kiss the bride."

Mary dabbed at her eyes with the lace corner of her hankie. The past twenty-four years had been incredible, and she hoped the woman whom her firstborn was named after had a life even half as happy.

San Luis Obispo, California
June 21, 2038

"HAPPY TWENTY-FIRST birthday, son," John said, handing Roy the small box.

Roy shook it, then turned it from one side to the other, examining it with studied thoroughness.

"Roy," his sister said impatiently, "open it. I want to see."

Alanna smiled, watching her children. Roy and Mary were as different as night and day, and they spent half their time pretending to be mortal enemies—when they'd really always been the best of friends. Maybe because they were barely a year apart in age.

Roy finally undid the ribbon and tore off the paper. A huge grin spread across his face when he opened the box. "Is this for real?" He looked from John to Alanna, then back.

John nodded.

"Wow! Thanks, Dad, that's really great."

"Well, I can't take all the credit. It was actually your mother who came up with the idea."

Roy shot her a grin, then moved closer and gave her a hug.

"What?" Mary demanded. "What is it?"

"Oh, just some business cards." Roy casually handed her one.

"Vice President, Superior Software? Da-a-a-addy! You're making him a vice president of your company when he's only twenty-one? He's not even finished university!"

"Well, he'll start off as a summer-only vice president."

"But what about me?"

"Hey, you're not twenty-one for another year. Besides, your brother's the best man with computers I've seen since—"

"Since yourself?" Alanna teased.

John grinned at her, while Mary went on trying to sound outraged.

Actually, Alanna knew her daughter couldn't care less about being a vice president in John's business. Mary's interests were more like hers, and she'd probably end up as a professor someplace. Maybe even at California State, on the same faculty as her mother.

Of course, that would be years away, but time went by so fast....

Closing her eyes, she let her thoughts drift back to the past, wondering how twenty-four years could possibly have flown by like twenty-four days.

It seemed only yesterday that she'd looked in through the window of the Miner's Saloon and seen John McCully for the first time.

She smiled to herself, remembering her first impression of him—the most magnificent specimen of an apparition she'd ever seen.

"What are you smiling at?" he asked quietly.

She opened her eyes and gazed at him. He was still the most magnificent specimen she'd ever seen.

"I'm smiling," she whispered, "at the man who's made me happy for twenty-four years."

He draped his arms around her waist and pulled her close. "How 'bout we try for an entire danged century?"

HARLEQUIN SUPERROMANCE ®

COMING NEXT MONTH

#618 MEG & THE MYSTERY MAN • Elise Title (*Class of '78*)
Meg Delgado goes undercover as a wealthy socialite on the
cruise ship Galileo. Her mission: to catch a thief. Her suspect:
Noah Danforth, who's got the looks, the charm and the wit of a
Cary Grant. But if Meg isn't who she seems to be, neither is Noah.
And together they discover that deception and disguise lead to
danger...and to romance!

#619 THE COWBOY'S LOVER • Ada Steward
Lexi Conley kidnaps rodeo cowboy Jake Thorn because she
needs him to manage her family's ranch while her father's in the
hospital. It doesn't help that Jake, her sister's ex-husband, may be
the father of Lexi's adopted son—or that he's still the only man
she's ever loved.

#620 SAFEKEEPING • Peg Sutherland (*Women Who Dare*)
An unexpected snowstorm traps Quinn Santori and her two young
companions in an isolated mountain cabin. A cabin that's already
inhabited—by a man toting a gun. They make an odd foursome—
Quinn, the two little girls in her charge and ex-con Whit Sloane.
And chances are their number will increase to five before the snow
melts. *Quinn's about to have a baby!*

#621 THE LOCKET • Brenna Todd
Transported back through time, Erin Sawyer is mistaken for her
double, the adulterous Della Munro, whose husband is a powerful
and dangerous man. But Erin finds herself attracted to his partner,
Waite MacKinnon, a man whose compelling eyes have been
haunting her dreams for what seems like forever.

AVAILABLE NOW:

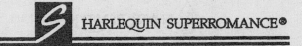

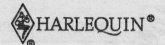

HARLEQUIN®

Weddings, Inc.

EDGE OF ETERNITY
Jasmine Cresswell

Two years after their divorce, David Powell
and Eve Graham met again in Eternity,
Massachusetts—and this time there was magic
between them. But David was tied up in a
murder that no amount of small-town gossip
could free him from. When Eve was pulled into
the frenzy, he knew he had to come up with
some answers—including how to convince her
they should marry again…this time for keeps.

EDGE OF ETERNITY, available in
November from Intrigue, is the sixth book in
Harlequin's exciting new cross-line series,
WEDDINGS, INC.

Be sure to look for the final book, **VOWS,** by
Margaret Moore (Harlequin Historical #248),
coming in December.

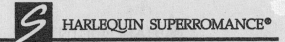

WHERE ARE THEY NOW?

It's sixteen years since the CLASS OF '78 graduated from Berkeley School for Girls. On that day, four young women, four close friends, stood on the brink of adulthood and dreamed about the directions their lives might take. None could know what lay ahead....

Now it's time to catch up with Sandra, Laurel, Meg and Kim. Each woman's story is told in Harlequin Superromance's new miniseries, THE CLASS OF '78.

> ALESSANDRA & THE ARCHANGEL
> by Judith Arnold (Sept. 1994)
> LAUREL & THE LAWMAN
> by Lynn Erickson (Oct. 1994)
> MEG & THE MYSTERY MAN
> by Elise Title (Nov. 1994)
> KIM & THE COWBOY
> by Margot Dalton (Dec. 1994)

Look for these titles by some of
Harlequin Superromance's favorite authors,
wherever Harlequin books are sold.

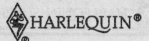

HARLEQUIN®

Don't miss these Harlequin favorites by some of our most
distinguished authors!
And now you can receive a discount by ordering two or more titles!

HT#25483	BABYCAKES by Glenda Sanders	$2.99	☐
HT#25559	JUST ANOTHER PRETTY FACE by Candace Schuler	$2.99	☐
HP#11608	SUMMER STORMS by Emma Goldrick	$2.99	☐
HP#11632	THE SHINING OF LOVE by Emma Darcy	$2.99	☐
HR#03265	HERO ON THE LOOSE by Rebecca Winters	$2.89	☐
HR#03268	THE BAD PENNY by Susan Fox	$2.99	☐
HS#70532	TOUCH THE DAWN by Karen Young	$3.39	☐
HS#70576	ANGELS IN THE LIGHT by Margot Dalton	$3.50	☐
HI#22249	MUSIC OF THE MIST by Laura Pender	$2.99	☐
HI#22267	CUTTING EDGE by Caroline Burnes	$2.99	☐
HAR#16489	DADDY'S LITTLE DIVIDEND by Elda Minger	$3.50	☐
HAR#16525	CINDERMAN by Anne Stuart	$3.50	☐
HH#28801	PROVIDENCE by Miranda Jarrett	$3.99	☐
HH#28775	A WARRIOR'S QUEST by Margaret Moore	$3.99	☐
	(limited quantities available on certain titles)		

TOTAL AMOUNT	$	
DEDUCT: 10% DISCOUNT FOR 2+ BOOKS	$	
POSTAGE & HANDLING	$	
($1.00 for one book, 50¢ for each additional)		
APPLICABLE TAXES*	$	_____
TOTAL PAYABLE	$	_____
(check or money order—please do not send cash)		

To order, complete this form and send it, along with a check or money order for the
total above, payable to Harlequin Books, to: **In the U.S.:** 3010 Walden Avenue,
P.O. Box 9047, Buffalo, NY 14269-9047; **In Canada:** P.O. Box 613, Fort Erie, Ontario,
L2A 5X3.

Name: _____

Address: _____ City: _____

State/Prov.: _____ Zip/Postal Code: _____

*New York residents remit applicable sales taxes.
 Canadian residents remit applicable GST and provincial taxes.

HBACK-OD

"HOORAY FOR HOLLYWOOD" SWEEPSTAKES

HERE'S HOW THE SWEEPSTAKES WORKS

OFFICIAL RULES — NO PURCHASE NECESSARY

To enter, complete an Official Entry Form or hand print on a 3" x 5" card the words "HOORAY FOR HOLLYWOOD", your name and address and mail your entry in the pre-addressed envelope (if provided) or to: "Hooray for Hollywood" Sweepstakes, P.O. Box 9076, Buffalo, NY 14269-9076 or "Hooray for Hollywood" Sweepstakes, P.O. Box 637, Fort Erie, Ontario L2A 5X3. Entries must be sent via First Class Mail and be received no later than 12/31/94. No liability is assumed for lost, late or misdirected mail.

Winners will be selected in random drawings to be conducted no later than January 31, 1995 from all eligible entries received.

Grand Prize: A 7-day/6-night trip for 2 to Los Angeles, CA including round trip air transportation from commercial airport nearest winner's residence, accommodations at the Regent Beverly Wilshire Hotel, free rental car, and $1,000 spending money. (Approximate prize value which will vary dependent upon winner's residence: $5,400.00 U.S.); 500 Second Prizes: A pair of "Hollywood Star" sunglasses (prize value: $9.95 U.S. each). Winner selection is under the supervision of D.L. Blair, Inc., an independent judging organization, whose decisions are final. Grand Prize travelers must sign and return a release of liability prior to traveling. Trip must be taken by 2/1/96 and is subject to airline schedules and accommodations availability.

Sweepstakes offer is open to residents of the U.S. (except Puerto Rico) and Canada who are 18 years of age or older, except employees and immediate family members of Harlequin Enterprises, Ltd., its affiliates, subsidiaries, and all agencies, entities or persons connected with the use, marketing or conduct of this sweepstakes. All federal, state, provincial, municipal and local laws apply. Offer void wherever prohibited by law. Taxes and/or duties are the sole responsibility of the winners. Any litigation within the province of Quebec respecting the conduct and awarding of prizes may be submitted to the Regie des loteries et courses du Quebec. All prizes will be awarded; winners will be notified by mail. No substitution of prizes are permitted. Odds of winning are dependent upon the number of eligible entries received.

Potential grand prize winner must sign and return an Affidavit of Eligibility within 30 days of notification. In the event of non-compliance within this time period, prize may be awarded to an alternate winner. Prize notification returned as undeliverable may result in the awarding of prize to an alternate winner. By acceptance of their prize, winners consent to use of their names, photographs, or likenesses for purpose of advertising, trade and promotion on behalf of Harlequin Enterprises, Ltd., without further compensation unless prohibited by law. A Canadian winner must correctly answer an arithmetical skill-testing question in order to be awarded the prize.

For a list of winners (available after 2/28/95), send a separate stamped, self-addressed envelope to: Hooray for Hollywood Sweepstakes 3252 Winners, P.O. Box 4200, Blair, NE 68009.

CBSRLS

OFFICIAL ENTRY COUPON

"Hooray for Hollywood"
SWEEPSTAKES!

Yes, I'd love to win the Grand Prize — a vacation in Hollywood — or one of 500 pairs of "sunglasses of the stars"! Please enter me in the sweepstakes!

This entry must be received by December 31, 1994.
Winners will be notified by January 31, 1995.

Name _____

Address _____ Apt. _____

City _____

State/Prov. _____ Zip/Postal Code _____

Daytime phone number _____
(area code)

Account # _____

Return entries with invoice in envelope provided. Each book in this shipment has two entry coupons — and the more coupons you enter, the better your chances of winning!

DIRCBS

OFFICIAL ENTRY COUPON

"Hooray for Hollywood"
SWEEPSTAKES!

Yes, I'd love to win the Grand Prize — a vacation in Hollywood — or one of 500 pairs of "sunglasses of the stars"! Please enter me in the sweepstakes!

This entry must be received by December 31, 1994.
Winners will be notified by January 31, 1995.

Name _____

Address _____ Apt. _____

City _____

State/Prov. _____ Zip/Postal Code _____

Daytime phone number _____
(area code)

Account # _____

Return entries with invoice in envelope provided. Each book in this shipment has two entry coupons — and the more coupons you enter, the better your chances of winning!

DIRCBS